GENERATIONS
of Love

GENERATIONS
of *Love*

PATRICIA SMITH JANSSEN

iUniverse, Inc.
Bloomington

GENERATIONS OF LOVE

iUniverse books may be ordered through booksellers or by contacting:

iUniverse
1663 Liberty Drive
Bloomington, IN 47403
www.iuniverse.com
1-800-Authors (1-800-288-4677)

ISBN: 978-1-4620-7097-8 (sc)
ISBN: 978-1-4620-7149-4 (hc)
ISBN: 978-1-4620-7098-5 (ebk)

Printed in the United States of America

iUniverse rev. date: 01/04/2012

TABLE OF CONTENTS

Chapter One 1
Chapter Two 4
Chapter Three 12
Chapter Four 18
Chapter Five 25
Chapter Six 31
Chapter Seven 38
Chapter Eight 42
Chapter Nine 47
Chapter Ten 52
Chapter Eleven 61
Chapter Twelve 70
Chapter Thirteen 78
Chapter Fourteen 86
Chapter Fifteen 95
Chapter Sixteen 106
Chapter Seventeen 123
Chapter Eighteen 132
Chapter Nineteen 147
Chapter Twenty 159
Chapter Twenty-One 172
Chapter Twenty-Two 181
Chapter Twenty-Three 187
Chapter Twenty-Four 198

PREFACE

Generations of Love follows the lives of three couples, their families and how each live through happy and difficult times. Each family is the next generation of the previous and they learned from the generation before them. Not only is *Generations of Love* a love story between husband and wife, but the bonds shared by grandparents, parents, and children.

The story begins with Matilda and Jeremiah as they lived in Ireland, a country they loved. Unfortunately, due to the demise of the linen industry, Jeremiah takes Matilda and their five children to America. After a long, strenuous ride on a ship across the Atlantic, they arrive in New York City. Although Jeremiah promised a better life in America, the family is met with even more hardships forcing Matilda and Jeremiah to wish they had remained in Ireland.

The second couple we are introduced to are Rose and Edmund. Rose is the daughter of Matilda and Jeremiah. As Rose becomes older, she falls in love with the theater and begins acting. This is where she meets Edmund and the two fall deeply in love. No matter how much Rose loves the stage, she loves Edmund more. Therefore when Edmund insist the couple move upstate to Albany, Rose agrees to follow her husband. There they have seven boys and one girl, Hannah. Through a number of ups and downs, the couple remains strong until an unfortunate death.

Hank and Hannah are the final pair of the three generations in *Generations of Love*. Hannah is the beloved daughter of Rose and Edmund. Not only is Hannah their youngest, she is her parent's only girl. Hannah and Hank meet in an unusual location. From the start they are plagued with hurdles they most overcome to be together. Once they are able to marry, they do so, and it becomes apparent to everyone how much love the two share. Through their love, we see a unique type of love rarely shared by others.

Throughout *Generations of Love*, the reader will experience love, loss, hurt, sorrow and joy. Each generation turns to the previous for help and guidance. Through their connections it is apparent how strong the bond between the generations becomes.

DEDICATION

Without the guidance and patience of my daughter, Laura Delehanty, I would never have completed this book.

ONE

The sunlight was streaming across Matilda Dunniff's face. There was a smile and slowly she uncoiled and stretched. Matilda felt happy and at peace with the world. She reached over and gently nudged her husband, Jeremiah.

He opened his eyes and said to Matilda,

"Someone is in a good mood."

No sooner the words were out than it all came rushing back to her. They were broke, had no hope of making money and an eviction notice was sitting on the dresser. Jeremiah turned to Matilda,

"Sunshine, why the sudden long face?"

"I just remembered our nightmare. What are we going to do?" Matilda replied.

"Haven't I've always taken care of you and the children why wouldn't I now?" said Jeremiah.

Matilda questioned Jeremiah, "How?"

About a year ago, the linen business died in Northern Ireland. Jeremiah had always been a flax farmer. The flax he grew was spun into linen. The flax blight made the market so depressed, Jeremiah was forced to give up growing flax.

Matilda tried to help the family by selling eggs, milk, and vegetables to the locals. Life was getting so terrible they were forced to slaughter the cow and chickens so they could put food on the table.

Throughout day Matilda went about doing her housework. She could not shake the fear in the pit of her stomach; Matilda knew something was about to happen.

During dinner that night Jeremiah made an announcement,

"I've done some inquiring in town and I think our solution is to go to America."

Immediately the children were excited with thousand questions. Matilda was speechless. She never dreamed she would leave her beloved Ireland.

"Jeremiah," she said, "There has got to be another way. How will we afford such a move?"

"I have some money saved and it's enough to pay our passage to America. There are no jobs here and if we stay we will starve. I know a man in America, Jim McCann, who is willing to help us until we get on our feet. I know this is difficult, but it is important we decide quickly."

Matilda was still not convinced. One thing that bothered her was what she had heard of the "coffin" ships. She honestly did not know if they could survive such a journey. With Jeremiah's insistence, eventually Matilda agreed. That night when they went to bed they held each other praying they made the right decision. Matilda thought as she drifted off to sleep,

"Jeremiah will provide."

Jeremiah was confident he could take care of his family.

The following week Jeremiah and Matilda made preparations. Matilda heard food was scarce on the ship so, she dried some meat and prepared a few vegetables. It was heart wrenching saying good-bye to family and friends, knowing they would probably never see them again.

It took them a better part of a day to get to Dublin. One of the local farmers gave them a ride in his horse and wagon. The five children and two adults rode in the back. The children were excited; this was a real adventure for them. They were delighted for the adventure.

"Jeremiah are you sure we'll be all right?" Matilda asked.

Jeremiah reassured her once again.

Once they reached Dublin they made their way to the docks where Jeremiah arranged for their passage to Liverpool, England and from there to America. They were taken by ferry to Liverpool.

In Liverpool, Jeremiah found a boarding house for the night. Matilda thought the room was disgraceful. It was just that, an empty, dirty room. It was so small they had to try and sleep sitting up.

Thankfully the following day the family boarded the ship, The Wanderlust, destined for America.

The ship appeared small for the number of people boarding. This worried Matilda. Once on the ship, Matilda's worse fears came to light, how was she going to keep her five children healthy? Because they were the first to board, and Matilda spread their mats around the ladder leading to the deck. She thought it was the best place to breath in sea air.

The trip was long, days ran into weeks. Each child got sick, but thankfully they did not get the fever. Matilda was exhausted. The mats were so close one could barely turn over. There were so many unclean bodies, the smell was overwhelming. Food was putrid. Matilda would dole out small pieces of dried meat and scant amounts of vegetables. Clean water was worse, one pint a day. Jeremiah's emotions went from guilt for putting his family through such an ordeal, to excitement of what laid ahead. He could see New York City in his mind.

"Matilda you will be amazed at the tall buildings that make up New York City, along with millions of people."

In Jeremiah's mind, he could see the city even though he had never been there. As each day passed he became more and more excited for what lay ahead.

TWO

For what seemed like forever, the ship arrived just off Castle Gardens, an island outside of New York City. An officer came aboard the ship separating the sick, infirmed, and insane and sending them to a hospital on Ward Island. Jeremiah and Matilda were lucky, although their family was weak from weeks at sea; they were candidates to go on to Castle Gardens. A barge brought them from the ship to Castle Gardens. Once there, they were led into a large room lined with wooden benches. Matilda hugged Jeremiah. She was so happy to be off the ship breathing fresh air and drinking fresh water. The registering clerk questioned Jeremiah. He asked their names, the Dunniff's, and all their surnames, Jeremiah, Matilda, John, Padric, Will, Elizabeth, and Martha. They also had to prove where they were from and where in the USA they were going. To Jeremiah's delight, Jim McCann was there to greet them and take them to his home, in a New York City tenement. Mr. McCann showed them where they would live. It was a tenement flat.

There were four rooms with only the first room and the back room had windows. Not only was the flat unventilated but also it was filthy. Matilda and Jeremiah, with their five children, managed to live in a windowless, unventilated room. Matilda encouraged John, Padric, and Will to try to find work immediately. Matilda and Jeremiah's main goal was to get a place to live.

Matilda was in awe of the huge city. To her, it was just as Jeremiah described. She would have loved to walk around the city, but pressures kept her at home. Matilda's days were filled taking care of her family.

Two of the boys got jobs relatively quickly as domestic servants. For Jeremiah the job search was a lot more difficult. Jeremiah heard of a company on Fulton ant Nassau St. where cotton was processed. This was opposite to what Jeremiah experienced while searching for work. On many occasions he would walk up to apply and a sign usually blocked the entrance,

"Irish need not apply."

With three of them working the Dunniff's were able to move to a place of their own. With only so much money they were forced to move into a tenement house, but this one seemed better than the one they shared with Jim McCann. The first thing Matilda noticed was the dirt throughout the flat. Matilda and her daughters literally scrubbed the walls, ceilings and floors. Sanitation conditions were primitive. Their tenement had a privy that was shared by other tenement occupiers; therefore Matilda and the family used chamber pots.

Delusion was setting in for Jeremiah. He realized streets were not paved in gold. The family was only slightly better off than they had been in Ireland. He constantly complained to Matilda about little things.

"Matilda my meal is cold."

"Matilda my clothes are not clean yet."

Matilda mostly ignored Jeremiah, but could not help feeling hurt. In many ways she felt like she did on the ship. It was hard to hold them all together.

Matilda's day began about four am and ended in exhaustion around nine pm. The more apparent it became that life was not going get much better, the nastier Jeremiah became. Much to Matilda's dismay, Jeremiah started to drink. At first it was a drink at the end of the day to relax. Now though, Jeremiah drank to get drunk and wallow in his memories of Ireland. On a good night he would play his fiddle and sing Irish songs, some in English and some in Gallic.

Food was still limited. For an atypical day they had coffee and bread for breakfast, potato sandwiches for lunch then for dinner some meat, cabbage, and potatoes. Occasionally, John and Padric managed to sneak leftovers home from the households where they worked. Matilda thanked God for what they had, especially hearing other women in the tenement complaining how much they were suffering.

On a rare night Matilda and Jeremiah would cuddle. Matilda always tried to reassure Jeremiah and said,

"You wait and see it things can only get better."

Jeremiah still had physical needs and Matilda did her wifely duty. They had been married twenty years and some of the passion was gone. But Matilda got a sense of security when they made love. She got a glimpse of her old husband.

After a couple of months, Matilda realized she was pregnant. Matilda had been pregnant a total often ten times as a result they had had three boys and two girls who survived. The pregnancy should not have concerned her because Jeremiah and Matilda always felt one more mouth was manageable. The fact that she was forty-five concerned her, but Matilda always had faith in God. Matilda told Jeremiah, she and was floored by his reaction.

"How am I going to provide for another child?" he shouted.

With all their other babies he had been happy and proud. Unlike Jeremiah, he was angry and turned to drink even more. A simple question nagged him. What would happen if Matilda got sick or worse died? Jeremiah always wanted to give his family a good life and now he had failed. That night when they went to bed he said to Matilda,

"I'm sorry Matilda I can't be happy about this baby. It scares me."

Matilda touched his arm and said,

"Jeremiah we will be fine."

On a cold windy night in December of 1879, a little baby was born into the life of impoverishment in the tenements of New York City. She was tiny, 5 pounds, and had a strong cry. Matilda was exhausted. She had been in labor 48 hours. Had it not been for the wonderful midwife it was doubtful either mother or baby would have survived.

Jeremiah had spent the 48 hours fortifying himself with a bottle of whisky. Although relieved Matilda and baby were ok it did nothing to ease his anguish. After a while, he peeked in to find Matilda asleep with the baby besides her. Jeremiah tiptoed in and stared at his wife. It had been a long time since he had seen her like this. Gently he brushed her hair from her forehead.

Quietly he said, "I love you Matilda."

As he was about to leave he noticed the baby staring at him. He answered her stare with a stare and left.

Rose turned out to be a serious baby and caused little trouble. Matilda tried to nurse often to strengthen Rose. After four months of nursing Matilda's milk dried up. The lack of meat and enough food were the causes of Matilda's milk to dry up. In Ireland they always had plenty to eat. Her other children were fat happy babies. Matilda worried about Rose.

As tiny as Rose was, she sat up and walked early like she was in a hurry to get somewhere. Jeremiah was either working or drunk. He literally ignored Rose. Rose's brothers and sisters were too busy working or doing housework to pay attention to Rose.

Matilda took in wash to give them a little more money. Elizabeth, Rose's oldest sister helped Matilda with the washing and ironing. Day after day, clothes would be hung on lines in the house. On good days they hung them outside.

The sibling nearest Rose's age was Martha. Martha was four, and barely more than a baby herself. Martha was in charge of Rose. Matilda always kept an eye on her beautiful baby. Rose's had beautiful auburn, curly hair, her eyes were hazel and her skin pale almost porcelain, with a blush on her cheeks. However it concerned Matilda that Rose was slight and so intense. As much as Jeremiah ignored Rose, she was drawn to him. Often when Jeremiah sat in his chair, Rose would crawl over to him and sit on the floor next to her father. When Jeremiah realized Rose was there Jeremiah would bellow,

"Matilda, take this baby away".

Matilda could not abide by the change in Jeremiah. He had been so good with the other children. If he would only look at Rose he would see some of himself in her or maybe he had. It seemed the more he drowned in his whisky the more distant he became. Nothing Matilda tried to do seem to help. He was determined to escape reality and thus escape his family.

Finally, one day Matilda confronted Jeremiah.

"Jeremiah something has to change. You're nothing like you were in Ireland. For the sake of the family and your health please do something to return to your old self."

Jeremiah seemed better for a couple of days, within a week he returned to the bottle.

By Rose's first birthday, she was walking. She was an adorable baby who openly displayed affection toward her family.

Martha continued to look after Rose. They were lucky to have a park nearby and when Matilda was free, she would take Martha and Rose to play. They played while their mother worked, usually mending her families' clothes. Martha and Rose made up games only the two could understand.

When Martha was younger, she did not mind taking Rose with her. As Martha got older and had more of her own friends, she resented Rose as a "tag along." Rose became aware of Martha's feelings as she turned six.

"Mama, I don't want to go with Martha anymore," Rose said.

Therefore, Rose stayed home most of the time. She would play with her doll. Even at six Rose had an active imagination.

At ten Rose started to help Matilda with the laundry. Her older sister had gotten married and her mother needed help.

Jeremiah was no longer working, he was sick. His skin was shallow, his eyes had a yellow tinged and his abdomen distended. Often, he was barely lucid and acted as if he was back in Ireland. Jeremiah was so out of it, he was completely unaware Rose was helping to take care of him. Matilda was aware of the physical and mental changes with Jeremiah. Deep down she knew he was dying.

At night as he slept in his chair she would say,

"My handsome husband, I love you."

Sometimes Matilda would say,

"You're a good man and we're going to get by."

As her father was dying, Rose found a new love, the theater. Her sister Elizabeth married a man who was the manager of a local theater. Elizabeth would sometimes take Rose to see a play. For a few hours, Rose's troubled home disappeared and she lost herself within the play. When alone Rose would act out parts of the play and secretly imagine herself as an actress.

Rose went to a Catholic school, which permitted less fortunate children to attend. Although Rose was Catholic, religion was rarely discussed in the home. Through her schooling, Rose found out many things were sins. Often, she would ask Matilda,

"Why don't we go to Church?"

Matilda wanted to tell her in the northern part of Ireland, where they were from, there was great hostility between the Catholics and Protestants. But, Matilda merely said,

"If you're good, pray to God and are kind to people God will love you."

Unsatisfied, Rose began attending Church on Sundays. As much as possible Rose tried to do as the nuns taught. She was developing a devotion to the Catholic faith, which she relied on all of her life.

In school, Rose did just enough to get by. If she failed a test, the sisters would tell her she would probably end up as a domestic. Little did they know, Rose was planning on becoming an actress. Rose knew not to cross the nuns. The nuns were known to use rulers in a way that did not appeal to Rose.

Rose managed to get through the sixth grade unscathed. Aside from school and helping her mother, Rose would play with her friends in the neighborhood. Sometimes they would watch the boys play stickball. However what Rose loved the most, was when they pretended to act out plays. Rose always played the lead, knowing she was good.

Throughout this time in her life, Rose had some scary things happening at home. Her father was sick and getting worse day by day. Matilda finally called the doctor. Upon examining Jeremiah, the doctor just shook his head. So often the doctor had witnessed Irish men in the terminal stages of alcoholism. He told Matilda,

"His liver is enlarged and probably not working."

He cautioned Matilda Jeremiah could have seizures and there was nothing that could be done. The doctor's advice was notifying the priest.

"How long will he live?" Matilda asked the doctor.

"Maybe a night or maybe a week, surely not more than a month" the doctor replied.

When Matilda went to pay the doctor he refused saying,

"I did nothing to help you."

Matilda and Rose took turns being with Jeremiah. Now his ranting's were few and he would just lie there struggling to breathe. A few days after the doctor's visit, Jeremiah had his first seizure. It was frightening for the family. When Martha got home from work, she assumed some of the duties of the house. Martha refused to help with her father. Martha insisted she could not bear to see her father in this condition. During the final stages of his disease, Jeremiah had no control of his urine or bowels. As a result of Jeremiah's illness, Rose grew up in a quickly, more than she should have.

There was just her sister Martha and her brother Padric at home. Rose was a great help to her mother. Matilda had to give up taking in laundry in order to take care of Jeremiah. Sometimes while sitting with Jeremiah, Matilda would hold his hand and allow her thoughts to return to the happier times of their marriage in Ireland. Although he could not respond, Matilda talked to him.

"We had a good life, especially in Ireland."

Matilda believed talking to Jeremiah some how reached him, and then he would know he was loved.

To Rose, it seemed Jeremiah had been critical forever. In reality it had only been three weeks.

One day Jeremiah was more restless than usual. He had been having one seizure after another. His breath was foul and he soiled himself constantly. Jeremiah was unable to take even the smallest amount of broth. Matilda finally summoned the priest. Usually Matilda thought the Last Rights would calm the sick, but nothing calmed Jeremiah. All they could do was watch him and pray he wasn't suffering. Jeremiah opened his eyes, and looked at Matilda and died.

They all grieved deeply. Elizabeth's husband paid for the funeral.

They tried to remember Jeremiah as he had been. For Rose, her father's death was devastating. She always hoped he would someday acknowledge her before he died. Rose was hopeless to feel the love of her father. As she lay in bed, Rose cried herself to sleep. Rose longed for something she never knew and now would never have, her father's love.

THREE

It had been six months since Jeremiah's passing and as a result, Matilda and Rose were forced to move in with Elizabeth, Rose's sister, and Ian, Elizabeth's husband. Matilda continued to mourn Jeremiah, with each day she seemed to become more depressed than the previous day. Rose mourned the death of her distant father, but she worried constantly about her mother's well being. Due to her intense grief, Matilda practically refused to eat, spending most of her days in bed. The family called for the doctor, due to their growing concerns. The doctor reassured everyone, especially Rose, that Matilda would be fine. She just needed to go through a period of grief in her own way, at her own pace. Rose noticed when her mother did speak, she often reflected upon Jeremiah and Matilda's life prior to New York City, when they were happy living in Ireland. As days turned into weeks, Matilda obsessed about her former life with Jeremiah in Ireland.

As Matilda became the more recluse, Elizabeth's husband Ian became resentful. Ian had a good job in the theater district that allowed him to support Elizabeth's family.

Rose now seventeen demonstrated her skills as a seamstress. With much joy and surprise, Ian got her a job at the theater, in costume fittings.

Rose loved her job being involved with actors and actress. She worked long hours and was paid very little. Rose gave the majority of her earnings to Ian. She kept a small amount to buy her mother small gifts in hopes of cheering her up. Matilda usually would put Rose's gift off to the side with a weak "thank you".

As Matilda's health declined, Rose became desperate for her mother to become stronger. She recited all the prayers she could remember from Catholic school. She had already lost her father, so she could not bear the thought of loosing her mother too.

As a result of her parent's misfortunes, Rose became very mature for her age. During the day Elizabeth took care of their mother. After work, Rose sat with her mother trying to encourage Matilda to eat. Rose often would read poetry to her mother. Every time Rose read Tennyson's poem "Tears Idle Tears", especially a specific stanza,

"Tears, Idle Tears, I know not they mean,
Tears from the depth of some divine despair
Rise in the heart, and gather to the eyes,
In looking on the happy autumn-fields,
And thinking of the days that are no more."

Her mother would silently weep. No matter how the poem made Matilda feel, Matilda asked Rose to read the poem again and again.

One day Rose came home to find her sister Elizabeth upset. Matilda had not awakened in the morning and still appeared to be asleep. Elizabeth had bathed her mother but Matilda did not respond. Elizabeth begged Ian to call the doctor and he refused stating,

"I am not going to waste money when the outcome is inevitable."

Rose went to Matilda's bedside and kept a vigil. It was a long night and when dawn came there was no change in Matilda's condition. Elizabeth notified Matilda's children. At some point someone brought Rose food, but Rose could eat very little. Repeatedly Rose read to her mother, including her favorite poems and prayers. That morning a little after ten Matilda simply stopped breathing. Matilda had gone to meet Jeremiah where she could rest in peace.

After Matilda's death Rose stayed on with Elizabeth and Ian. Her work in the theater made her happy. Although Rose continued to work as a costume fitter, she still dreamed for her big break, to become an actress. She was working on the costume of a leading actress when she got up the courage to share with her about her dream of becoming an actress. Rose discussed her dream because she was eighteen and she knew she needed an opportunity soon before she was considered too old. Unlike other girls her age, Rose did not obsess about finding a husband or having children; she wanted a career in the theater, which was her priority.

As Rose was working on a costume, one day the director of the theater asked Rose if she would do a walk on part for two dollars. Rose was elated and performed her part with great poise. Soon with each production, Rose was asked to act in small walk on parts.

After two months, Rose was offered a small part with two speaking lines. Every time she rehearsed the lines she would fumble over them. An actress, who had befriended Rose, said,

"I have a solution for you Rose."

Although Rose was receiving small parts, she was still responsible for fitting costumes for the actress just before final rehearsal. Joan, was the actress, who offered Rose a glass of champagne. The champagne tasted strange and made Rose flush, but at the same time she felt more confident. Later that day in rehearsal Rose had no difficulties with her lines. In fact she felt more relaxed and self-assured as if she could be the star of the play. After that, parts became more frequent. Rose needed to find a positive way to resign from costume responsibilities so she could focus more on her acting. Before each performance Rose always had a glass of champagne.

Rose's big opportunity finally came along. Although others might not see her opportunity the same way, Rose was ecstatic. Rose was told if she performed well she could be offered an acting position. The best part, as far as Rose was concerned, was she would be able to give up costume fitting. Rose rehearsed her lines constantly. Not only did Rose nail the audition, but also she was sensational. From that moment on Rose's parts became more substantive and essential to the play.

During Rose's new found opportunities in the theater, she began to date Bill, the manager. Only there was one issue neither Rose or Bill could ignore, Bill was married. At first it was just simple dinners after the show and Rose could see no harm as long as it was platonic. Gradually it became flowers before each opening, which lead to more and more attention from Bill.

Elizabeth and Ian went on with their own lives and allowed Rose her freedom. While Rose enjoyed her right to make her own life choices, she had no one to confide in. If she rejected Bill's attention her career could be at stake. If she went along with his advances, her acting parts might become bigger. So for the time Rose went along with the flow, resisting all forms of intimate contact. Unfortunately this was not enough for Bill. Bill often said to Rose,

"You don't care, you are just using me."

Rose consented to kissing but repeatedly told Bill,

"It will never amount to anything, you are married."

With the relationship she found herself involved in, Rose increasingly became unhappy. Rose trapped in a web unable to free herself.

One night during a play, Rose locked eyes with a rugged looking man. At the time Rose thought little of it. Slowly, Rose realized the stranger was in the audiences nightly, always in the same seat staring at her. One night the stranger appeared back stage, Rose was confused because Bill was in her dressing room. As the stranger approached he stated,

"You are a wonderful actress. You have the ability to make your character appear real."

During the man's visit, Rose simply thanked her admirer.

The next night her admirer was back again only this time he introduced himself as Edmund Wright. Rose felt more at ease speaking with the stranger because Bill was away. After the exchange of innocent pleasantries, Mr. Wright left. Rose thought no more of Edmund Wright.

Mr. Wright became a nightly visitor. Once before a new play he sent flowers. Rose found herself smitten with Mr. Wright. Mr. Wright asked if he may escort Rose home. On the first date Edmund told Rose about himself.

He said,

"I was born in New York City and am thirty years old. My parents were immigrants from Wales. For two years, I lived in Wales trying to trace my roots. While in Wales, I met a woman and married. We had a healthy baby boy, but within two days my wife was dead. I've an older Aunt Kitty; she moved in to help me take care of the baby. When my son was two, we all moved to New York City including Aunt Kitty. My son's name is Edmund Jr.. By the way do you think you could call me Edmund and I call you Rose?"

Through Edmund's words, Rose sensed his sorrow. Continuing,

"I also have two brothers, Albert who lives in Albany and Patrick who moved west and I haven't heard from since. I worked as a demolition contractor and make a good living."

As the two dated more frequently, Rose began to share with Edmund parts of her life. She explained to Edmund how her parents left Ireland and relocated in New York City as his parents had. Rose told Edmund she was the baby of her family and out of her many brothers and sisters she was the only Dunniff child born in the United States. Rose also shared how close she had always been with her mother. Rose found it difficult to describe how painful it was to watch her mother die of a broken heart after her father passed away. Rose decided to spare Edmund from the abandoned relationship she had with her father. Rose couldn't share with anyone the rejection she received from her father. For Rose that rejection was too painful.

After sharing each other's stories their relationship intensified. Rose finally broke things off with Bill. It had not been difficult because another beautiful actress came along; therefore Bill lost interest in Rose. And, her career did not come to an end.

Rose began seeing Edmund a couple times a week. She was noticing more and more about him. Edmund had piercing blue eyes, a straight nose and a chiseled jaw. Neither tall nor short, he was built like a bull. The only flaw was Edmund was almost bald, what little hair he had was bright red. They made a handsome couple with their contrasting features, Rose was willowy with curly auburn hair and Edmund with his husky good looks. When they walked down the street Edmund hooked Rose's arm in his and strutted like a peacock. What Rose liked the most about Edmund was his sense of humor. He loved to laugh and make her laugh.

Gradually their dates became more than an escort home. Edmund and Rose took walks in the park and sometimes Edmund took Rose to different theaters to see plays. Rose thoroughly enjoyed seeing other performances. Her dreams were still of acting. When she thought of a serious relationship she never excluded acting.

Elizabeth and Ian were delighted that Rose had someone courting her. They encouraged Rose to invite Edmund for Sunday dinners. Neither seemed to mind that Edmund was a widower with a young child. Nor were Elizabeth and Ian concerned with the age difference. In reality they wanted Rose out of the house. Rose was very much aware of their feelings and was beginning to think it would not be a bad idea.

After their first kiss, Edmund said to Rose,

"I am getting serious and want you to date only me."

Rose had many admirers, but something about Edmund made her heart flutter. She found herself thinking of him often and being disappointed when he was not in the audience. As the kisses became more passionate Rose began thinking of a family.

After about six months of courtship Edmund asked Rose to sit on a park bench.

"Rose I love you very much. Will you marry me and be a mother to my son?"

Rose immediately said, "Yes".

Edmund presented her with a beautiful yellow diamond ring. Rose was speechless. Never had she seen such magnificent ring. He also assured her she would not have to give up her acting career.

Subsequently, Rose met Edmund Jr. and was enchanted with him. The feeling seemed to be mutual. Edmund Jr. resembled his father in his build. Otherwise he was blond with big brown eyes. The little boy obviously adored his father and he was the center of Edmund's world.

Meeting Aunt Kitty made Rose the most anxious. After all, Aunt Kitty had been the woman of the house and Rose was not sure how she would like an intruder. Rose's fears were unfounded; Aunt Kitty was taken with Rose and would prove a great asset in the future.

On a cold crisp sunny day in December, Rose and Edmund were wed. Rose had just turned twenty and Edmund was thirty-one. The year was 1899.

FOUR

T he wedding was held in the rectory of St. Gregory's Catholic Church. After her mother's death, Rose never wavered from her faith. Edmund was not Catholic, although he agreed to raise their future children as Catholics. Rose looked beautiful in a simple green suit. Rose thought Edmund was handsome in his new suit. Rose and Edmund did not have the means to hold a large reception; therefore, they had a nice dinner at Elizabeth and Ian's home. Albert was Edmund's best man and Martha was Rose's matron of honor. Aunt Kitty and Edmund Jr. were also in attendance with Edmund Jr. stealing the show.

After the reception, the bride and groom boarded a train for Albany with their final destination being Niagara Falls. On the train ride to Albany, Edmund noticed a change in Rose. She seemed nervous and was babbling about nothing significant.

Edmund finally said,

"Rose what is wrong?"

Rose hesitated then confessed to Edmund what was bothering her.

"Edmund, as you know I am an actress and actresses do not have a reputation for high morals. The truth is I have never been with a man. Sure I have heard a lot of stories, but what if I displease you?"

Edmund laughed, hugged Rose and said,

"Don't worry my love, we will teach each other everything we need to know about making both of us happy. Trust me, it will be the beginning of a wonderful experience for both of us."

Rose smiled and knew immediately how lucky she was to find a man like Edmund. That night in their hotel room Edmund was true to his word. Not only did he show Rose how to explore his body, but also he pleasured her in ways that were deeply exciting. More importantly, he told her how wonderful she was and how much he loved her.

By the time they reach Niagara Falls, the scenic wonder of the falls no longer interested them. They wanted to be alone, make love and explore with all the fire and passion that they possessed. Although they wanted to remain in their room, they did manage to slip out to see the massive falls during their five-day honeymoon. However, the majority of their time was devoted to getting to know each other, physically, emotionally and psychologically.

On the day of their return to New York City there appeared to be some sadness. Rose did not want the spell of the previous five days, their honeymoon to end. Reality scared Rose because she would be moving in with Edmund, Edmund Jr. and Aunt Kitty. The thought of her future seemed a bit intimidating. Could Rose be successful in her new roles as wife and mother while continuing to become a successful actress?

The day of their return Rose began rehearsing for a new play. Did Edmund really mean what he said about her acting?

"He would not interfere with her career."

Rose was questioning herself now. Did she want the career she loved so dearly, or did she want to be Edmund's wife? Did Edmund need a wife who attend to the house, master cooking, and take care of Edmund Jr. and their future children? Many children were to come and fill their house, hearts and lives. Rose found herself in tears as she held the script wondering what she would do.

The brownstone where Edmund and Rose resided was in Harlem. It was far more impressive than any other place Rose had known. The new home consisted of three bedrooms, a parlor, dining room, and the kitchen. But the one part that really impressed Rose was the bathroom, located inside the home with the toilet, sink, and a huge bathtub. Rose smiled and thought if only mother could see me now. Sometimes, Rose wished her mother lived with them rather than Aunt Kitty. It wasn't that Rose disliked Aunt Kitty, it was because Rose ached for her mother. Plus, Matilda having six children of her own, would have been a great help when the time came for Rose to have children. Matilda would have taught Rose the love of motherhood like no one else could have understood.

Married life was blissful for Rose and Edmund. Edmund's business was thriving and Rose's acting career seemed to be heading toward the big time. Both were very happy with each other. One night after eight months of marriage, Edmund and Rose were relaxing in the parlor.

"Edmund I would like to ask you a question but it feels a bit embarrassing. Actually, I probably should ask one of my sisters."

"What is it Rose, you should never be embarrassed to ask me anything?"

"Why haven't we gotten pregnant yet? Does it have to do with you never completing the act inside me?" asked Rose.

"Well" said Edmund,

"You're right. I never finish lovemaking inside you so you won't become pregnant. I didn't know you wanted a baby. It would mean giving up your career at least for a couple of years."

"Edmund, my love, promise me to always plant your seeds within me and let things happen as they will."

Edmund gave Rose a devilish smile and replied,

"Then I'll start tonight".

Rose giggled and retired to the privacy of their bedroom.

Soon after their conversation, Rose announced she was pregnant. Edmund insisted she take a leave from theater. Edmund was very solicitous. He insisted that Rose live healthier than she had been while working. They took frequent walks in the park and Edmund monitored what she ate. Rose often wondered if Edmund's over protectiveness for her and the baby was due to the tragedy of Edmund's first wife. So, Rose went along with his protective behavior. Upon learning Rose was pregnant, Edmund pressured Rose to see a doctor, but Rose wanted a midwife. Her mother used a midwife, but in this day and age more women were turning to doctors for childbirth. Although Rose's feelings about doctors were opposite to Edmund, she made an appointment with Dr. Hansen solely to pacify Edmund. Rose was quite embarrassed when Dr. Hansen examined her. Edmund had been the only man to see her naked. Dr. Hansen's demeanor and kindness put her at ease. After the examination, Dr. Hansen told Rose she should have no difficulty delivering a healthy baby. Rose decided to agree with Edmund and Dr. Hansen would deliver their baby.

The pregnancy was unremarkable. Rose felt wonderful until the seventh month. By then Rose was getting huge. She had she gained forty-five pounds throughout the previous six months. As time went by, simply things such as sitting, tying her shoes, or walking any distance were becoming difficult. A week before her delivery date, Edmund decided he would stay home until she gave birth. He loved Rose so much he wanted nothing to go wrong. Two days prior to her due date, Rose's water broke. Edmund immediately called for the doctor. Rose laughed because the contractions were mild. When Dr. Hansen first arrived, he expected it would be at least eight hours before Rose gave birth. Subsequently, Dr. Hansen examined Rose, changing his mind stating the baby would arrive within an hour or two. Rose was lucky because the delivery went smoothly, especially since this was her first child. When Dr. Hansen told her to push, Rose pushed twice and all of a sudden appeared a healthy, crying baby boy with bright red hair. Upon hearing the crying, Edmund rushed into the bedroom. Rose held their baby and then proudly held him up for Edmund to see. Although Edmund was thrilled with his son, he was still concerned for Rose. Edmund questioned Dr. Hansen thoroughly until he was satisfied Rose would be fine.

For Rose everything seemed easy. The delivery was easy. Then nursing and motherhood seemed instinctive for Rose. Rose decided being a mother greatly out weighed her acting career, which made everything worth it. Edmund and Rose chose the name Joseph for their first son. Joseph was a happy, content baby. Rose had concerns because he was not a pudgy baby, he was long and thin, and in her mind healthy babies were chubby. Taking him for walks delighted Rose. She thought he was the most adorable baby in Harlem. Each Sunday, Edmund would join his family on walks. Even though Edmund already had a son, he could not have been happier with Joseph. Joseph had clear blue eyes that seemed to laugh when he looked at his parents. Life was good and Rose often thanked God for her family and everything she had been given.

It was four years before Rose got pregnant again. They wondered why it took so long for Rose to conceive again, but no one had the answers. During those four years Rose and Edmund's love intensified for each other and their little family brought them great joy.

In 1902, Rose and Edmund were blessed with Adam who neither resembled Rose or Edmund nor anyone from either family. Adam had dark hair and dark eyes. He had a face that was always changing expressions. His birth was easy like with Joseph. Rose and Edmund consider themselves blessed. Adam was a good baby who also brought much happiness to their lives.

For the next couple of years, Rose and Edmund enjoyed in the delight their growing family provided them. Edmund Jr. was so gentle with his younger brothers. He often enjoyed playing with Joseph. Rose loved hearing them play and how their laughter traveled through the house.

During the spring of 1905, Rose was going through her third comfortable pregnancy. By the fall she experienced a smooth delivery. The third baby was also a boy. Rose was a little disappointed, although she would never admit it aloud, she had hoped for a little girl. However, she loved her baby boy. Edmund was thrilled with their new son, but there was one dilemma. What to name this baby. Rose had a brother William and liked Billy. Edmund had other names in mind. He wanted Edward, to be called Eddie. Rose did consent after awhile. Eddie was also born with red hair, but instead of being a placid baby like his brothers, Eddie had a fiery disposition. He not only got frustrated easily, but would scream rather than of cry. Eddie was difficult to calm and demanded a lot of attention. With Eddie, Rose was so grateful to have Aunt Kitty's help. Aunt Kitty looked after the older boys while Rose spent her time caring for fussy Eddie. Once Eddie became a year old and could walk, his temperament changed and he became one of the clan. Rose and Edmund were so proud of their family.

Four years went by before their next baby, Walter, was born. Walter chose a sweltering day in the summer of 1909 to make his presence known. He was a small baby with auburn curly hair, resembling Rose. Rose and Edmund were very happy with their latest addition to their family, but this made five boys including Edmund Jr. Although Rose was not Edmund Jr.'s biological mother, Rose never thought of him as someone else's son, he was always hers. She was honored when he called her mother.

Rose said to Edmund,

"Wouldn't it be nice to have a girl for a change?"

Very seriously Edmund told his wife,

"All I want is for you and the children to be healthy."

Shortly after the birth of Walter, Rose became pregnant for the fifth time. Rose was not as exuberant with this pregnancy. Every day she thanked God for Aunt Kitty. Rose doubted she could have managed a house full of boys without her.

December of 1910, as if to reward Rose for her hectic life, God blessed Rose and Edmund with a tiny baby girl. She looked so dainty and frail compared to her brothers. Her cry was weak and Rose and Edmund were worried. They christened their baby Kathryn. Kathryn inherited her father's red hair and had startling grey eyes.

As soon as Kathryn was strong enough, Rose and Edmund took her to the doctor. They explained Kathryn's health issues to the doctor. Very gently he examined Kathryn. When he was listening to her heart his facial expressions changed. Rose squeezed Edmund's hand. The doctor completed the examination of Kathryn. He was very somber with his diagnosis. Compassionately, he told Rose and Edmund,

"I am sorry to have to tell you, but your little girl was born with a serious heart condition. I wish I had you positive news for you, but nothing can be done. Try not to let Kathryn cry or get overly excited because it will put a strain on her heart."

Rose was devastated and could not speak. Edmund asked the most difficult question,

"Will she die?"

"Yes, she could live a year, but I can't be sure. You may bring her back as often as you like, the doctor responded.

On the way home Rose and Edmund were silent, each lost in their own thoughts. Kathryn was asleep when they reached their house, so they put her in her bassinet. The two just stared at her. How could such a beautiful baby be so sick?

In bed that night Rose and Edmund talked. They decided to treat her like their other children except for when she cried. Also, they were determined to make the most every day they had her.

Kathryn was slow in developing. It was four months before she smiled. What Kathryn lacked in physical development, she made up for mentally. She knew she didn't have to cry much to be fed or held. Everyone pampered her. Aunt Kitty adored Kathryn and would hold her for hours. Rose spent many nights rocking Kathryn. She was determined to prevent anything from straining Kathryn's little heart.

After five months, it became obvious Kathryn was becoming weaker. Her lips and finger nail beds had a bluish tint. Still, she seemed free of pain and was always smiling. During a visit with the doctor, he reassured Rose and Edmund that Kathryn would not suffer when the time came the doctor said,

"Kathryn would pass in her sleep,"

Rose spent most nights either holding her or sitting by her bassinet. Often Edmund would either join Rose or relieve her, encouraging her to try and sleep. Shortly after, on a night Kathryn was fussy, Edmund rocked her and sang to her. Quite suddenly, Kathryn gave a shutter and simply died. Edmund sat holding her for what seemed like hours, tears streaming down his face. Eventually Rose came in, took one look at Edmund and rushed to him taking Kathryn in her arms. Edmund relinquished the rocker and went into the kitchen.

Rose, Edmund, and their family buried Kathryn. Their grief was overwhelming. Though they were still in denial and mourning, Rose and Edmund had to pull themselves together so they could continue to care for their five sons.

FIVE

ife resumed as best as it could for Rose and Edmund. They
focused on their most important problem, their need for
more room. Instead of moving to a larger home in New
York, Edmund wanted to make a geographic change. His brother
Albert, also a building contractor, lived in Albany. Albert strongly
encouraged Edmund to relocate his family and join Albert in the
construction business. Albert was sure that the two brothers would
have a thriving business in Albany. Edmund talked to Rose. Rose
was hesitant because New York City was the only home she had ever
known. She was not sure of making such a drastic change. Edmund
tried to reassure Rose about relocating. Edmund entice Rose with the
idea of buying a new home.

Edmund told Rose of a magnificent home. It has five bedrooms
in an area of Albany called Pine Hills. This is where Edmund and
Albert would be building homes.

Rose finally, with slight fear, agreed. In June Edmund moved his
wife, five sons, and Aunt Kitty to Albany. By now Aunt Kitty was in
her 80s and slowing down. Nevertheless, she was part of the family
and was dearly loved.

When they arrived at their new house Rose said,

"Oh my goodness this is magnificent."

She was in awe of what laid before her eyes. This new city did
not resemble New York City. There were trees everywhere, fields
surrounding homes and wide streets. As Rose saw the house, it took
her breath away. Their new home was white with yellow shutters.
There were two floors besides an attic and a cellar. The first floor

consisted of the parlor with the brick fireplace. Pocket door separated the parlor from the dining room. Rose was very pleased with the large kitchen. In the kitchen was a new icebox, coal burning stove and a breakfast nook. Off the kitchen was a porch, almost the same size as the kitchen. From the porch was a clothesline attached to a pole in the large yard. Rose thought how ideal for huge loads of wash. On the second floor there were three bedrooms, all good size, but the master bedroom was enormous. There was a bathroom between the bedrooms. This bathroom was grander than the one they had in Harlem. Edmund built two very large bedrooms and another bathroom in the attic. He thought Edmund Jr., Joseph, and Adam could sleep up there. What really took Rose's breath away was the backyard. It was so easy imagining her children playing in such a space. There was a large maple tree perfect for a swing. The only drawback with the backyard was it was nothing but dirt. Edmund sensing some dismay said,

"I promise there will be a lawn in no time and I will buy you flowers so you can plant a garden."

The Wright family settled in Albany with little trouble. Eddie and Walter shared a bedroom on the second floor and Aunt Kitty had the remaining bedroom. Aunt Kitty's bedroom overlooked the street. Rose hired a man to wallpaper the parlor, the dining room, the master bedroom, and Aunt Kitty's bedroom. The wallpaper for the rooms was all different floral prints. Rose purchased a rocking chair for Aunt Kitty, who really was appreciative. Edmund and Rose felt it was the least they could do for Aunt Kitty who was so instrumental in their lives. Not only was Aunt Kitty Edmund's aunt, she became a surrogate mother to Rose and a grandmother to the boys. The Wright household would be very different if Aunt Kitty had not been a part of their lives.

Rose came to the conclusion that Edmund's choice of moving to Albany had been wise. Just as Albert predicted, the construction business was booming. Edmund made a large profit when he sold his business in New York City. Edmund used the profits from selling his business in New York City to purchase the Albany home free and clear. With the money he had left, he used for necessities the family needed.

The years in Albany flew by. The older children had begun school and Rose was delighted keeping house and tending her family. To Rose's surprise, the longer she lived in Albany the less she missed the city, her friends, and her acting career.

Things began to change in 1913. First, Rose was pregnant again and feeling sick. This pregnancy was different from her other pregnancies. Rose spent most afternoons resting, unlike with the other pregnancies, Aunt Kitty wasn't able to help Rose as she had in the past. Aunt Kitty was becoming weaker and weaker as the days passed.

Much against Rose's protest, Edmund hired a woman to come in daily to help Rose with the housework, cooking and the boys. Her name was Gertrude; she was twenty-six years old, a large strapping girl who proved to be a great help to Rose and the family.

Like her other pregnancies, Rose was under the care of a doctor. The difference though was this doctor specialized in delivering babies. Due to Rose's previous pregnancies he continually tried to reassure Rose and Edmund the baby would be fine. He was right. On May 2, 1913 after two hours of labor a beautiful baby with auburn hair and green—blue eyes was born. Rose and Edmund named him Johnny because Rose thought he looked like a Johnny. As with the others, Rose and Edmund were thrilled with the newest member of their family.

During July, in 1913, Albert and Edmund's business began to slow down. They were a small construction company that sustained a comfortable income for the both of them. At first, they were puzzled with what was happening to their business. Albert and Edmund had a fine reputation, but they could not compete with the larger construction companies when bidding for new jobs. Edmund was determined to tough it out as long as he could provide for his family.

Over time, Edmund saved a large sum of money. After talking to some business associates, Edmund invested in the real estate market. He bought three old brownstones in south Albany and renovated each. He was told if he was selective in choosing tenants, he could rent them for a nice price. This distracted Edmund from the reality of his constructive business.

In the spring of 1914, the handwriting was on the wall. Finally, Edmund and Albert sold their business to a competitor, Conway contractors for a considerable amount of money. Edmund again invested his profits in real estate. He chose the New Scotland Ave. area of Albany. After the sale of their company, Edmund and Albert went to work for Conway construction. Edmund now had set hours. The headaches of owning a business were gone. Edmund was able to effectively work for Mr. Conway and maintain his real estate investments. Edmund seemed happier because he had more time to spend with his family. Daily life for Rose went a long pretty much the same.

By October of 1914, Rose found herself pregnant again. Although she was getting older, this pregnancy was easier than the last. As with all the other pregnancies, Edmund was pleased.

Rose did say to Edmund,

"This time I promise it will be another boy!" and laughed.

This seemed to be a likely prediction. Low and behold, on February 2, 1915 an infant boy was born. Rose and Edmund were dumbfounded when deciding what to name their newest addition. The family names had been used. With much haggling and with the help of the rest of the family, the family decided upon Harry. Harry was a happy, content baby who was always smiling.

After the birth of Harry, Aunt Kitty's health began to fail. On July 4, 1915, Aunt Kitty passed away in her sleep. Edmund was upset and mourned her death. Aunt Kitty had been part of his life for over twenty-five years, she had been with him through the tough times, and especially when he lost his first wife in Wales. Aunt Kitty came with Edmund leaving her family behind in Wales. Not only had Aunt Kitty been a tremendous help to Edmund but after he married Rose, she had been a saint to Rose and the family.

When it came time to burying Aunt Kitty, Edmund bought a burial plot. He also bought an area with 10 plots for Rose, their children and Edmund. Rose and Edmund knew they had to have Kathryn exhumed and buried in the family plot.

Rose loved living in Albany, but felt isolated from her siblings. Her family remained in New York City due to their commitments. Every couple of years, the Wright family would take a trip to New York City to visit Rose's family. During one of Martha's visits to Albany, she and her husband fell in love with the city.

Rose and Martha wrote many letters discussing the possibility of Martha and George moving to Albany. Martha loved Rose, Edmund and the boys. She and George had never had children and Martha often wish she could be closer to Rose and her nephews.

When George lost his job, as a tailor, Martha and George decided moved to Albany. By the summer of 1916, Martha and George moved into one of Edmund's brownstones on Dove Street. Edmund assured George he would help him find employment. Even though Edmund no longer had his own business, he still had connections with many influential people in Albany. After a few inquiries, Edmund procured employment for George in a new department store on Pearl Street. This store was in need of an expert tailor and George fit the bill.

Once again the Wright home was running smoothly. This didn't last long because Edmund and Albert lost their jobs. Conway construction was being investigated for illegal business practices and embezzlement. It was difficult for Edmund to find work. He put his cards on the table for Rose. Edmund always consulted Rose when major decisions were to be made. Edmund's objectives consisted of first listing their assets,

"I own land on New Scotland Avenue, the three brownstones on Dove Street, and our home in Pine Hills."

Next he listed his problems,

"No job and to arthritic to do manual labor anymore."

Possible decision Edmund said,

"Sell their present home, and move into the biggest brownstone he owned. Since the real estate market was strong, selling some of the property was a practical solution."

The discussion on went on for a week. At last Rose agreed with Edmund's plan. What made her acquiesce was the knowledge Martha would be next-door.

After the decision to move to Dove St, Edmund said to Rose,

"I'm going to take you for a ride around our new neighborhood."

He pointed out the park nearby for the children to play. Then they stopped at the empty brownstone and went in. On the first floor was a kitchen, with modern appliances, dining room, large parlor, and like her other home there was a large porch on the back of the house. The upstairs had three bedrooms with a beautiful bathroom. On the third floor there were three smaller bedrooms. The house also had a large unfinished attic. The cellar was damp and would be of little use.

After visiting their new home, Edmund took Rose for a surprise. There was a theater on North Pearl St., having a theater close by Rose felt the move could remind her of her life in New York City.

The move to Dove Street was uneventful. Edmund had been able to sell their home in Pine Hills for a large profit along with the land in New Scotland. The first thing Edmund did was buy a safe to store the money and important papers. Years earlier he had made a will leaving everything to Rose. He had heard of the difficulty some families had when the husband died and left the wife with many investments. Therefore, Edmund only saved his stock investments. The stock market was doing well and he hated selling his stocks now. Their new home was large enough to accommodate all the Wright children and their housekeeper Gertrude would be nearby. After much thought Rose suggested she take care of their children and the house. The older children always had chores and that was help for Rose.

Fortunately, Edmund found a job as a milkman. Although this job was hard physically he was grateful to get it. He worked long hours and his salary was a third of his Conway job. Edmund was satisfied because this job meant he could still support his family.

Edmund and Rose viewed themselves to be fortunate. They had a roof over their heads, food on the table, and seven healthy boys. More importantly they had love and passion for each other. Every day they professed their love for each other. The only difference was every time they made love they were careful to take precautions to avoid future pregnancies.

SIX

Things were progressing nicely. Between Edmund's job and the rent from the two brownstones, they were getting along financially.

In 1917, Martha's husband, George, was called to duty in World War 1. Family obligations required Edmund to provide Martha with a place to live rent-free. Edmund was pleased to help Martha however he did mind losing the income. Edmund felt bad that he was too old to enlist. So, ensuring Martha a place to live was Edmund's contribution to the cause. The war ended in 1918, George returned home, and the rent was resumed much to Edmund's relief. Raising a family on a milkman's salary was difficult.

During April 1918, the telltale signs of spring were all abound. It had been a mild winter with the promise of a warm spring and hot summer. Birds started singing early in the morning, the air smelled sweet, and the buds on the trees were beginning to swell. Rose and her family felt a sense of renewal. Everyone was enjoying the spring days while Rose began feeling ill. Most days Rose was only able to keep small amounts of food down and a moderate amount of liquids. Rose recalled the terminal illness of her father, Jeremiah. Edmund too was worried.

"Rose you are going to see the doctor!" Edmund insisted.

The doctor was very thorough in examining Rose. At the end of the exam he called Edmund in and talked to both of them. First, to put Rose's mind at ease the doctor assured Rose she was not terminally ill. But, what Rose had was serious and he suggested they see their obstetrician, Dr. Smith. The family doctor felt Rose was pregnant!

Both Edmund and Rose were shocked. They could not believe Rose was pregnant again. This made eight pregnancies.

"Oh Rose, we were so careful. I don't know what went wrong," Edmund said.

After the initial shock Rose cautioned,

"Wait until we see Dr. Smith".

It was unusual for a husband to go to the obstetrician with their wife, but Edmund always worried about Rose when she was pregnant, especially this time. The obstetrician, Dr. Smith, agreed that Rose was pregnant. Rose had concerns about this pregnancy but Edmund was happy just as he had been with all the other pregnancies.

Rose's nausea continued and occasionally she vomited. She attempted to eat small meals despite how sick she felt. At six-month, Rose started to feel better. Dr. Smith was pleased. She had gained weight and the color in her cheeks had returned. He assured Rose that the baby would be fine.

Early on January 4, 1919, Rose went into labor. This delivery was long and painful and Rose experienced heavy bleeding, much more than with her other babies. Dr. Smith said,

"If the bleeding does not lessen and/or Rose does not deliver soon I will have to hospitalize her."

Very few Cesarean Sections were done in 1919, but in emergencies an obstetrician would not hesitate. A sudden urge to push overwhelmed Rose. She was still bleeding, but delivery appeared eminent. At one o'clock on the dot a beautiful baby girl was born. She weighed 9 lbs. 2 oz. and the doctor laughed while declaring,

"The baby's size caused all the trouble."

Rose was beside herself.

"Edmund come here quick," Rose shouted.

The doctor was still delivering the afterbirth when Edmund shyly entered the room. He feared something was wrong. When he looked into Rose's arms and saw a beautiful vision he knew everything was fine. A baby girl, he was spellbound. Slowly, he put his arms around Rose and gave her a tender kiss. Next he took the baby from Rose and held her very gently. Edmund undid the blanket and checked his baby. She had all her toes and fingers. What little hair she had was curly and still wet, plastered on her head. Naturally her eyes were blue but not the dark blue of a newborn, but aqua blue. Long dark lashes surrounded her stunning eyes.

"Oh Rose, she is magnificent," whispered Edmund.

In the meantime, Dr. Smith was able to get the bleeding under control.

"Now listen carefully,"

Dr. Smith said, "No more babies."

"We won't our family is complete," Edmund replied. And, so it was.

Dr. Smith went on to explain to them that if Rose started bleeding heavily again he would have to remove her womb, uterus. This news concerned Edmund but for the now he tried not to focus on what Dr. Smith said, but to immerse himself with his new baby girl.

As days passed, Rose became stronger and bled very little. Baby girl, as the baby was called, was more alert. She had a strong cry and slept two to three hours at a time. Sometimes baby girl just wanted to be held and rocked. Martha and Edmund took turns rocking her. Edmund could not get enough of his baby girl. At the time of their daughter's birth, Edmund was fifty-seven and Rose was forty-six.

The problem facing Edmund and Rose was what to name their baby girl. They decided not to name her after a relative. Rose and Edmund thought she should have a name all her own. Finally, three weeks after baby girl's birth, she was christened Hannah Marie Wright, a pretty name for a pretty baby.

Hannah was smiling and goggling by the time she was two months old. Her brothers adored her. The boys as soon as they returned from school would run to wake up Hannah. Rose would say,

"You better not wake up Hannah."

The boys then argued over who would hold Hannah first. Rose was worried Hannah was becoming spoiled. Hannah was never allowed to cry, without someone picking her up. The brother most intrigued with Hannah was Harry, who was four and a half years old. He was not in school yet so he supervised all her care. He even watch Hannah's diapers being changed when they were soiled, which was more than could be said for the other brothers.

By 1919 Edmund Jr., was twenty-two and working as a laborer. Joseph was twenty and an apprentice machinist. Adam, sixteen, the one who looks like none of them, worked as a clerk in a grocery store. Eddie, who made them laugh, was fourteen. He was still in school and did odd jobs in the neighborhood. Walter ten and Johnny seven were still boys and aside from their daily chores, they went to school and played. The one that Rose and Edmund thought would be the youngest was Harry. Harry had been pampered and was known to throw a tantrum if he did not get his way. Then there was Hannah. Edmund and Rose were surprised from the start and when she was born.

Hannah was becoming such a good baby. She cried a little and laughed a lot. Also, Hannah began sleeping through the night. Rose was overjoyed. She was pleased that Hannah ate well and was a fat baby. The only concern Rose had in regards to Hannah was thumb sucking. Perhaps that's why she was so content.

In early April 1919, Rose took Hannah out for walks in her carriage. They walked to Lincoln Park, where they sat and enjoyed the sun. When Edmund accompanied them, he would talk to Hannah even though he knew she was too young understand. He loved to point out the various birds. Hannah often responded to her father in her own language. Rose and Edmund were so impressed with their baby girl's ability to try and communicate with them.

Where Hannah thrived was in communicating, however Hannah was slow to crawl and walk. She had little need to. Her brothers would fetch anything she needed. Rose commented how she never used baby babble with Hannah. Her brothers loved to teach her words, including at times, bad words. Throughout Harry remained her protector. Once Rose figured out why Hannah refused to crawl or walk she put an end the boys getting everything for Hannah. When Hannah wanted something she would point and say,

"Want."

Patiently she would wait. Eventually Hannah started to crawl, when she realized her brothers were no longer granting her wishes. Then one day, Edmund looked up, and saw Hannah shocking herself, by taking a step. Edmund later told Rose,

"Hannah crowed like a rooster."

From then on there was no stopping her. Slowly, everyone discovered Hannah was getting into everything. By now Hannah knew what "no" meant, but rarely obeyed when she heard the word. It seemed Rose was the only person able to discipline Hannah.

At eighteen months, Hannah's hair started to grow. It was very curly and so dark it almost appeared black. Adam was the only member of the family with hair as dark. He was so happy, he told them,

"At last I look like someone else, Hannah."

In the evenings, as Hannah grew older, Edmund and Hannah would sit on the stoop together. Lovingly he would tell her about the stars. Hannah loved this time with her father. While they gazed at the stars, Hannah would tell her father ridiculous stories to make him laugh. The bond between them was growing strong.

Martha was becoming ever present in Hannah's life also. She loved to read to Hannah. Martha would read Hannah nursery rhymes and poetry. Like Matilda, Martha and Rose's mother, Martha loved poetry. She hoped to share that bond with Hannah one day. When Hannah was three, Martha's husband George, died of lung cancer. Hannah saw little of Martha after George's death. Without George there no longer seemed a need for Martha to remain alone in the brownstone. She could not afford the rent and she had never worked. Therefore, the plausible answer was for Martha to move in with Rose and Edmund. With all the children, no one was sure which bedroom would be Martha's. After a brief discussion, Martha was thrilled to share a room with Hannah. Thus, began the intertwining of Martha and Hannah's life.

At forty-eight Rose went through a personality change. Edmund figured the irritability was because she was so busy taking care of their large family. The boys all had assigned chores to do but those were trivial tasks. The cooking, cleaning and laundry fell upon Rose's shoulders. Rose no longer felt it an honor to take care of her family; she considered it a curse. Martha looked after Hannah and helped with small things such as the mending, but she did little else to aid Rose. Eventually Rose's behavior became a serious problem.

Rose and Edmund's sex life had become non-existent since Hannah's birth. Edmund attributed this to Rose's fear of becoming pregnant again. He tried to talk to Rose only to be unsuccessful.

Edmund noticed Rose's demeanor with Hannah had also changed. If asked, Rose denied any problems and stated how much she loved her little girl. Slowly, Rose started to withdraw from the family. This was especially hard on Edmund and Hannah. If Hannah turned to her mother for comfort, Rose often shunned her and told her to seek out Martha. At times, Rose would yell at Hannah, causing the little girl to cry. Edmund noticed Rose seemed to care less and less, often yelling at everyone, accusing them of not loving her.

Finally, Edmund could stand no more and took Rose, practically by force, to the doctor. Edmund explained the circumstances while Rose kept trying to deny his statements. The doctor asked Rose,

"Are you still having your period?"

Rose wept. This had been her secret. Quietly, she shook her head no. The doctor turned to Rose and Edmund and explained how Rose was going to through the change. Although this would not be an easy time for everyone in the family, Edmund and the children would need to provide Rose with patience, love and help.

Upon their return from the doctor Edmund called a family meeting. He told the children,

"Everyone will help your mother without being asked!"

When the oldest questioned what was wrong with their mother, Edmund responded,

"Her body is tired from raising all of you and taking care of everyone needs, it is time we do the same for your mother."

Edmund turned to Martha asking her to assist with the housework and cooking. Martha was more than happy to help. Martha took her sister aside and explained she too had experienced the same symptoms, but only less intense. Martha leaned to Rose, gave her a sweet kiss on the cheek, and let her know she was there for her.

Edmund became distressed. How could afford to hire someone to help Rose. Money had always been tight, even though he owned three homes. He considered selling one of the brownstones, then decided against it. Edmund at sixty-one, knew he was aging, and was cursed with severe arthritis. He found it difficult to manage his milk route. Common sense told him, the day was soon approaching when he would have to retire. At that time, he might be forced to sell his homes. Edmund decided for now, he could only help Rose by holding her at night. He often expressed his love for her. When he tried to comfort Rose she seemed to relax often followed by tears.

As everyone tried to help Rose, she remembered what use to calm her in the past. Rose and Edmund invited Albert and his wife to dinner. Shortly after their guests' arrival, everyone was offered a cocktail. Edmund was taken back when they all replied they would enjoy a drink, including Rose.

Rose noted how the alcohol made her feel. She felt more relaxed and like her old self. Edmund noticed this slight change in Rose and subsequently offered her a drink each night prior to dinner. For those around her, the nightly cocktail was known as Rose's tonic; a habit she continued throughout the remainder of her life. Rose never exceeded more than one drink per evening mainly because deep in her heart she knew alcohol had caused the demise of her father.

SEVEN

H annah's first day in kindergarten was a joyous event. Rose outfitted her baby in her Sunday's best with a beautiful bow gathering her hair. Rose proudly walked with Hannah to school. At first, Hannah clung to her mother, but then Sister Paul took her hand and told Hannah,

"Your mother is leaving for awhile and then will return later."

Hannah understood. She didn't scream for her mother, as other children did, but let a few tears fall as she watched her mother leave.

Rose was pleased Hannah adored being with the nuns. Hannah constantly talked about them.

"Sister Richard said this." "Sister Vincent said that."

Hannah always believed everything the nuns told her. Like her mother, Hannah developed a strong Catholic faith. Rose always followed the teachings of the Church. In turn, she was determined her children would do the same. Surprisingly Edmund did too, although he never officially converted.

Hannah soon felt like her brothers attending school. Joyfully, she went off with Harry to school everyday. Edmund had taught Hannah to read and calculate simple arithmetic before she started school. Therefore Hannah was well ahead of her peers academically, finding the lessons easy. This never kept Hannah from enjoying school, often telling her parents she was going to be a nun and a teacher. Occasionally, Hannah would dress up like a nun, enfold her arms very piously, and teach. Begrudgingly, her brothers became her students. Hannah would mimic the nun especially when talking sternly to one of the boys. Unfortunately Harry was often cast as the disobedient student. Harry, a good-natured child, would go along with Hannah's role-play until the day she threatened him with a ruler. It was then Rose decided to step in explaining to Hannah,

"In our family no one gets hit by anyone or anything."

The most interesting and humorous time for Rose was Hannah's preparation prior to making her First Communion. Although Hannah was of the right age to make her First Communion, she lacked any concept of the holy event. One day Hannah came home from school asking her mother about mortal sin. Rose tried to explain such a difficult theory to such a young child. Rose began,

"Hannah you know when someone is acting badly?"

"Yes," Hannah replied. "It's when you stick your tongue out at someone."

"In some ways it is. Hannah, little ones usually commit small sins, such as forgetting to say their prayers or not minding their mother and father. Most children don't commit big sins and big sins are mortal sins."

With relief, Rose relaxed when Hannah seemed pleased with the explanation. Cheerfully Hannah replied she would be a saint because she would never sin. Rose chuckled to herself as Hannah walked away.

On the day of Hannah's First Communion, she was dressed all in white and looked radiant. The entire family was in the Church. During Mass, Rose whispered to Edmund,

"We have no more babies."

Both Rose and Edmund took a deep breath, proudly looked at Hannah then smiled at each of their boys.

Following Hannah's First Communion, Rose seemed to become more calm. She still remained a bit distant from her family, but was not given to fits of rage or crying. Hannah wanted her mother's attention, but most of the time was disappointed with Rose's lack of response. Thank goodness for Martha. She nurtured Hannah until Edmund came home. Edmund was very attentive to her. The more time Martha spent with Hannah, the more she fell in love with the little girl. Not having children of her own, Hannah became Martha's surrogate child. Knowing how touchy Rose could be, Martha was careful not to usurp Rose, taking over only when Rose wasn't able. Rose did not seem to be bothered or notice Martha's feelings for Hannah.

Hannah was very popular in school. Two of her friend's moved into her father's brownstones. One was Izzy Adler, whose parents immigrated from Russia. He loved baseball and taught Hannah how to play. Their favorite game was ledge ball. Hannah had a wicked throw. She would hit the stairs with such force the ball often flew over Izzy's head becoming a home run. They also played baseball in the vacant lot with the other neighborhood children. When Hannah and Izzy played baseball, she was the only girl. The neighborhood boys begrudgingly allowed her play, solely because of her brother Harry. When he played, he made sure Hannah was included. Every so often, while playing, a baseball hit Hannah in the eye. Edmund was concerned every time Hannah came home with a swollen, black eye. He finally had enough and refused to allow Hannah to play baseball. Fortunately, she was permitted to play ledge ball with Izzy. Hannah remained the neighborhood tomboy, with much encouragement from her brothers.

The second friend of Hannah's was Margaret Palmer. Her house was next to Hannah's. Unlike Hannah's house, where there was one family living, Margaret's brownstone was designed for three families. The Palmer's resided on the top floor. During the summer months it often felt like a furnace at Margaret's. When it became really hot Margaret and her family sat on the stoop, along with Hannah and Martha. Rather than play sports, Margaret and Hannah liked to play was house. Margaret would pretend to be the mother and Hannah the father. They used their dolls as children. If Margaret was in good humor, she would play school. Without any arguments Hannah was always the teacher. Some times Izzy would play with the girls. He absolutely refused to play house; Hannah would never let him be the father. Of the three friends, Hannah often dominated the others.

Margaret and Hannah were two beautiful little girls who enjoyed many of the same things. There appeared to be one difference the two could not agree on, how little girls should look. Margaret was conscious of her appearance. She liked to wear dresses and curls in her hair. Hannah was the opposite. She begged her mother to wear pants. Hannah wanted to dress like the boys. Rose would not give into Hannah. Hannah often pleaded, but Rose remained steadfast. Rose felt the least she could do was remind her daughter she was a girl; little girls wore dresses. Hannah knew when she was defeated.

By the time Hannah was nine, Edmund had made decisions affecting their lives in the years to come. Edmund's arthritis was crippling him. He could barely pick up a glass without experiencing extreme pain. His doctor recommended he take aspirin, but the time had come when aspirin did not ease the pain. Thus, Edmund was forced to retire. Edmund worried how he would support his family. He always had been frugal, which allowed him to save some money over the years. Edmund knew he had not saved nearly enough though. He determined there was enough money to last a year. The brothers were providing their share for household expenses, but for Edmund their part was not sufficient. Edmund Jr. worked in elevator construction. Joseph was a machinist. Adam became a newspaper reporter, Eddie was a laborer and Walter worked as a laundry helper. Edmund after much thought, decided the market seemed strong so he would sell the two brownstones. He turned to his brother for assurance and advice. Albert agreed it was an opportune time to sell and he recommended Edmund to invest the profits in the stock market. Edmund was uneasy with the market; therefore he put the money in his safe until he chose a financial strategy.

Edmund learned quickly, once he retired, to stay out of Rose's hair. He became more active in Hannah's life. His daily routine consisted of reading the paper and smoking cigars. Edmund did decide the home was lacking an essential, a radio. Although he did not like to waste money on needless expenses, he thought everyone would enjoy the entertainment. Rose and Hannah were delighted. Thus, Edmund knew his money was well spent.

EIGHT

I n 1928 the country was calm. However in the Wright household, there were changes. Hannah grew out of being a tomboy and blossomed into shy, young girl. Her health was a concern for Rose and Edmund. Hannah was often sick with chest ailments. When Hannah got sick the whole house became chaotic. Rose was very protective of Hannah. Rose worried because the boys were rarely sick and if one became ill it was always minor. Hannah was different. She ran high fevers and coughed until it hurt. Rose tried mustard plasters on her chest and rubbed her down with alcohol. Edmund thought to himself, he would always be concerned about his little girl no matter the circumstances. When Hannah was sick during the night, Martha always sat with her. She would tell Hannah about Ireland and her grandparents, Jeremiah, and Matilda. Martha usually made up most of what she told Hannah. If Martha could remember a tale, she often exaggerated.

Due to constant illnesses, Hannah's appearance changed. She continued growing tall and thin, instead of having a healthy glow, her skin appeared translucent. Throughout her hair remained thick, curly, and dark, and her aqua blue eyes were still striking. Hannah's overall appearance became unusual.

On Sundays, Hannah could be heard shouting to her father,

"Dad are we going to Uncle Albert's house?"

As always, her father would respond,

"Yes precious, at twelve o'clock."

The family would take the trolley to Albert's house in West Albany. Edmund had sold the car the year before. There Hannah would play with her cousins and enjoy a fried chicken dinner. These were happy times for Hannah and her family.

Due to the frequencies of Hannah's illnesses, she had fallen behind in her schoolwork. In turn, this led to a blasé attitude regarding school. Also because her health required her to remain home, Hannah enjoyed listening to the radio. Amos n' Andy program was her favorite. Hannah could be heard laughing throughout the house. Edmund enjoyed the radio as well. He favored listening to the orchestras preforming the classics. Perhaps the biggest fan of the radio was Rose. She would listen intently to the dramas, close her eyes, and pretend she was back on the stage. She knew she would always remain an actress in her heart.

Hannah turned ten in 1929. This was a very important birthday for Hannah; she would never have a one-digit age again. Following Hannah's birthday, Edmund made a financial decision. In March he decided exactly what to do with the proceeds from the sale of the brownstones. Edmund divided the money, half deposited in the bank and the other half remained in the home safe. Although Edmund was uneasy with his choice, he decided he made the best financial maneuver.

April of 1929, a surprise came to their house. A strange man in peculiar clothes arrived asking for Edmund. Rose was about to tell the stranger to leave when Edmund appeared behind her. At first, Edmund did not recognize the man. Upon closer inspection, he sensed a family resemblance. Feeling awkward, the stranger spoke,

"I'm Patrick, Edmund".

Edmund was shocked and overwhelmed. He pulled his brother in and giving him a bear hug. Patrick was invited into the home. Before Edmund introduced Patrick to the family, he brought Patrick into the parlor. As much as Edmund loved his brother, he was a little suspicious by the unannounced visit.

"So Patrick, how long has it been, forty years? I remember you left suddenly, without so much as a goodbye."

Patrick's hesitation provided Edmund the opportunity to take in Patrick's appearance. He had a handlebar mustache, funny looking shirt, and vest. Patrick's wide belt and tight pants confused Edmund.

What Edmund found the strangest part of his brother outfit were Patrick's boots. They were different from any others Edmund could think of, these had heels and pointed toes.

Edmund thought Patrick looked like an overgrown cowboy. Startling Edmund, Patrick finally said,

"I'm sorry I left so suddenly. Let's just say the demons were after me. It was important that I tell no one I was leaving or where I was headed. You can probably tell from my attire I headed west. I bought a ranch, married, and had a family. After many successful years I lost everything. My wife, my children, and the ranch are gone. I realized the only family I had were you and Albert. I knew Albert was in Albany and naturally looked him up first. He told me how to find you, so here I am. You may not be happy to see me, but Edmund I'm thrilled to see you."

Edmund and Patrick remained secluded, until dinner, catching up on their lives. Patrick was not aware Edmund once lived in Wales. Patrick was introduced to all during dinner and everyone took a liking to him. When Edmund and Patrick returned to the parlor, Edmund found out the reason for Patrick's unannounced visit.

"Patrick it's not that I am unhappy to see you, but I get the impression your sudden visit was for a reason."

"You always were perceptive Edmund, you're right. Albert told me you might have some money to invest. It so happens, I might have the investment for you."

Edmund immediately had doubts. At the same time, Edmund was furious that with Albert. How could Albert have betrayed him so easily?

"I will listen Patrick with the understanding I will not agree to anything."

"As I was saying I have an investment that has the potential to make us very wealthy. It does entail some risk, I won't lie to you Edmund."

Silence loomed as Edmund thought. Edmund was hesitant because he wondered how Patrick lost his ranch and family.

"Patrick before you tell me your scheme, I'd like to know more about why you lost everything, especially your family."

Patrick knew Edmund would ask this question, but he was determined Edmund would never find out.

"What happened to me has nothing to do with here and now," said Patrick.

"Patrick, I don't know anything about you. Haven't laid eyes on you in decades, you show up at my door and expect me to invest with you. I think I'll pass on your idea, infact I'd rather not hear the details. My main concern is the well being of my family. As I told you, I am no longer working and I need to be very careful in choosing investments. Losing it is not an option," Edmund fumed.

"Well brother, if that's how you feel perhaps, I should be on my way. Just for your information, Albert was interested," said Patrick.

Edmund couldn't resist asking Patrick,

"How much are you investing?"

"Well as I told you, I am down on my luck, so I thought I would manage everything." Patrick replied.

"Sorry Patrick, but the answer is thank you, but no."

With that, Patrick left without saying goodbye to the family. Edmund felt bad, but he knew this would be a regretful mistake. Edmund shortly after, appreciated how wise his decision had been.

The summer of 1929 was very hot and humid. Windows were always open, but still everyone suffered. Thank goodness September brought great relief. Hannah enjoyed her summer vacation. Mainly she read and played cards with Martha. Martha was becoming more of her mother than an aunt for Hannah. Martha introduced Hannah to the library. Hannah boasted she would read every book in the fiction section.

Each day Hannah seemed to be healthier, but she was still troubled. Hannah would spend time with Martha rather than go out with her friends. It was almost if she was afraid of something. September and the return to school were not greeted with great enthusiasm. During, school Hannah daydreamed which forced a nudge by her teachers to remain on task. Rose and Edmund talked to her, but Hannah's downward spiral continued. The only class Hannah excelled in was English, especially writing. In other subjects, Hannah did just enough to pass.

Edmund began to act strangely since the visit from Patrick. October 24, Edmund decided to withdraw all his money from the bank. He told Rose he had a premonition something was going to happen and wanted all the money in his safe.

NINE

Without warning on October 29, 1929 the Wright's world, as they knew it would change forever. Albert came and talked to Edmund. The stock market had crashed and Albert was broke. It appeared Albert had lost everything. Without hesitation Edmund insisted Albert and his wife move in with them. Edmund thought back to Patrick's visit and was thankful he had not invested. He often wondered how Patrick was doing. Edmund knew Patrick would be fine; he was sure Patrick landed on his feet.

Naturally, things at the Wright home changed. Even though there was money for food, many markets had gone out of business. In desperation, Rose tried to plant a garden. She had little experience gardening, compared to her mother Matilda. Matilda had splendid gardens in Ireland.

In the early years of the depression, the boys still lived at home. Edmund Jr. and Joseph had jobs, but their salaries had been cut. The others took odd jobs. All the boys, with the exception of Edmund Jr., gave their money to Rose. Edmund Jr. was engaged and would be marrying shortly therefore needed to save his money. After Edmund Jr. and his fiancée married, they needed a place to live. It was decided he would live with his in laws.

Money in the Wright household, as with other families, was scarce. Although Edmund had retrieved his money from the bank and kept it in the safe, he would take money when absolutely necessary. Rose had to make adjustments. Meat was served once a week, on Sundays. The family ate oatmeal twice a day. Lunches consisted of whatever could be scraped together. Clothes were patch, mended, and patch again. Hannah was growing very tall and hems could be let down just so much. Rose frequented church thrift shops that virtually gave away clothes. Hannah was not always gracious with the clothes her mother brought home. She particularly hated her winter coat. While throwing a tantrum, Edmund sat Hannah down, explained their financial circumstances.

Everyone was thankful for Martha. Somehow she was able to get yarn and knitted everyone warm sweaters, mittens and slipper booties. As winter grew closer, Martha was appreciated by all even more because without her talent for knitting, the frigid temperatures would have been difficult to survive. The price of fuel, along with everything else, was so high; Edmund made sure the heat was on only when necessary.

Due to their financial problems, Rose and Edmund were forced to remove Hannah from parochial school and place her in public school. Hannah was crushed with the change. All her friends attended parochial school. Hannah's only friend at the new school was Izzy Adler. Although they were close, he preferred to hang with the boys. Also at her old school, Hannah wore a uniform and in the public school the students were allowed to wear whatever their parents could afford. Hannah did like the teachers at her new school. She felt they did not get on one's case because of grades. The teachers seemed to wait until a student failed before contacting parents. Even though Hannah was smart, her grades remained in the 70's. Prior to changing schools, Rose and Edmund gave up trying to get Hannah to improve academically. They simply had too many other issues to be concerned with rather than constantly argue with Hannah.

Hannah made few friends at her school and always came directly home. Even though her father had spoken to her about the depression, Hannah kept to herself and was sheltered from the world. She knew money was always a problem. She also knew something horrible had happened to Uncle Albert.

Hannah was upset because Edmund Jr. left. This bothered her most of all because he was the first in the family to leave.

As withdrawn as Hannah was, she did notice little things, her father no longer smoked cigars and the radio was moved from the kitchen to the living room. Edmund, the older boys, and Albert constantly listened to the radio. It no longer played dramas or music, but world events. Often she heard a groan from the parlor. Slowly, Hannah became curious as to what was happening. She began to sit in with the group around the radio. When she was puzzled or did not understand what was happening, she kept her questions to herself. Edmund was not oblivious to Hannah's new interest and smiled when he saw her.

As times changed, so did Edmund. Mentally he was sharp, and physically he had deteriorated. His hands were painful and knotted. His hip and knee joints worked with great effort and pain. What little hair he had was white and he often had chest pain with exertion. Still his disposition remained cheery. Edmund would not complain when there were so many other, more important things to focus on. Just living day by day was an effort for Edmund. He was very aware that his chest pain was an ominous sign. He visited the doctor, without Rose's knowledge, and the doctor gave him little pills to take for the chest pain.

As the 1920s came to a close, everybody was optimistic that the New Year would alter their lives. Christmas had been bleak. Most of the gifts were from Martha's knitting. Hannah could not think of what to give her family. She had developed an interest in poetry. She decided to write a poem for her parents and Martha. She gave her father a poem on aging. Her mother, she wrote a poem about spring. Finally for Martha she wrote a poem about night and the fear of night. With each poem she hand decorated the edge of the paper with colored pencils. Rose, Edmund, and Martha were each very moved with Hannah's presents and treasured them until their deaths.

1930 came about with little change. Albert and the boys partitioned the attic from scrap lumber. Albert made a little apartment in the attic for him and his wife. Although they froze in the winter and roasted in the summer, they were happy. Heat continued to be a problem. Harry, Johnny, and Walter would go to the railroad yards, in West Albany, searching the tracks for coal that had fallen. Edmund still had contacts in the building industry and received odd pieces of wood for a nominal fee.

In the middle of 1930, a homeless drifter came to the back door. Rose always tried to give them something. Often the men did little jobs to help pay for their food. This particular day was different. When Rose opened the door she recognized the drifter.

"Rose" he said, "It is Patrick."

Warmly Rose welcomed Patrick in. Edmund was napping in his chair by the stove and Rose did not want to wake him. She also did not want Edmund to be shocked when he saw Patrick. Patrick had long greasy hair, a full beard, and tattered clothes. Rose ushered him into the dining room. She could not bear to have him in her parlor. They still had many fine pieces from their days in Pine Hills. Rose did not question Patrick, although retrieved the scissors and cut his hair. She then handed Patrick some of Edmund's clothes and steered him into the bathroom to bathe, shave, and discard his clothes. Patrick handed out his clothes to Rose and she promptly put them in the fire. She shuttered as she envisioned Patrick crawling with lice. Rose gave Patrick lye soap and instructed him to scrub himself from head to toe.

As Patrick emerged from the bathroom Edmund was waking. Rose gently told Edmund that Patrick had arrived. When Patrick entered the kitchen Edmund greeted him warmly. Rose gave him a big bowl of porridge with honey and a strong cup of tea. For a while no one said a word. Patrick ate his food with great relish. It had been two days since he had eaten. Sometimes he thought he would never arrive at Edmund's. Patrick felt if he could reach his brother, things would get better. Edmund asked Patrick to share his tale. This time however, Rose also remained listening while sipping her tea. Edmund knew he had to remain calm as he listened to Patrick. His chest pains were more frequent and he insisted on keeping this to himself. Patrick nervously began.

"Well, after I left, I went to Texas to chase my dream. I worked on the oilrigs until there was no more work. Next, I hitched a ride to Colorado in hopes of reuniting with my wife. There I found out she had divorced me and had moved on. My sons were grown and living in California according my wife, they too had washed their hands of me. It's time I'm honest with you, Edmund. I lost my family and my worldly goods due to drinking and gambling. There were many tough years for them. When I drank too much, I became a monster. After I realized what a bum I'd become I started jumping trains, heading east. During my travel, I met many people who were like me. It has taken me at least a month to reach Albany. I do not come with another rich scheme, but to beg shelter, until I can get on my feet."

As Edmund listened to Patrick, he realized Patrick had age too. Patrick had stained fingers from smoking, his eyes were dull, and his teeth rotten. His skin was covered with age spots and he was as thin as a rail. Yet Patrick was his brother.

"Well Patrick let me speak with Albert. He and his wife live here too."

The brownstone Edmund and Rose called home there was a kitchen, dining room, and a parlor on the first floor. The second floor had three bedrooms, one for Rose and Edmund, one for Hannah and Martha and one for Joseph and Adam. On the third floor there were three small bedrooms. One was Eddie and Walter's the other was Johnny and Harry's. The third bedroom had been Edmund Jr's, but was now used for storage. Conceivably there was a room for Patrick.

When Albert came home, he and Edmund retreated to the parlor. Edmund told Albert of Patrick's tale. Both agreed, he was blood and if they could they should help him. The brother's were in agreement about one other issue when it came to Patrick, they would help Patrick provided he did not drink or gamble. Having made up their minds, they called Rose for her opinion. Even though it meant more work for her, she was glad to open her heart and home to Patrick. Patrick was called to the parlor and given the decision.

"You are welcome to stay as long as you do not drink or gamble."

Patrick was so moved he started to cry. He understood if he drank or gambled he was out. Patrick moved into the little room on the third floor. Patrick already had a fan in his new home, Hannah.

TEN

By 1933, tension had subsided some in the Wright household. FDR was President and his administration was working on the New Deal. Although the men of the Wright family weren't lawyers or doctors, they were ambitious and hard working. Money was still tight but with his sons' contributions, Edmund found he was turning to his safe less often.

Patrick began to drink shortly after he moved in. True to his word, Edmund demanded Patrick to leave. Unfortunately, Patrick was never able to sober up, therefore became a homeless derelict. He could barely survive panhandling and relying on soup kitchens. As anyone would predict differently, Patrick did not survive long living on the streets. Over the winter, Patrick was found frozen to death in an abandoned car. He had identification and Edmund was contacted.

"Please come and claim the body of Patrick Wright."

Edmund, although not surprised, was disappointed with his brother. Still, Patrick was family; Edmund provided a proper burial.

Edmund Jr. moved home along with his wife Mary. He was working as a laborer for Local 106 on the Dunn Memorial Bridge. Edmund Jr. and Mary lived in what had been Patrick's room. The room was small, but this allowed them time to save money. Edmund insisted they pay room and board, which amounted to ten dollars a month.

A great occurrence took place when Eddie and Adam went to work for the Civilian Conservation Corps in 1933. Each was sending home twenty dollars a month. The rest of the boys worked when and where ever they could and continued to contribute to the support of the family. Compared to other families, Rose and Edmund's family remained together through the depression, except for the brief time Edmund Jr. moved out. The Wright's remained united. They cared for each other and made room for extended family.

One day, Edmund was sitting in the parlor letting his mind wander. For the past couple of weeks he was trying to figure out something special he could do for Rose. His heart began to skip beats and the pain could be overwhelming at times. He knew his days were limited, which urged him to do something for Rose. Out of nowhere it came to him. After her family, the one thing Rose loved the most was the theater. Now Edmund needed to figure out how to get them to the theater and back. He decided to ask Edmund Jr. to drive them. Edmund Jr. was more than willing. Edmund Jr. picked up the tickets and would drive Rose and Edmund. Edmund gave his son money for the tickets and gas. Over the years Edmund had watched his money very carefully. He still had quite a large sum. Now he was trying to preserve the remainder for Rose after he died. Still, surprising Rose with a trip to the theater was worth every penny. Martha agreed to help. On the day of the play, Martha managed to sneak into Rose's closet and take out her best dress. At five pm, Edmund said to Rose,

"Put on your favorite dress and be ready to go out at seven."

Rose was beside herself wondering what Edmund was up to.

"Edmund where are we going?"

"It's a surprise and that's all I can tell you," replied Edmund.

At seven pm Rose was eagerly ready.

"You look like my beautiful bride," Edmund said upon seeing Rose.

Edmund Jr. had the car ready and was in the parlor when Rose came down the stairs. He gave Rose a big hug. Out they headed in Edmund Jr.'s car. Rose was on eggshells not knowing where they were headed. As they approached the theater, Rose started to laugh. She gave Edmund's hand a squeeze and kissed him on the cheek. Edmund was so pleased with the night. When Edmund Jr. drove up to take them home Edmund was beaming.

"You do know I love you Edmund Wright," said Rose.

The night was a complete success and Edmund was free of any chest pain.

Hannah was beginning high school and for the first time loved school. Rose was so happy to see Hannah change from the shy introvert to a happy outgoing teenager once again. Hannah was beautiful and popular at school. She became somewhat vain and like her mother became enthralled with actors. Hannah loved makeup and Edmund was always telling her,

"Hannah you looked like a floozy, wash your face."

Hannah would laugh at her father and say,

"You have no idea what's popular".

Edmund was concerned with the word "popular". Edmund knew how a young lady should appear to others. Granted, he had rather Victorian style in mind, but Hannah paid little attention to this.

While in high school, Hannah's health was much better therefore she missed little school. Rose was surprised because providing healthy meals was still difficult. Regardless, there was color in Hannah's cheeks and her eyes sparkled.

Hannah started keeping a journal of her high school years. There was so much to write about. She wrote about her friends and teachers, pep rallies, and much more. She had her favorite teacher Miss Ryan.

Edmund was very strict with Hannah. She was limited as far as evening activities and especially dating boys. At fourteen he felt Hannah was too young. When he did relent, he made Harry go with her. Hannah complained bitterly, but went along with it. Harry never minded tagging along with Hannah and her friends thought Harry so sophisticated because he graduated from high school and worked for the local paper.

Edmund at the age of seventy-four was an old man and very infirmed. Any movement he attempted was made with pain. He suffered chest pain with exertion or emotional upset. A cough now plagued him. The doctor called it a heart cough.

Rose at fifty-four was tired. Menopause symptoms had abated, but worry had taken its place. Rose worried constantly about running the home, having enough food and clothing for the family. Most of all, she worried for Edmund. Rose's biggest job was to shield him from any tension. When they were younger, they had a very fulfilling and active sex life. Over the years, between Rose's troubles and Edmund's declining health, this had ceased. Their love and closeness had remained strong. Edmund was still her great love and Edmund felt the same for her. Perhaps the uniqueness of their relationship was they demonstrated and verbalized their feelings. Edmund still patted her on the backside when she went by and cuddled with her every night. Rarely, did they have a disagreement and if they did it was always settled quickly and fairly.

Rose and Edmund loved all their children, but Hannah was special. There wasn't any jealousy among the Wright children. In fact, they all still spoiled Hannah. Hannah was very close to her father. They enjoyed listening to the radio together. If Hannah had a question, it was Edmund she sought out. Hannah turned to him for help her with her homework. Although she was indifferent to her studies as a child, in high school, she wanted to excel for her father. Edmund was so proud of her. Hannah enjoyed sharing her poetry with him. She was talented and very proud of her writings. Edmund told her it was her Irish heritage. Although Edmund's health was declining, Hannah was oblivious to this. With his encouragement, Hannah entered her first poetry contest at school.

Hannah's poem was about aging, she hadn't realized it's meaning. She worked on it feverishly, often writing, tearing it up, writing again, correcting, and finally, it was just right. Timidly, she handed it to her English teacher crossing her fingers. Edmund was sure she would get first price. Anxiously, Hannah waited the outcome. The day arrived and the whole student body was assembled when the winners were announced. Later that day, Hannah came home in tears. She went directly to her father to tell him what happened.

"It's not fair. My poem was the best and I didn't even get honorable mention."

She sobbed to her father.

Hannah had not shown the poem to her father until now. Edmund's critique was kind and honest.

"Hannah did you read any of the winning poems?"

Hannah showed him the copies they had been given. Quietly, he read them. He concluded the others were uplifting, while Hannah's was sad and remorseful. Still, he thought her poem was excellent. As he praised her poem he pointed out to Hannah, the others were most likely chosen because of their tone rather than the quality of writing.

One day Hannah was walking home from school when a boy caught up to her and started talking. Hannah was glad to see it was Izzy Adler, her old friend. Gradually, they started walking home from school every day. No one thought any thing of this because he was Hannah's childhood friend. One day Izzy asked,

"Hannah would you like to go to the movies with me on a Saturday afternoon?"

Excited, Hannah asked her father. Edmund agreed as long as there was a group going. Hannah managed to gather a group to meet at the movies. Izzy came to pick her up and off they went. During the movie Izzy shyly took Hannah's hand. At first Hannah was startled, because they were always friends, but it was nice holding his hand. Occasionally, she would turn to him and smile. From then on, Izzy and Hannah often went to the movies, held hands and smiled at one another. The only one who realized something was occurring was Harry. Whenever Hannah returned from a movie, Edmund would ask about the movie and if she had a nice time.

In her junior year of high school, Edmund agreed to let Hannah go to a school dance with Izzy. He still thought of Izzy as a family friend and not a perspective boyfriend. Hannah thought differently about Izzy. Hannah was so excited; the dance was all she could think about. She was concerned,

"What will I wear?"

"Mother I needed a new dress and new shoes. Something special one would wear to a dance. "

Edmund Jr. surprised Hannah with a new dress. It was a pale yellow, Hannah's favorite color. The dress looked stunning on Hannah with her dark hair and pale complexion. Still, Hannah did not own dress shoes. Rose and Hannah wore the same size shoe. Rose had an idea. She had never disposed of her clothes from when she was acting. Rose had a specific pair of shoes in mind. Although it took Rose some time to find the shoes, when she did they were perfect. Hannah was thrilled. The shoes were gold with a little heel. Martha knit Hannah a fancy evening bag and she wore ribbons in her hair.

The day of the dance, Hannah fussed and primed all day, by evening, she was ready. Izzy arrived at six and was in awe by how beautiful Hannah looked. Rose and Edmund likewise admired their only daughter. The entire family gathered to see Hannah and Izzy off. Every aspect of the dance was magnificent! Hannah and Izzy danced to every song. Everyone was dressed in their finest attire. Soon the selection of King and Queen was made. Hannah held her breath. Everyone had told her how beautiful she looked so Hannah thought she should win. Izzy gave her a hug as the announcements were made. Even though she lost, Izzy told her she was the prettiest girl there. This seemed to appease Hannah and she managed to enjoy the remainder of the evening. Maybe it was the excitement of the evening, but Hannah knew she was crazy about Izzy. He had been infatuated with her for a long time. During the last dance of the night, Hannah experienced her first kiss. Later, she would describe it in her journal as divine.

After the dance Hannah and Izzy's life went back to normal. They would go to the movies and for walks. Sometimes Izzy would visit Hannah and they would sit in the parlor and talk. Changing in Hannah was her poetry. She wrote poems describing feelings of love without mentioning the word love. Hannah was talented at writing poems while Izzy wrote prose. Eventually, Rose became concerned. She observed them and realizing things between the teenagers seemed serious. Rose sat Hannah down for mother daughter talk.

"Hannah there is some thing I need to explain to you. First, as you know Izzy is Jewish. His family would probably not accept you because we are Catholic. Your father and I would like to see you start dating other boys. You realize Izzy graduates in June. He probably will go to work. We like Izzy, but can sense problems. Please trust us, think about what I have said."

Hannah did think about the conversation with her mother. On their very next visit, Hannah shared with Izzy her parent's concerns. Izzy looked at Hannah,

"I'm glad we have a chance to talk. In the fall I will be going to New York City to live with my uncle and his family. Shortly after, I will enroll in City College. Naturally, I will have a part-time job but for the most part my uncle will be supporting me. Apparently my uncle is a successful diamond broker."

Hannah was surprised. Things did appear to be changing. Her reliance on Izzy would come to an end. Neither spoke except for a few pleasantries then parted with a hug rather than a kiss.

The summer between Hannah's junior and senior year, she and Izzy spent most of their time together. They discussed their future. Izzy would be leaving in September, and Hannah had a surprise for him. She was knitting him gloves for the cold winters in the City. Martha was pleased with Hannah's skill at knitting. Finally, their last night together came. Like always they went to the movies and sat in the back. This time Izzy did not hold Hannah's hand but put his arm around her. As the movie played, Izzy would kiss the side of Hannah's face and stroke her hair. Just before the movie ended, Izzy pulled Hannah toward him and kissed her fully on the mouth. Hannah was surprised with the emotions she felt, and kissed him back. On the walk home, they were desperate to share and talk about their futures. Hannah assured Izzy she would never care for any one the way she cared for him. She promised to visit him when she saved enough money. Before they said goodbye Hannah gave Izzy his gloves. He was very touched and in return Izzy gave Hannah a locket with a picture of them at the prom. They parted as each sheds some tears.

During her senior year, Hannah got a part-time job at Whitney's Department Store on Pearl Street. She was a sales woman and enjoyed the job very much. Although, she didn't make much money she gave most to her mother.

Hannah thought she would never get over Izzy. She started to date other boys. Hannah wrote to Izzy and at first his letters came weekly. Gradually though they stopped. Hannah realized a part of her life had ended.

Hannah's senior year was full of changes. Due to her job, she felt grown up. At home her brothers still treated her as their baby sister. Surprisingly, Hannah did not mind. She liked being the youngest; lot of perks came with it.

A serious issue the family was forced to acknowledge was Edmund. He was very sick. Rose and the boys turned the parlor into a bedroom. There was a comfortable chair in the parlor, Rose often slept in it at night. Rose was scared. Edmund had taken care of her for years. He was facing his own mortality and had accepted his illness. Due to his constant pain, the doctor ordered morphine. Rose administered it, but often Edmund would refuse. He did not want his mind clouded. In the evening the family sat with him. Sometimes, Hannah would turn on the radio, so he could listen to music. Edmund tried to prepare each for life without him. It was particularly difficult talking to Rose. Leaving his love would be the hardest thing for Edmund to accept.

"Rose" he said, "I've made sure you and the children will be taken care of financially. You know where the safe is, use the money wisely."

All Rose could do was mourn. The money, he said, should last a year or more. She also had her boys to help support her and Hannah.

To Edmund Jr., his father said,

"I expect you to take care of your mother."

When he completed addressing each child, Edmund began to relax. He drifted into deep sleep. Hannah was full of emotions. She knew something awful was happening to her father. Hannah didn't know how to prepare herself for what was to about to occur. Rose was so engrossed with Edmund's pending death, she had little time to be supportive for Hannah. Hannah turned to Martha. Martha held Hannah trying to explain to her what and why things were happening. She encouraged Hannah to pray to God. Rather, Hannah blamed God for what was occurring to her father. She wondered if she could believe in Him should her father die. Deep in her heart she willed her father to be well and life would be back to normal. Every day Hannah saw her father she would make a comment about how he was improving. The others could not bring themselves to tell Hannah her father was getting weaker day by day.

On a mild spring day in April 1937, Edmund seemed more alert than usual. He declined morphine; although it was obvious he was in great pain. When his entire family was by his side Edmund requested his morphine then fell into an unresponsive sleep. The family spent all their time with Edmund. Everyone taking shifts so he would never be alone. Rose relented allowing Hannah to miss school so that she too was with her father. Still in denial, Hannah was oblivious as to how close her father was to dying. Edmund was not Catholic, but Rose had the priest come to the house anyway. During the latest stages of his illness, Edmund expressed the desire to convert to Catholicism. The priest said the prayers and baptized Edmund. Now Rose was happy because Edmund received Sacrament of The Last Rights. Slowly Edmund slipped away. He looked very peaceful and at rest. After the Mass for Edmund he was buried in our Lady of Angels Cemetery next to Kathryn, Aunt Kitty, and Patrick. For Edmund's family, they could grieve in a way they knew how, together.

The Wright household began to change. Albert and his wife moved. Rose chose to swap bedrooms with Edmund Jr. and Mary his wife. Rose, no longer could be in the bedroom where she had shared so much with Edmund. Martha and Hannah each had a room to themselves. Rose grieved for her love, and she was able to provide love and guidance for her grieving family. Hannah had taken Edmund's death the hardest, crying often. At first Rose had a difficult time with Hannah returning to school. Hannah healed and the pain lessened, she began to participate in life again. She still was sad and withdrawn.

Just when Hannah began to return to a normal schedule: school, chores, boys she became sick. At first, Rose thought Hannah had the flu. She ran high fevers and developed a terrible cough. Eventually, Hannah's illness passed and she returned to school. Rose noticed Hannah still coughed and started to lose weight. Rose decided it was best Hannah give up her part-time job. Rose was beginning to worry about Hannah. This time she, Edmund was not here to be the voice of reason.

ELEVEN

H annah attended school all of May. Her cough had lessened; she was not as tired. Rose was relieved as Hannah's physical health improved but Rose became concerned with her psychological wellbeing. At home, Hannah appeared sad and depressed. She no longer went to the movies with her friends. The prom was fast approaching, the second week in June, and Hannah never mentioned it to her mother. Finally, Rose asked Hannah about the prom. Meekly, Hannah said she was not going.

"Not going?" said Rose.

"Did anyone ask you?"

Hannah faced her mother; it appeared as if she had somehow changed.

"Honest Mom, don't you think having fun so close to dad's death is wrong. To answer your question a couple of boys did ask me but I would not dream of going."

With this reply, Rose's concern increased as she tried to convince Hannah that her father would want her to go and have fun. Hanging around the house would not bring Edmund back.

Rose called upon Mrs. Adler, Izzy's mom. Explaining Rose's concern for Hannah, she wondered if Izzy could come home for the prom. Having Izzy around might perk Hannah up. Without hesitation Mrs. Adler agreed with Rose. Izzy's mother always liked Hannah and thought Izzy could help Hannah through her grief. Mrs. Adler wrote Izzy and informed him of the situation. Izzy was just finishing his first year of college, and had a break before he started his summer job. He was happy to come home for a visit and see Hannah. While Hannah continued with her daily routine, Rose and Mrs. Adler prepared for Izzy's surprise visit. Martha decided she would sew a new dress for Hannah: one appropriate for a special night.

Hannah's senior prom was scheduled for the twelfth of June. On the fourth, Izzy returned home. After a brief visit with his father he went to Hannah's. Hannah opened the door speechless. The last Hannah had heard from Izzy was when she received his letter of condolence. After the initial shock, Hannah, laughed for the first time since her father's death. Rose was thrilled to hear her daughter so happy. Immediately, Izzy stated,

"Lets go to the movies this evening."

At first Hannah hesitated, Izzy gentle persuades Hannah to agree. Somehow, Hannah knew her father would allow her to be happy spending time with Izzy.

That night they saw a romantic movie starring Katharine Hepburn, and as always held hands. On the walk home, Izzy, without hesitation asked,

"I would be honored if you would allow me to escort you to your prom."

Hannah thought about her father for a moment and decided she would love to go especially since Izzy had asked. Secretly, she had tried on her yellow dress weeks earlier. Much to her dismay it was too big.

Hannah smiled as she and Izzy walked up to her home. She couldn't wait to tell her mom the news. Even though Rose was asleep Hannah woke her and told her how Izzy had asked her to go to the prom with him. Rose gave Hannah a big hug and ushered her to bed. Relived, because Rose had concerns whether Hannah would actually agree to go. As Rose returned to bed, she felt Hannah might just be okay.

Hannah woke the next morning excited about the prom, but nervous because she had nothing appropriate to wear. At breakfast Hannah asked Rose if she would be able to alter her prom dress from last year. Regretfully, Rose told Hannah she didn't think she would be able to but told Hannah,

"Talk to Martha."

Hannah sheepishly asked Martha if she would take in the dress from last year's prom. Martha led Hannah to the closet and pulled out a beautiful aqua blue dress. Hannah stood there confused and shocked; she could hardly believe her eyes. The dress was magnificent. It had a full skirt and a fitted bodice with small cap sleeves barely covering the shoulders.

"Oh, thank you Martha. I can't believe you made this for me. Why you didn't even know if I was going?"

"Oh I knew you would go and your mother requested I make something special for you," replied Martha. Hannah's brothers chipped in to buy the materials. Eagerly, Hannah tried it on. Martha called Rose. Rose was speechless; Hannah looked beautiful. The aqua color accentuated Hannah's eyes. As Rose gazed upon her daughter, she noticed how exquisite Hannah's eyes were especially her long thick lashes. Rose thought Edmund would have been speechless, as he took in his little girl all grown up. Except for some minor adjustments the dress was a perfect fit.

Izzy arrived for Hannah in his cousin's old car. As soon as he saw Hannah, he was mesmerized. Not only had she grown up in the past year but was more beautiful than he ever remembered. Hannah no longer resembled a young girl, but a young lady. Izzy surprised Hannah with a car, a corsage, and a camera. Rose pinned the flowers on Hannah's dress. Just prior to their departure, Harry took a photograph of Hannah and Izzy.

This year Hannah was more mature and enjoyed the dance. Hannah and Izzy were no longer sweetheart but friends. Therefore Hannah relaxed and focused on having fun. Still, a part of her heart thought she was disrespecting her father by enjoying herself. Hannah no longer cared about prom queen. When the queen was announced, Hannah congratulated her with genuine feelings.

While Hannah was never one hundred percent healthy, the acuteness of her illness had passed. Following the prom, Hannah was focused on graduation. Rose told Hannah,

"I'm so proud of you completing high school. Your father is proud of you also even though he is not here to tell you himself."

On a beautiful June day, Hannah graduated from high school. The event reminded Martha of the poem,

"What is so rare as a day in June."

Hannah had her picture taken, by a professional at his studio and with this came recognition of Hannah's completion of high school. At the ceremony graduates were seated in the front and listened patiently to the guest speaker. It was a typical high school graduation speech,

"Go forth and conquer your dreams."

Hannah's dream was to get a job as a secretary and help take care of Rose. Hannah always had a sense of innocence and was not expecting any awards during graduation. Her name was called during the ceremony, and Hannah received an award for proficiency in secretarial skills. With the award she was given, five dollars. At home, they had a small party in Hannah's honor. The entire Wright family attended. Hannah decided she would give the five dollars to Rose as support for the family. Rose thanked Hannah for her generosity and told her,

"Hannah, you need an outfit when applying for jobs. Therefore tomorrow we'll go downtown shopping".

Hannah was feeling so happy and a bit guilty because her brothers and Martha had given her gifts for graduation. They were all so proud of Hannah because besides her, Harry and Edmund Jr. were the only others of Rose and Edmund's children to graduate from high school.

Edmund Jr., who worked for Local 106, as a laborer, was promoted to foreman. He heard of a job opening in the office. Although it was not secretarial, it was a position that required answering the phone and running errands. Edmund Jr. spoke to his boss and inquired about the position. He mentioned Hannah and how she received the secretarial award during graduation. Edmund Jr.'s boss agreed to give Hannah a chance. Stressing if Hannah did not do well he would have to let her go, no matter who's sister she was.

Hannah was ecstatic. The next day, dressed in her new clothes, Hannah started her new job. As expected, she was very proficient and impressed her boss. With her first paycheck Hannah gave Rose ninety percent and kept the remainder. Hannah did not have specific plans for her savings, but she allowed herself little splurges such as make up. Slowly, Hannah began making slight changes to her appearance. She would tend to her nails, constantly shaping them and using brightly colored polish. Hannah wanted to make a change with her hair, but she was nervous as to what to do. She had only cut her hair twice while in high school and never was it a drastic change. Now it was very long and curly to the point of being unmanageable. One day after considerable though, Hannah asked Rose to cut her hair. Hannah immerged with a very becoming shoulder length cut she wore stylishly.

Life seemed to go along smoothly for the Wright family until Rose realized she was facing a financial situation. As Edmund said the money was spent in a year and now was gone. Hannah had been working for six months and always gave Rose money, but Edmund Jr. and Mary moved after having their first baby. Unfortunately, they were no longer able to help. Most of the other boys had likewise left and were living their own lives, providing Rose with little money. Everyone's help was appreciated, but it was not enough to feed the family and take care of the house. Harry still lived at home contributing as always but it still was not enough. The house was need of repairs putting Rose in a predicament.

Then a thought came to mind, which might remedy Rose's financial need. There were two empty bedrooms and the attic. All of which she had no use for since her boys had moved out. With help from her family, she tidied up the rooms and decided to rent them. At Church was a bulletin board with notices attached to it, and Rose placed room for rent flyer on it. Within two weeks, she had renters in both bedrooms and attic. The tenants, young men, allowed Rose to finally feel she could manage again.

Rose never considered the work that accompanied the role of landlord. Along with room came board, where she served breakfast and supper. Although she was used to taking care of a large family, this was different because rather than family, she was taking care of strangers. During supper, Hannah would help and always did the cleaning after for her mother. Rose's motto, "early to bed, early to rise," seemed to help, but for Hannah, she preferred staying up, listening to the radio while she knitted, wrote in her journal, or worked on her poetry.

A year went by, Hannah never missed a day of work. She began showing signs of becoming ill. Hannah kept how she felt quiet, but Rose was aware. Again came the fevers and cough. Rather than listening to the radio in the evening, Hannah took to "early to bed." Often, upon returning from work, Hannah would nap although still helping her mother. Even people at her job noticed a difference in Hannah. She had lost her spunk, but still did her duties. Hannah could control her fevers and cough with medicine, but by summer, Hannah was becoming sicker and started to missing work. Rose increasingly worried, but was at a loss as what to do. Rose thought Hannah's illness would pass as previous ones did because there had not been any sign of blood when coughing. Although no one in her family ever had tuberculosis, Rose knew of those who had. With this illness, Hannah's symptoms were similar to those of the past illness, cough, fever, malaise and loss of weight. Hannah was so thin it was impossible to imagine becoming any her thinner.

Eventually though Hannah's symptoms became worse. Hannah took a leave from her work until she was well. Hannah knew she would improve, but Edmund Jr. was not so sure. He spoke with Rose and said

"Hannah needs to see a doctor."

Rose was confidant she could take care of Hannah, she always had prior. This time was different and Rose knew it.

Hannah tried to eat but would vomit. Besides high fevers, night sweats had started. Hannah tried to keep the severity of her cough from her mother as much as possible. The sputum she coughed up was now was blood tinged and she was getting short of breath. Still, Rose thought if Hannah rested and ate she would get better. Rose didn't want to admit there was no money to take Hannah to the doctor. Determined Rose believed since she had always taken care of Hannah, she could do just as well.

Unknown to Rose, Hannah's days were a blur. Never had she felt so sick. Her eyes developed brightness due to the fevers. Hannah always tried to eat with each meal but rarely was able to succeed.

She could drink water. She was so thirsty because of the fevers. Rose now needed to wash Hannah's sheets daily, brought on by the night sweats. Martha tried to help Rose but she had aged too and could only do so much. Rose prayed to Edmund to give her the strength to take care of their daughter.

One evening, Hannah had a severe coughing spell. She coughed up a large amount of blood. Hannah turned very pale with a blue tinge around her mouth. Rose trying to keep herself calm got a message to Edmund Jr. that she needed his help. He came right away. Immediately Edmund Jr., Rose, and Harry brought Hannah to St. Peter's Hospital. In the emergency room as soon as the staff was told of Hannah symptoms, they put her in isolation. Rose wore a mask when she sat with Hannah. Hannah had fallen into a deep sleep and Rose feared the worst. Silently Rose prayed to God,

"Please spare my baby girl."

With in hours, the doctor entered Hannah's room explaining to Rose Hannah was critical and had tuberculosis. He stated the immediate concern was to stabilize Hannah. She would eventually need to go to a tuberculosis sanitarium, a hospital that specializes in treating tuberculosis. Immediately following the diagnosis a doctor began an intravenous and moved Hannah to a private room, solely for isolation. Rose stayed by Hannah's side until Edmund Jr. urged,

"Come on mom, let's get you home to rest. Hannah is sleeping and there is nothing you can do for her other than keep yourself healthy."

The nurse pulled Rose aside, prior to her visit the following day, explained how contagious tuberculosis was and she should immediately clean Hannah's room with Clorox. Later in the week Rose visited Hannah, she was shocked to see Hannah resting with the head of her bed slightly raised surrounded by an oxygen tent to aid her breathing. Rose smiled at Hannah demonstrating confidence to assure Hannah things would be better soon, while knowing deep inside she was afraid for her daughter.

Hannah said to her mother in a weak scared voice,

"They took a chest x-ray and collected sputum today."

She wanted to go home and pleaded to her mother to find out when she would be released. Also, Hannah expressed concern the longer she remained hospitalized, the more money it would drain on the family finances. Rose reassured Hannah that she was just to rest. Rose demanded, Hannah was not to worry about money; her only concern was to get better.

Days passed when the doctor approached Rose in the hall. The doctor told Rose his original diagnosis was confirmed by the tests. He stated,

"Hannah, as you know, is very ill. The plan is to treat Hannah at St. Peter's Hospital for the next three weeks in order for Hannah to build strength prior to transporting her to the tuberculosis sanitarium."

Right then, he did not know which sanitarium Hannah would go to. When Rose asked him how long Hannah would be at the sanitarium the doctor did not know except it would be a while. Rose turned to the doctor and asked,

"How long in your terms is a while?"

Reluctantly the doctor replied,

"At least two years although the length could change depending upon how fast she responds to the treatments."

Rose couldn't believe her ears, two years, how could she tell Hannah? When Rose told Edmund Jr. the prognosis he suggested they not tell Hannah, only let her know she would be released when she was better. Until Hannah was strong enough to transfer she spent all her time in bed surrounded by the oxygen tent. Most days Hannah slept, which the doctor assured Rose rest was nature's way of healing. The third week came and the medical staff prepared getting Hannah ready for her transfer to Homer Folks State Tuberculosis Hospital in Oneonta, New York. Gradually, the nurses' began to sit Hannah in a more upright position surrounded by the oxygen tent. Slowly they dangled her legs over the side of the bed. Lastly Hannah was moved to a chair. Thrilled because she no longer layed motionless in a bed surrounded by an oxygen tent. Though, excited with her achievements, every effort exhausted her.

The day came for Hannah to travel to Oneonta. The doctor informed Rose and Edmund Jr. that the hospital opened in 1935. It offered the latest methods of treating tuberculosis. The doctors warned Rose some of the treatment provided bordered on experimental. Also because it was state run those who could not pay were admitted free. Rose wasn't sure if what she was about to do was right. She still felt she could take care of Hannah. What bothered Rose the most was the distance between Albany and Oneonta. Rose had no idea how often she could visit Hannah. They had never been separated with the exception of Hannah's stay in St. Peter's Hospital.

Rose and Edmund Jr. arrived at the hospital early. As Rose help Hannah get dressed, she had to refrain from taking Hannah in her arms and never releasing her. However, Rose remained positive and confidant if only for Hannah. Hannah's concern was the clothes Rose bought from home. Rose reminded Hannah,

"You will be in pajamas for the first four weeks and graduate to regular clothes."

Her brothers pooled their money for material and Martha made Hannah three pairs of pajamas and a bathrobe. Martha also knitted Hannah slippers. Rose packed Hannah's cosmetics hoping Hannah would soon feel well enough to enjoy them.

The trip to Oneonta took three hours. The road was bumpy making it impossible to drive quickly. During the beginning of the trip, Hannah seemed to be okay. Unfortunately halfway through the trip, Hannah began to cough and became short of breath.

"God," thought Rose "what are we going to do?"

Edmund Jr. reassured Rose and Hannah they would get there soon enough then sped up as fast as he could. Rose told Hannah to lie back and stretch out on the backseat. Although Hannah was not comfortable, her breathing became better. At last, Oneonta came into view; a small town with intriguing hills all around it. When they departed from Albany it was overcast, but as they arrived the sky was beautiful and serene. Hannah seemed to perk up especially since she had never been out of Albany. On the far edge of town, a grouping of multistory brick buildings could bee seen. They had reached Homer Folks!

TWELVE

annah felt as if she were dreaming, Rose was kissing her good bye and she was sitting in a wheelchair in the waiting room. Hannah held on to the suitcase holding all her worldly goods. Hannah tried to be brave, but her eyes were filling with tears; she was so scared because she never saw Rose cry. Even though Hannah was hospitalized for three weeks, she still didn't understand why she was here. Hannah glanced around the room, noticing everyone looked ill. She thought this is where one is sent to die when there is an infection in the lungs.

After what seemed like an eternity, a woman approached Hannah. She asked Hannah if she thought she needed the wheelchair. Hannah, not knowing what to say, answered "no." The woman instructed Hannah to follow her to an office. Hannah had not walked in three weeks and was very weak. She glanced at the woman and did a quick mental evaluation. Hannah saw were friendly eyes, mask, white uniform and white shoes. Hannah finally realized the woman across from her was a nurse. The nurse asked to see the envelope Hannah had brought from St. Peter's Hospital. She spent the next five minutes reading the contents. Occasionally, she would look up at Hannah trying to comprehend the information provided with Hannah. After what seemed like an eternity, the nurse summoned an attendant to get a stretcher. Next she looked at Hannah and with a stern voice scolded Hannah and said,

"You should have told me you had hemorrhaged."

Hannah looked at the nurse as if she spoke a foreign language. Hannah had no idea what hemorrhage meant. Before she knew what happened, she was lifted onto a stretcher with two pillows under her head. For a moment Hannah closed her eyes and relaxed. She was so tired and was having difficulty breathing.

As Hannah was being moved on the stretcher, the nurse began asking questions. At first, the questions were easy; Hannah answered them with her eyes closed. Eventually the question became more difficult about her breathing. Hannah answered the best she could. Hannah noticed during this interview she didn't seem as scared. Finally the nurse asked Hannah a simple question,

"How do you feel?"

Hannah misunderstanding the question and told the nurse how scared she was. Hannah explained,

"I've always had family to look after me. I don't know what I'm doing here, I don't want to be here."

The nurse smiled under her mask. Hannah reminded the nurse of a little girl, a very sick little girl.

The nurse began explaining to Hannah the process she would be going through. First Hannah would be taken to an examining room. Her temperature, pulse and respirations would be taken, along with her weight if she could stand. Then the doctor would come in and do a complete exam.

"Do you have any questions," asked the nurse.

Hannah shook her head no.

The nurse did the preliminaries. She tried to weigh Hannah, but Hannah got too dizzy. Next a doctor entered. Dr. Jones was very kind and smiled a lot. Outside his mask Hannah could see his eyes crinkle. After listening to Hannah's lungs and hearing her cough Dr. Jones ordered oxygen. He told Hannah there were many patients at Homer Folks and she would have friends in no time. Subsequently an attendant came and brought Hannah to the third floor. When they arrived the attendant stopped at the desk, was told to wheel Hannah to the ward and leave her on the stretcher next to her bed. It seemed like she was there for hours. Eventually Hannah fell asleep.

After what seemed like hours, a portly nurse startled Hannah. It appeared as if what she experienced earlier disappeared. This nurse focused on the tasks ahead.

"Come now, off the stretcher and into the bathroom for a shower. Hannah wash your hair with this soap; we don't want bugs. We know where people like you are from."

Hannah was shocked. Hannah wanted to tell her she did not have bugs and ask her just where did she think Hannah came from. Unknown to Hannah, many thought people with tuberculosis were from the depths of society and were lice infestation was common. Rather Hannah slowly got herself off the stretcher, with no assistance. She retrieved a pair of pajamas, from her suitcase, along with her comb and brush. Before entering the bathroom the nurse informed Hannah,

"Hannah you are to brush your teeth over the toilet, to avoid spreading germs."

It felt as if showering along with washing her hair took forever. Twice Hannah nearly passed out, but she caught herself on the railing in the shower. Following the shower, Hannah did exactly as told and climbed into bed. Exhaustion hit and Hannah began coughing more than before, causing difficulty breathing. She felt like a brick rested on her chest. Not knowing what to expect, Hannah looked out the window by her bed. Hannah could see a large barn surrounded by pastures. Hannah was interrupted before she could be distracted by the view. The same nurse entered explaining some things.

First, "You are not to get out of bed for any reason. If you need something use the long cord to call for a nurse."

Second, "You must use a bedpan no exceptions."

Third, "You'll have oxygen started."

The nurse started the oxygen. This did not frighten Hannah because she had been in an oxygen tent at St. Peter's. When the nurse came toward her with a small tube she resisted. Hannah began to question what was occurring.

"What are you going to do?"

The nurse tried to calm Hannah fears, explaining to her, the tube would be passed through Hannah's nose to the back of the throat and hooked to oxygen. Assuring Hannah the tube would not hurt allowing Hannah more freedom compared to the tent. Hannah cooperated and with in a minute the nurse secured the oxygen to her nose with tape.

At last Hannah thought the orientation was finished. She was so tired and wanted to sleep. The oxygen made breathing easier. Unfortunately the nurse returned.

"Now" the nurse said, "I will explain the rules of the ward. If you cough up sputum you are to spit it into a sputum cup. Your sputum contains the germs that make you sick."

"Meals are served at eight am, twelve noon and five-thirty pm, and snacks at ten am, three pm and eight-thirty pm. Every meal and snack includes milk which is important for your recovery".

The word recovery would be spoken again and again at Homer Folks. Lastly the nurse told Hannah,

"The doctor will be in in the morning to check on you".

"Cooperation will make your life easier," cautioned the nurse.

Overwhelmed by all she had been through Hannah closed her eyes and fell asleep.

At the sound of a racket, Hannah awoke, startled at first not knowing where she was. Slowly, she remembered her day. Hannah wanted to cry. She felt lost and deserted, but refused to cry in front of these strangers. As she looked around, she realized the noise was dinner being passed out. While waiting for her tray, she noticed that she was in a large room with nine other patients. It was difficult to determine anything about them other than they were patients because they were in bed not wearing masks. When her tray arrived Hannah looked over the food and decided she'd eat the custard and Jell-o. She also drank the milk remembering the nurse's warning. Hannah leaned back on her pillows waiting for an attendant to take her tray. When Hannah opened her eyes, it wasn't the attendant standing beside her, but the same nurse taking her tray away.

"Now look dear, if you want to recover you have to eat. If you don't eat, we will feed you and by force if necessary. Do you understand?"

"Yes," Hannah said meekly; thinking never had she been spoken to in such a manner. Fear swept over her.

When night came, snacks were given, and the patients were settled in for sleep. Without warning the lights went out. Hannah never felt so lonely, even though she shared a ward with nine other patients. Except for the coughing, which was nonstop, it was quiet. Nightlights were scattered about and when nurse's rounds were made flashlights were used. The dark seem to magnify Hannah's fears and loneliness. She turned toward the window and thought about praying, but she felt abandoned by everyone, especially the God she'd grown to love. Over and over Hannah would say she wanted to go home. Most of all, although she was nineteen, she wanted her mother. Soon Hannah's thoughts turned to tears then sobs. Hannah pulled a pillow over her head, letting her feelings flood through her tears. Unconsciously Hannah fell asleep.

Startled around six am Hannah was awakened by the ward coming to life. Still confused she was curious as to what to expect. A nurse in a blue uniform, different from the night before, brought Hannah a basin of warm water to bathe. Hannah brushed her teeth over a kidney basin. The nurse made Hannah's bed while she laid in it. Hannah willed herself to use the bedpan twice, deciding while it was crude, and she had no choice. The breakfast trays were served. Hannah remembering the other nurse's threats did her best to eat most of the food on the tray. Making sure no one was watching, Hannah took a bunch of tissues wrapped what she couldn't eat, and buried it under the used tissues in her bag taped to her bed. When the nurse reached Hannah she commented on how much she had eaten.

"Remember recovery is the aim," said the nurse.

Again "recovery" was used and this puzzled Hannah.

Hannah wondered what the remainder of her day would be like. In her suitcase she had paper, pencil, and stamps. Hannah thought she would write her mother letting her know she was fine. Timidly, she put on the call light and the nurse came. When Hannah asked for her suitcase, Hannah never expected to hear what she was told. She was not to do anything but lay as still as possible, talk little, and sleep or rest. This was to encourage the lungs to heal.

"Oh my God," thought Hannah.

"How will I ever manage this."

Scared Hannah asked the nurse,

"How long before I can write my mother?"

Surprised, this nurse seemed to show some compassion and her eyes appeared kind.

"Well" she said, "Typically patients are ordered strict bed rest for at least two weeks. Then the x-rays are done to see how you're lungs are healing. If there are signs of healing and your temperature is normal, you will be allowed to sit up in bed. Gradually you will permitted to read and write letters. Everything depends on how rapid you recover."

The nurse straightened Hannah's bed, fluffed her pillows, and checked the tube in her nose. Hannah thanked her, relaxed a little, and closed her eyes. Sleep came quickly and Hannah dreamed distorted things about Homer Folks.

Hannah had only been asleep about fifteen minutes when she awoke to a familiar face staring down at her. He gently touched her hand to assure she was awake. It was Dr. Jones from the day before. Patiently he gave her a couple of minutes to wake up, helping her get a drink of water from the pitcher by her bed.

Dr. Jones started to talk to Hannah,

"I will answer your questions and tell you what to expect. First however, I want you to tell me about your self."

Hannah was taken back. Dr. Jones seemed nicer than the others she had been acquainted with since her arrival. After a moment Hannah, began to tell Dr. Jones all about herself and her family. Hannah talked for thirty minutes before Dr. Jones interrupted her asking her to save some for his visit tomorrow. Dr. Jones knew how patients felt alone, scared, and unsure what to expect. He had been treating tuberculosis patients for twenty-five years and had his own theories relating to treatment. Hannah's first question for Dr. Jones was,

"What is wrong with me? I know I'm very sick and will I die?"

Having heard all these questions many times, Dr. Jones was guarded when he answered Hannah.

"Tuberculosis is caused by a germ that makes the lungs sick and causes a lot of pus and holes in the lungs," said Dr. Jones.

He also explained to her what it meant to be contagious and why the staff wore masks. Hannah asked questions until she understood.

Dr. Jones knew from Hannah's paper work, she was very sick, but the extent he could not be sure therefore, he tried to explain how tuberculosis was treated. He told Hannah some of the same things the nurse had said stressing bed rest would probably be for a month. The basic treatment was rest, fresh air, and nutritious food. He explained to her that the barn and fields she saw from her window were the hospital's. That was where cows, pigs, chickens, were raised along with huge gardens.

Dr. Jones explained to Hannah the types of tests that would be done. He told Hannah to expect the following, frequent chest x-rays, a test called a bronchoscopy, in which a tube would be passed into her windpipe, collections of sputum and others depending on the results of the ones he listed. Each of the tests would be preformed the next day. Hannah was not as scared or nervous as she thought she would be prior to the doctor's explanations. Dr. Jones explained each so thoroughly and simply Hannah understood what was to going to happen. Then he told her something personal. He contracted tuberculosis when he was an intern. He went to a sanitarium similar to Homer Folks and recovered. This gave Hannah hope and a more positive attitude. Before Dr. Jones left, he reminded Hannah the best advice he could give to help her recover was to cooperate. Some how as Dr. Jones was walking away Hannah felt a bit more at ease.

The remainder of her first day passed quickly because this was all so new. She seemed more optimistic after speaking to Dr. Jones and recited "cooperation" over and over. Before lunch was served Hannah was able to rest, which she needed. As with breakfast, Hannah hid some of her food because she couldn't imagine how one could be expected to eat so much. Hannah awakened about three pm, the nurse took her temperature and she had developed a fever. As with everything she needed to drink large amounts of water. Hannah had resisted drinking too much because she was embarrassed to use the bedpan. Now, however, she remembered Dr. Jones's words and began to drink more water.

The rest of the afternoon she filled her time looking over the ward. Her bed was metal and a light was fixed to its side. Next to her a woman was sleeping. Hannah had noticed this women prior because she was often walking around and wearing regular clothes. Sensing she was being stared at, she awoke and smiled at Hannah. She introduced herself as Carol Higgins and welcomed Hannah to Homer Folks. In time Carol and Hannah would become best friend during their stay.

When dinner arrived, promptly at five-thirty, Hannah needed to rely on her trick of hiding food. As the trays were removed, Hannah noticed the nurse from the previous evening. She approached Hannah with three little bottles, explaining, she told Hannah to fill each bottle with sputum. She then said,

"If you don't not comply, I'll have no choice but to stick a tube down your throat."

Normally this would have frightened Hannah, but she knew she could do as she was asked.

As the nurse left, Hannah tried to recall the happenings of the day. Unfortunately, Hannah's exhaustion got the better of her and before she could remember her visit with Dr. Jones, Hannah slipped off into a deep sleep.

THIRTEEN

annah awoke the next morning before the ward activities began. Hannah was anxious about the tests being performed that day. The chest x-ray she was getting used to, but it was the bronchoscopy that made her nervous. Dr. Jones discussed the tests the day prior and attempted to reassure Hannah it was necessary in order to treat her condition. As the morning progressed, it appeared as if the events of the day would not differ from normal; until Hannah was told to dress in a hospital gown rather than her own pajamas. Also, Hannah was not allowed breakfast, including anything to drink. About seven am Nurse Riley, the nurse Hannah was leery of, came in and gave Hannah pre-op medication. Soon after an attendant came and took Hannah to a small building which housed treatment rooms, two operating rooms and doctors' offices. Hannah was transferred to a treatment room and placed on a stretcher. A new doctor appeared Dr. Martin, and said,

"I will explain to you what you can expect during this test." Hannah had expected to see Dr. Jones this morning not someone new. While sitting on the side of the stretcher, having her throat numbed, Hannah started to become scared. The medication they had given to calm her wasn't working. Hannah was told to lie down with her head hanging off the top of the stretcher. Then they covered Hannah's eyes and restrained her arms.

"What were they going to do?" was all Hannah could think. She tried to say something, because her throat was numb she couldn't. Hannah heard Dr. Martin say,

"Hannah we are about to begin. You might feel some pressure in your throat but you will be able to breathe at all times."

Unbeknownst to Hannah two strong nurses were standing on either side of her. The procedure began and Hannah's fear rapidly turned to panic. As the hollow metal tube reached the back of her throat Hannah felt as if she could not breathe. She started thrashing her head and tried to kick her legs, but her legs had also been restrained. Dr. Martin realized he could not continue because of Hannah's out burst, he signaled for the nurses to hold her head and her legs still. The procedure took fifteen minutes and when Hannah was freed from her restraints all she could do was cry. One of the nurses noticed her tears and wondered if Hannah had been given the pre-op medication. The nurse gently patted her hand and Hannah slowly turned to look at this woman whose eyes appeared to be sympathetic. By the time Hannah returned to her room, she was exhausted and wanted sleep desperately.

Soon Dr. Jones approached with a large folder in his hand. He kindly woke her and said,

"I'm sorry the bronchoscopy was so difficult. We were able to get a lot of sputum and sent it to the lab for testing. Your chest x-ray was very revealing. I am going to show it to you and explain what you see."

Dr. Jones got out the x-ray and held it to the light.

"The dark areas you see here,"

he pointed to areas around the base of the right lung.

"Represents pus in the chest cavity and it's pressing on the lung making it hard for you to breathe. The spots here and here are large cavities that the tuberculosis germ has eaten away. We will be putting a tube in your chest cavity that will allow the pus to drain into a bottle. Our hope is this will bring your temperature down and you will begin to feeling better."

Hannah, exhausted from the earlier procedure, was only concerned if it would be as bad as the bronchoscopy. Dr. Jones reassured her it wouldn't be as bad.

By lunchtime the numbness had disappeared in her throat and Hannah could swallow again. After sipping water she was brought her lunch tray. To Hannah's relief her lunch did not contain the usual foods; there were soft foods like custard, soup, and Jell-o. Hannah was surprised she felt a hungry, eating all the food on her tray. That afternoon Hannah was left alone and slept. Dr. Jones explained to her if her arm was broken they could rest it in a cast but with sickness in her lungs she had to rest and sleep as much as possible.

When Hannah awoke, Carol, her friend and a patient on the ward, snuck over and explained more about life at Homer Folks. Carol told Hannah,

"Most of the patients form a close community. Some patients never receive visitors so at times I might take another patient with me when I have a visit. It's a way to make others feel as if they are not alone in the world."

Hannah asked Carol about the two o'clock whistle she had heard. Carol explained,

"Those patients who were up and around participating in various activities must return to their rooms for absolute bed rest when the two o'clock whistle sounds. Everyone must then rest for one hour and thirty minutes. This meant, no talking or eating, but in bed with little movement"

Carol always seemed to pick up Hannah spirits when she came to chat.

Hannah had a restless night, mainly due to the night sweats. The next morning, she awoke to a second round of pre-op medication and brought back to the treatment room. Like the day prior, Dr. Martin was performing the procedure. With Hannah sitting on the side of the stretcher, Dr. Martin injected novocaine, a medicine to deaden nerves going in her chest cavity. Hannah was more cooperative today because this procedure did not require a scope going into her throat. Hannah was told if she felt any pain the doctor could increase the novocaine. Before Hannah realized the procedure was completed. Hannah was back in bed with a tube coming out of her chest. It was hooked to a bottle that sat on the floor. Hannah was afraid to move. Initially because she was anxious the tube would fall out. If the tube fell out she would have to go through the procedure again. Gradually through, with reassurance from the nurses, Hannah began to move around in bed.

As the days passed after each procedure Hannah's breathing became easier. Dr. Jones was also pleased because her temperature was also down. Hannah started feeling better causing her eagerness to get up and move around. Hannah was sore from lying in bed constantly and wanted to be allowed to use the bathroom rather than the bedpan. Before long, Hannah was permitted to sit on the side of her bed, dangling her feet. Finally she thought, a start.

Hannah received mail. She was given a letter from her mother and one from Harry.

Rose described changes that had taken place. The tenants remained even after Hannah's diagnosis and Rose had even rented to a new person. It was difficult for Hannah to read the new tenant had rented in her room, but decided not to dwell on the news. Rose mentioned each of Hannah's brothers had agreed to give Rose ten dollars a month and each of the tenants paid fifteen per month therefore things at home had improved. Also Rose mentioned Martha had sent her love and promised she would send yarn and needles for Hannah shortly. Hannah read how Edmund Jr. and Harry made many needed repairs around the house. Rose was sure they would be comfortable during the winter months. Rose explained how much everyone missed her and things were so quiet without her around the house. Hannah seemed a bit unsure when her mother mentioned the special Mass being said especially for her, but she also felt some comfort by the notion. She ended the letter by encouraging Hannah to be cooperative in everything to speed along her recovery. Rose's letter cheered up Hannah but at the same time made Hannah homesick and a little jealous because she wasn't home.

Compared to her mother's, Harry's letter was cheerful and funny. Although it was short he included two good jokes and talked about visiting her once the doctor gave the approval.

Hannah's spirits had been lifted until she gazed up and saw Nurse Riley. In Hannah's opinion, Nurse Riley seemed to get a thrill intentionally scaring Hannah. Hannah remembered Carol's advice and began hiding her fears from Nurse Riley. Carol had told Hannah what really seems to frustrate Nurse Riley was just being nice. Hannah decided to spend her days trying, as hard as it was, to be nice to Nurse Riley. Surprisingly to Hannah, Nurse Riley reacted differently to Hannah's kindness and over the course of several days their relationship seem to improve.

After two weeks, with her temperature remained normal, her chest tube was draining very little, and her color was better, Hannah's appetite also improved. While making his rounds one day Hannah begged Dr. Jones,

"Please let me do more".

Dr. Jones agreed she had shown signs of improving, so he placed an order in her chart stating Hannah could write letters and have visits from other patients. There was one exception; Hannah still was on complete bed rest. Hannah was delighted and eagerly wrote a long letter to her mother. Hannah stressed how she was improving but decided to leave out topics such as her chest tube or the bronchoscopy. After completing her first letter she called Carol over and exclaimed,

"I've had great news. I can start having patients visit." So excited the two laughed like schoolgirls talking about boys.

The medical staff seemed sincerely happy for Hannah because they recognized a patient's morale positively affected their recovery.

Following the two o'clock mandated rest; Carol appeared with a group of people who were all patients. Hannah was introduced to Vera, Pearl, Ann and Mike. Hannah was shocked to see a man among the women. They all seem pleased to see her and shared stories regarding their treatments. They all agreed the bronchoscopy was the worse procedure they had endured. Mike turned to Hannah, and said,

"If you didn't fight it wasn't that bad. The doctor was right you could always breathe."

Listening to Mike, Hannah asked him how many he experienced and he answered three times. Each patient stressed the nice attributes about Homer Folks. Occupational therapy was where you could make all sorts of things. Hannah shared her love of knitting. Vera replied,

"Hannah if you let them know the occupational therapist will provide you with yarn and needles."

Hannah was thrilled. To make Hannah's first visit the with other patients more momentous, Carol had brought her camera along taking a picture of just Hannah sitting up in bed and then a second of all of them surrounding her. Carol assured Hannah she would have copies made for her. As the group was leaving, Mike teasing Hannah suggested when she was able they would see a movie provided by Homer Folks. Hannah smiled shyly as Mike caught up to the others.

Hannah continued improving a little each day. Although Hannah was happy with each small achievement, her thoughts were focused entirely on when she could go home. Dr. Jones stressed,

"Hannah it is much too early during your recovery to contemplate discharge."

Her new friends visited daily with Carol spending a great deal of time trying to heighten Hannah's spirits. All in all, Hannah was as content as she could be, but she still pushed Dr. Jones to at least let her out of bed.

Finally Dr. Jones discontinued her oxygen, which permitted Hannah to stand along side her bed. It was progress, but not what Hannah had wished. Dr. Jones informed Hannah the chest tube was going to be removed. He assured Hannah the removal would be much less painful and no medication was needed. Hannah, reassured, could not wait to be free of the tube and bottle. After the procedure, Hannah felt great. Eagerly, asked the nurse to help her out of bed. Hannah took pleasure with the ability to stand without restrictions. Later Carol came with the same group of fellow patients. They said,

"Congratulation! Hannah soon you you'll get more and more privileges."

Carol, in a mothering way, made sure Hannah did not get too excited about the future. True to their word, more privileges did follow. Hannah was finally allowed to use the bathroom. This lead Hannah to believe she would be going home soon. Hearing this her friends tried to convince her to be realistic with hopes and plans.

A month passed and Hannah began to notice subtle changes in her health. She noticed first her breathing. It was becoming labored.

At night, her perspiring was increasing. The thought of night sweats terrified Hannah. Hannah refused to call the nurse, but lay in her damp bed. What frightened Hannah the most was the return of her cough; Hannah refused to inform the nurses but there was no need because upon taking her vital signs, Nurse Riley realized Hannah was becoming feverish. Nurse Riley told Hannah.

"Your temperature is up, and you will remain in bed until Dr. Jones comes on the ward."

Hannah's crushed morale made her tearful. In the morning the food trays arrived. Hannah unable to eat, she only picked. Carol tried cheering Hannah up by reminding her of the progress she made before.

"You took two steps forward and one step back and eventually you will continue to progress."

As Carol spoke, Hannah for the first time thought about dying. Maybe because a few nights prior she was told another patient had died. She felt terrible and worried.

Dr. Jones came in late that day, and pulled up a chair, and talked to Hannah. He stressed that it was a setback that could be treated.

"Tomorrow they will collect sputum first thing in the morning looking for blood."

Hannah wanted to tell him they would not have to look very hard.

"Then a chest x-ray would be taken, read immediately, and if pus has reaccumulated they will reinsert the chest tube."

What distressed Dr. Jones the most was Hannah's appearance of bluish tinged lips and dark circles around her eyes. Gently, Dr. Jones told Hannah,

"We will also be restarting the oxygen."

The one positive thing he was able to tell Hannah was there would not be another bronchoscopy performed at this time. The following morning they collected sputum and she was taken to the treatment building. Where Dr. Martin inserted a chest tube. Back on the ward Hannah resumed complete bed rest. She felt she had hit a spot where there was no climbing out. Hannah turned her head toward the wall and just let the tears flow. Hannah was so depressed she wondered,

"Why me?" and "What have I done to deserve this?"

Carol was aware of Hannah's discouraging feelings, as was Nurse Riley. Each showed concern. If Hannah gave up her fight, then there was little anyone could do. Carol decided to write Rose. Careful not to alarm Rose to the seriousness of Hannah's condition, but suggested she send pictures from home for Hannah.

Nurse Riley decided to have a long talk with Dr. Jones. Both decided Hannah needed something positive to focus upon. As Dr. Jones approached Hannah, she reminded him of a frightened deer. He sensed she had given up. Gently he stated,

"Hannah recovery is mostly in your hands. There is just so much medicine can do."

She needed to be convinced not let tuberculosis win. Hannah had to call up all her mental resolve to overcome the tuberculosis.

"I can't just lie here trying to get better. I need something, but I don't know what. How am I ever going to cope?" asked Hannah.

The despair in Hannah's voice touch Dr. Jones and he knew he had to do something. He went to the nurses' station and talked to Nurse Riley. He not only discussed Hannah with Nurse Riley, but Dr. Martin as well. By the conclusion of their discussion it was decided by the three strict bed rest could be modified. What they realized was if a patient gave up, then all the bed rest would not be beneficial for the patient. Knowing Hannah was critically sick, the realm of death was realistic, they concluded to allow her to sit up, write letters and continue limited visitors. Dr. Jones passed their decision on to Hannah and she merely smiled at him.

FOURTEEN

he doctors seemed pleased the modification from strict bed rest did not seem to interfere with her progress. In fact, after three weeks, the chest tube was clamped and Hannah was allowed out of bed. Gradually her activities increased. One day Nurse Riley smiling approached Hannah and told her she was permitted to go out on the porch. It was magnificent for a November day. The sky was robin blue, sun shining, full of glory, and there was a chill of wind. This was the first time Hannah was permitted outside, since arriving at Homer Folks. Hannah failed to realize how cold it was because the staff had bundled her clothing in layers. Once outside, Hannah joined other patients sitting in the "cure chair", a lounge chair with adjustments for back and foot. The chair was made of wood leaving Hannah to wonder how comfortable it could be. Hannah was thin when she entered Homer Folks and now she was even skinnier. "A bag of bones," Carol called her. An attendant helped Hannah with the chair so she could be comfortable. Hannah was then covered with a thick woolen blanket. Hannah looked at her neighbor and smiled. They introduced each other. His name was Jim Carey, rugged and handsome. Hannah guessed his age between thirty and thirty-five. Hannah liked he seemed easy to talk to. Each day there after, if the weather permitted, Hannah sat on the porch. Each day Jim Carey managed to sit next to her. Their conversations range from life at the Homer Folks, to Hannah's family. Jim told her about parties held at Homer Folks. He was surprised when Hannah told him she had not gone to on-campus movies. Jim was making a play for Hannah but she was too immature and innocent to realize it. Hannah thought of

Jim as a friend and nothing more. What Jim was trying to begin was a practice at the Homer Folks called "cousining". Cousining was a romantic interlude between patients. It was strongly discouraged by the staff. If patients were caught they were separated during free time and watch carefully.

Christmas time was approaching, Hannah's feelings homesickness resurfaced.

"How could it be Christmas when she was here without her family," she wondered.

At the Homer Folks, Christmas decorations were appearing everywhere. The staff put a tree up in each ward and the patients decorated it. Hannah became choked up when the groups of patients began singing Christmas carols. How this reminded her of home. Her family would read the bible, specifically relating to the birth of Christ. They would then sing Christmas carols. As tradition, everyone attended midnight Mass at the Cathedral. Now Hannah had learned to control her tears, especially in front of others, but still her heart ached. She asked the question,

"Why?" "Why is this happening to me?"

A couple of weeks before Christmas; Rose, Edmund Jr. and Harry came bearing gifts. Hannah was thrilled. Times were still difficult for the family but each had little presents for Hannah. Martha sent a holy card of St. Theresa with a prayer on the other side that was for the sick. Hannah recited the prayer every morning and slowly felt confident she would eventually get better. Hannah had knitted presents to give also. And, wrote a poem for all. Edmund Jr. was bubbling with news. He purchased a home and his wife was going to have another baby. Hannah was so thrilled for him. She was going to be an aunt again. Both Adam and Johnny were married and each had a child. Although all the brothers help their mother, the one Hannah relied upon the most, was Edmund Jr. to be there for Rose.

On Christmas day the patients' schedules were dismissed. There was still the necessity of taking temperature and meals but the rest of the time the patients were allowed to intermingle.

Jim came to Hannah's ward and said,

"I've brought you a little present".

It was a tiny ceramic bluebird. Hannah was so pleased, but also felt strange because she didn't have a gift for him. But, who would've guessed he would have given her a gift. Jim had devised a devious plan. While talking to her, he guided Hannah to the doorway where mistletoe hung. Before she knew what happened, he took her in his arms and kissed Hannah directly on the mouth. Hannah, shocked and very upset yelled, "Stop!" Carol had tried warning Hannah about Jim, but she thought he was just a friend. Hannah wasted no time informing Jim how she felt. Standing there with his mouth-hung open, not typically rejected by a woman, he turned and left.

After the holidays, life at the Homer Folks resumed to normal. The weather turned cold and snowy. Whenever possible, they were permitted to go on the porch. Hannah, told by other patients, in the spring everyone would be encouraged to spend their two o'clock rest on the porch. At times, Hannah felt it was so cold that she would freeze. When she complained and asked if she could go in she was told,

"This is necessary for your recovery."

She was reminded of the three-pronged approach for treatment; rest, fresh air, and proper nutrition. Quite frankly, Hannah was tired of hearing this, but she still tried to comply. Sometimes her positive attitude seemed remiss, but she internalized it and tried put on a brave front. It was so hard to do.

Spring came improving the mood of the patients. Patients went for walks around the grounds.

Some patients had jobs. The jobs consisted of light, medium, and heavy tasks. Light duties would be something simple such as dusting. All patients out of bed were expected to make their beds, dust their bed and the stand and change the paper bag hanging off the side of the bed. A heavy job was typically performing gardening or helping on the farm. Medium was considered everything in between. Hannah did the housekeeping duties around her unit.

Although she had been at Homer Folks for seven months, the doctors were not pleased with her lack of progress. While Hannah seemed oblivious, the doctors were genuine in their concern. She listened to what the doctors had to say, but she felt better and more energized. At meals she ate everything. The food was so fresh. Hannah's mother never had food like this to cook with. Also, Hannah rationalized her improving, with the fact she had begun to gain weight. The doctors knew there was little indication of her lung healing but because of her morale they permitted her the privileges she was most anxious to gain.

Hannah was allowed to go to the movies. Movies were shown in a big auditorium on the main floor of building three, Hannah's building. Most of the movies were quite old, but that didn't matter to the patients. The first movie Hannah saw was "I Like Your Nerve". It was funny and romantic. It made Hannah laugh and became the perfect distraction. Carol along with other patients of the ward went with Hannah. Little by little Hannah felt she was becoming part of the gang.

May began as a beautiful month. The weather was perfect, and the sun had warmth, leaves were budding, and everyone seemed in good spirits.

That was until a visit on the tenth. Rose and Edmund Jr. came. Rather than their usual deminer, they appeared somber. Immediately Hannah knew something was wrong. After a few pleasantries were exchanged, Rose told Hannah that her much beloved Martha had died. Hannah was shocked. She knew Martha's health was failing, but she had no idea how close to death she was. Hannah was told Martha had simply not awakened one morning. Her death was peaceful. Hannah could tell Rose was shaken from Martha's death because they shared a mother-daughter relationship. Hannah could not think of a time without Martha and everything she meant to her. She thought about the beautiful prom dress Martha made with love. Without noticing Rose handed Hannah a large bag. In it were all the knitting supplies Martha had, plus skeins of yarn. Later, when lights were off, Hannah spent hours with her memories of Martha.

When Hannah first arrived at the Homer Folks, her family sent her little gifts and letters frequently. Hannah believed in someway the attention was due to guilt. Hannah's tuberculosis progressed until she suffered a major hemorrhage, most likely because of denial and lack of resources. Rose once told Hannah how sorry she was she hadn't taken action sooner. Hannah had no malice in her heart; she loved them all. When Hannah was finally permitted to write letters, she wrote letters practically daily. When she was very sick, Carol wrote for her. Overtime the letters and small gifts became fewer and fewer, except those from Rose. In turn, as Hannah became more involved with the patients and life at the Homer Folks she too wrote less often. In fact Hannah pushed herself to write her mother once a week. In some ways this was therapeutic because it helped Hannah with homesickness.

With the added privileges Hannah had a setback, which concerned the doctors had. One morning Hannah awoke noticing she felt feverish and was coughing more than normal. While alarmed, she tried to hide her condition from the staff. As Dr. Jones made his rounds Hannah was sitting up in her chair. When she smiled weakly, Dr. Jones noticed her glassy eyes; he listened to her chest, and frowned. Calmly he asked Hannah to return to bed and remain there for couple of days. Dr. Jones hoped Hannah only had a cold. He told Hannah,

"I'm am only going to order a new chest x-ray for now, but you are to remain in bed until told otherwise, no porch or outdoor time."

Hannah felt awful, she was glad to be in bed for a couple of days. Hannah found it difficult to eat and on top of everything she'd become more emotional. She couldn't get Martha out of her mind. How many times had Martha taken care of Hannah through the years? How she wished she could have been there for her. During the day the ward was practically empty, this allowed Hannah private time to grieve and cry without causing attention.

Later in the afternoon Hannah had an x-ray. When she was finished and was back on the ward, Hannah was grateful to return to her bed. Between the wheelchair maneuvering and standing for the x-ray Hannah was exhausted. Hannah immediately fell asleep, barely waking for dinner. When she finished eating, what she could, Hannah immediately drifted back to sleep. As she awoke the following morning, Hannah noticed she felt stuffy, congested, and achy. Maybe she had a simple cold as Dr. Jones was hoping, so she thought.

Dr. Jones was late when he arrived for Hannah's examination. He sat in a chair next to Hannah's bed. Immediately triggering Hannah's nervous mind. Dr. Jones sat quietly for a minute then looked at Hannah,

"Hannah I just finished reviewing your x-ray with Dr. Martin."

"The x-ray showed no signs of pneumonia, so you probably have a cold or virus. What we need to do is collect some sputum and keep you on bed rest. I will order cough medicine for now and reevaluate your condition in a couple of days. In the mean time, drink plenty of water and juice to quicken your recovery from the bug you have."

Hannah felt relieved until Dr. Jones continued speaking,

"We were able to see how your tuberculosis is progressing. In your right lung there are large areas that are badly infected. Do you remember I told you cavities could form? We need these areas to heal. With bed rest and fresh air, these areas will begin to fill in. Unfortunately your x-ray shows lack of healing we'd wished for. Testing your sputum will allow us to see how contaminated the lung is with the tuberculosis germ. When you are feeling better from the cold we will discuss other treatments."

Hannah's eyes grew big with a look of panic. Every test except for the x-ray had been painful so to hear of more treatments Hannah immediately became anxious. Hesitantly she asked Dr. Jones what was the treatment and if it would be painful. Dr. Jones said he would discuss it with her when they were ready to do it. This reply did nothing but make Hannah very anxious.

About a week later Hannah began to feel better. Dr. Jones allowed her to get out of bed and visit with her friends. Hannah was not permitted to go outside or the movies yet. Hannah hadn't been disappointed because the last two movies had been westerns, which she never cared for that genre. What Hannah really liked about the movies was the social time.

Dr. Jones came by to speak to Hannah about the other procedure they briefly discussed weeks prior.

"Hannah do you remember when I mentioned performing an additional treatment. I told you I would tell you about the procedure we are ready to perform it."

Hannah was frightened, but tried to remain calm. What could she do? She would have to agree, as long as it was not a bronchoscopy.

"What we are going to do is an artificial pneumothorax. This is a procedure where we inject air in this space between your lung and the chest cavity. What this will do is make the lung collapse. With your lung collapsed, the lung can be at absolute rest and you will have still have your left lung to breathe with."

"Will it hurt?" Hannah asked.

"Yes it will but this should speedup your recovery. You'll notice a little more shortness of breath. After this procedure it is imperative you rest. Depending upon how you respond you will be able to resume porch rests and have limited visitors but I'm afraid no movies, and walks will need to wait. Do you have any questions?"

Hannah just shook her head no trying not to cry. The only question Hannah asked,

"When would they perform the procedure?" Dr. Jones rose slowly, turning toward Hannah, replying,

"The following morning."

Early the next morning, after a night of tossing and turning, a nurse gave Hannah a mild sedative. An attendant brought her to the medical building. When she entered the treatment room, Hannah smiled at Dr. Martin and said hello. Hannah tried to remain in control but what she needed was a sign from Dr. Martin telling her to,

"Fight, beat this disease Hannah."

Whatever they were going to do, Hannah wanted no part of it. Hannah was not only scared but also fed up with doctors. If this procedure was so great why did they not use it in the beginning of her treatment? Secretly Hannah wanted to fight them off but knew she wouldn't. Within minutes the doctor had numbed the area and was inserting a large long needle. Before Hannah knew what happened they were through. Dr. Martin listen to her lung to be sure there were no breath sounds. He complimented Hannah on her cooperation and advised Hannah she would be receiving oxygen for the next couple of days to help her breathe.

When Hannah returned to her room she was placed in bed with the head elevated. Immediately after the pneumothorax Hannah noticed a change in her breathing. She felt like a drowning person fighting for air. Dr. Martin assured her it would get better and elevating the head of the bed did help. Also Hannah got relief from the oxygen. Each day Hannah felt better. In just one week the oxygen was off and she was getting out of bed. Going on the porch did help raise Hannah's spirits too. All the time she was recouping her friends visited her every day. They all sat around Hannah's bed and Carol took more pictures.

"Pictures, just in case you ever forget Homer Folks and so you don't forget us," Carol said.

How could Hannah ever forget this! She did enjoy her friends.

There was a new member of the group, named Alex. Alex was even younger than Hannah. He was tall and his face was covered with acne. Like Hannah, his eyes drew you to him. They were very pale and washed out blue. Hannah felt protective of him and was always giving him words of encouragement. One day Alex did not show up. When Hannah asked where he was the group hesitated. Finally they told her he had a setback and was on bed rest. As soon as Hannah could she went to his bedside and was shocked by what she saw. Alex was on his back with oxygen going. His skin was ashen and shiny. He kept his eyes closed the whole time she was there. Hannah called him by name and he responded with the week hello and a smile. Trying to give him reassurance, Hannah said, "Fight" and she also told him,

"Don't let the disease win."

She sounded surer than she felt. Every day Hannah visited Alex. Sometimes he responded and sometimes it seemed like he was just asleep. The next time when she was going to his room the nurse stopped her and said,

"You can't go in."

"Why?" asked Hannah.

The nurse replied,

"Because Alex is no longer there."

Immediately Hannah knew what she meant. Hannah was aware of other patients who had died but she had not known them. By not knowing them Hannah did not have to face the reality of the death. Alex had been her friend. She had told him if he fought he would get better. All had been lies. Later that night Hannah lay in bed trying to put things into perspective.

"Why had God let Alex die?" Was this a sign that she should be preparing to die? Certainly she had been sick like Alex. Why hadn't she died? Was she going to die at Homer Folks too, alone without her family like Alex had? Was she ready to die? Once again Hannah was scared and like a child, wanted her mother. Hannah finally theorized life was not fair and often made little sense.

Although Hannah was in mourning the daily routine continued. She felt frightened whenever she experienced shortness of breath or felt she was coughing more. She worried about her own mortality. Many young people Hannah's age felt invincible except for those at the Homer Folks.

FIFTEEN

T he days began to run together, each just as the previous. Everyday Hannah visited the patients on the various wards. Besides patients who were too sick to leave their beds, they always introduced themselves to new patients. Their goal was to cheer up as many as would allow. Occasionally, there would be a patient who refused their kindness, but for the most part they were welcomed. On a typical day as they made their rounds, the group was introduced to a new patient, Hank Schmidt. He appeared pleased to have visitors, but he was a little shy, especially with the women, Hannah noticed. After a couple of visits he began to warm up and expressed how he looked forward to their coming. Hank would listen to their stories as he observed the group. He seemed to pay special attention toward Hannah, but did not direct any conversation toward her.

Socializing was very prevalent. In the evenings, everyone gathered in the recreation room to listen to the radio. Along with the radio, there were magazines, newspapers, and cards available. Hannah liked canasta and played often. Hannah would always bring her knitting while she talked and listen to the radio. Listening to music was her favorite pastime but many of men were more into the happenings associated with the war in Europe. While the majority of patients were in the recreation room, the staff usually congregated around the nurses' station where they smoked and drank coffee paying little attention to the patients' activities.

On one such evening Carol called Hannah aside.

"Hannah I am in love with a patient, his name is Joe."

Hannah had noticed them together and observed them disappear into the bushes but naively thought nothing more of the two. Hannah assumed they wanted privacy in order to talk or hold hands. Hannah did know anything more than that would lead to trouble. So when Carol approached Hannah, she was quite surprised. What Carol suggested next shocked Hannah.

"Hannah, Joe and I wanted to kiss and hug, but you know it's forbidden. Would you please stand guard briefly outside the linen room while Joe and I go in?"

Hannah stood speechless. What Carol was proposing was not only wrong, but it could get them all in trouble if caught. On the other hand, Carol had been very good to her. Infact Hannah loved Carol like a sister. In the end, Hannah agreed, but only for five minutes. Hannah's stomach ached with butterflies as she stood guard, longer than five minutes. Also the noises she could hear coming from the linen room sounded like more than kissing! Eventually, Carol and Joe exited looking a bit flustered, each with a sheepish smile, and both thanked Hannah. As Hannah walked away she hoped this would not happen again, however the meetings became a weekly occurrence. Hannah, overcome with guilt, stood guard. After a few weeks, Hannah finally figured out what was really happening between Carol and Joe.

Hannah was cautious to follow the directives that affected her recovery. The doctors reversed the pneumothorax when substantial healing took place. Every three weeks Hannah had a chest x-ray and needed to fill sputum jars for them to study. It had been a while since Dr. Jones been by to give Hannah bad news. Still, Hannah would not let her guard down because there was always a chance he would appear one day. Hannah religiously went to the porch every morning. After sitting on the porch, Hannah would walk the grounds often stopping to take in the sun. During the afternoon two o'clock, mandated rest Hannah slept soundly, usually sleeping over the allotted time.

Hannah's attitude, along with her appetite, changed. When Hannah first arrived she was hiding her food, now she ate everything provided enjoying every mouth full. This included the milk she was given. Hannah never cared for milk as a child but now she drank it faithfully. Hannah often thought about the times when food was scarce around the Wright household. It made her realize how lucky she was now, almost ironic. To eat healthy she had to be ill. This didn't make sense to Hannah but much didn't.

The question of her discharge was always in the back of her mind. Hannah also thought about what she would do after leaving Homer Folks guessing, she would most likely would live with her mother, get a job as a secretary, and take care of her mother as Rose got older. Occasionally, Hannah would ask,

"Dr. Jones when will you be able to predict my discharge?"

He always answered Hannah evasively. He refused to tell her, her progress was very slow, which could not allow him any predictions. For every two steps forward Hannah made often lead to one huge step backward.

Time seemed to drag by but when October came, Hannah wondered what had happened to summer. The weather was beginning to chill and the leaves with their brightness made each day seem unique. It was in the ever-changing month of October, when Carol came to Hannah needing to talk to her. Carol insisted they be alone and talk in private so they went for a walk. All of a sudden Carol turned to Hannah,

"I'm pregnant!"

Speechless, Hannah thought she heard Carol wrong, "Pregnant?" Carol continued in tears,

"Joe won't talk to me and he's accusing me of fooling around with other men. He insists the baby is not his."

To make things worse Carol had been vomiting. The staff felt it should be investigated, they never suspected Carol was pregnant.

A doctor was summoned, questioned Carol thoroughly. Carol admitted to having sex, there was no sense in denying it so the doctor quickly made his diagnosis. He said,

"Carol, while you seem healthy, but you are not ready for discharge."

"Hannah," Carol said,

"The doctor wants to do a therapeutic abortion."

As Carol was sobbing, Hannah, naïve as she was, asked Carol,

"What's an abortion?" By the time Carol could gather the strength to explain what the doctor ordered, Hannah was crying too. Until Hannah arrived at Homer Folks she knew very little about pregnancies. In fact, Hannah knew nothing about how a woman became pregnant, until Carol had enlightened her.

A few days later, Carol was taken to the medical building. Hannah knowing what was about to happen became restless and withdrawn. She wanted to be with Carol so Carol didn't have to face the abortion alone. During rest time, Carol returned, she was very pale, and tears were streaming down her face. Once Carol was settled in her bed, Hannah went to her, sat, and held her hand. It seemed almost inhuman to expect Carol to bear both the physical and mental pain of ending her pregnancy. Joe somehow managed to lie his way out of everything. Hannah could not understand how people who knew Carol could think of her as promiscuous. Carol told Hannah,

"Joe was the first and only man I have ever been with."

Carol went through the ordeal alone because no one believed her when asked who the father was. Hannah rarely saw the Carol she had grown to love as a sister. To appease everyone, Carol would go through all the motions of being her old self, but Hannah knew the inner spark was gone; and for good.

Along with the leaves and weather changing, October brought the yearly, highly anticipated Halloween party. Hannah volunteered on the planning committee. Naturally a costume party was proposed. To include the younger patients at Homer Folks, the adults would plan a special time for them for trick or treating.

The planning committee came up with various activities for the party and all insisted for bobbing for apples. A staff member, who was on the committee, squashed the idea. She reminded the group, even though she agreed it was fun, it would never be approved in fear of spreading disease. Disappointed, no one argued, they understood. The committee finalized their plans, including the music for the evening. Naturally to peak everyone's interest in attending the party, the group decided on various competitions relating to their costumes. The largest prize would be given for the most original costume. When everyone was getting ready to leave, return to their wards, one of the staff members and committee members announced the time the party would end at midnight. Normally, lights off were always at ten-thirty. Therefore, to make everything complete the committee reread their plans and who would be responsible for what. By the time the meeting was finished everyone, including Carol, had genuine smiles wishing the party was sooner than later.

Hannah thought long about her costume. Many of the ideas that came to mind were impossible to make due to the lack of supplies needed. At last, Hannah decided what she would dress as, a little girl. She borrowed a skirt from Carol because Carol was shorter than Hannah by about six inches, making Carol's skirt the perfect length. A week before the party, those who hadn't a costume scrounged through lockers for something to wear. Hannah was standing by Nurse Riley when she remembered she needed a doll. Hannah turned to Nurse Riley saying,

"Would it be possible to get me a doll from the children's ward, it's part of my costume?"

Nurse Riley had taken a liking to Hannah not only because Hannah was so polite, kind young lady but also because she felt sorry for Hannah, because of her prognosis. Nurse Riley gladly obliged by going to the children's ward to borrow a doll. Hannah decided to wear her hair in pigtails and put freckles on her nose with an eyebrow pencil. Hannah drew the line, she would not take off the blood red nail polish she loved, even for one night.

Halloween eve came and, as twilight was settling, the children made their presence known throughout each ward showing off their costumes. Each had a pillowcase to collect their treats. Shortly after the children returned to their ward, Hannah and friends were off visiting patients who were too sick to attend the party. Hannah was proud of her costume and decided at the last minute to bandage her knee. Carol was a teenager, although she was still pale and depressed. All night, it was obvious to Hannah Carol was trying to appear to be having a good time. She wished she could help Carol in some way even though she knew deep down there was nothing for Hannah to do, other than be Carol's friend.

When Hannah reached the auditorium she was thrilled with the decorations. Occupational therapy had been especially instrumental in making decorations. The party was already flowing with patients. As Carol and Hannah looked around they noticed patients with masks on, so they tried figuring out who was who. Soon after the music they chose, began. A strange looking person came over,

"May I have this dance?"

Who ever the stranger was, dressed like a woman wearing a mask, wig, false boobs, a dress that almost touched the ankles and a pair of flat nurse shoes. Hannah couldn't help but laugh. As they danced she tried to get him to talk, but he remained silent. If Hannah came up with a question he would need to answer, the gentleman made his voice sound high and strange. Hannah had a marvelous time with him. Hannah and her admirer danced to almost every song. Hannah finally was provided an opportunity to sit and relax; the stranger brought her refreshments.

At about nine-thirty, an announcement was made,

"Gather around, we are about to hand out awards." Hannah's admirer was standing next to her. When the winner for the most original costume was announced, Hannah's jaw dropped in surprise. The dashing stranger won. When the judges kindly asked the winner to reveal his face the stranger politely shook his head no. Hannah knew she would find out who she had been dancing with all night because having played a roll in the planning the party anyone masked would be asked to remove their masks during the last dance. As Hank removed his mask, he gave Hannah a huge smile and finished the dance. Hank Schmidt had turned her evening into something magical. After the dance, Hank asked Hannah,

"Would it be all right I if I walk you to your ward?" Hannah agreed and they said their goodnights. Hank was able to convince Hannah to go for a walk with him the following day.

Hannah could not recall an evening where she had such a wonderful time. Granted she attended at two proms with Izzy, but there was no comparing. As she fell into sleep, her mind filled with thoughts about Hank. He frightened her a little, but not in a creepy way. She thought of what happened between Joe and Carol, which made her decide anything with Hank would be friendly. Hannah awoke the following morning with a grin on her face.

She was smiling not only of the previous night's memories, but because it was a beautiful, Indian summer day. Hannah met Hank on the path named the "cure path". They walked a bit, sat on the bench, and watched the squirrels play in the trees. They said very little to each other. The silence was not awkward but natural. Finally, out of nowhere, Hank asked Hannah if she would tell him about her family. Hannah smiled,

"Would you like the long version or the time I've been here at Homer Folks?"

He chose the longer version, so he could listen to her rather raspy voice. He thought her voice was sexy but Hannah was sweet and gentle. Completely ignorant to Hank's motives, Hannah agreed and began.

Hannah thought, since he asked, she wouldn't leave anything out and began with her grandparents.

"My grandparents, Jeremiah and Matilda, immigrated to the United States from Ireland."

She decided to embellish some, when referring to life in New York City. Hannah shared touching stories about her grandparents, especially their trip from Ireland on the ship. Hank displayed particular interest when Hannah mentioned Rose's days performing in the theater. As Hannah remembered various times she had experienced or heard in relation with her parents, she would occasionally let a tear drop. Thinking of her father often had this affect on Hannah. She amazed Hank when she told of all her brothers. Hannah described the move to Albany. She bragged, with a smile ear to ear, speaking of her father's business. She introduced Hank to Aunt Kitty and Martha. Suddenly Hannah's tempo and pride began to fade when she told Hannah about the loss of her father's business. She included the need to sell their house and her father's occupation as a milkman. Then Hank was told how Edmund's illnesses were so severe he could no longer work, which led to the boys supporting the family. After a couple of deep breaths Hannah shared more about her personal life. Hannah described the years during the depression, forcing Hank to think Hannah's family were not as impoverish as others. He could decipher a substantial amount of cohesiveness through the family. Then she switched to her life, which to her was not as fascinating as her families. Hank never interrupted Hannah and when Hannah paused as if lost in a memory he let her be. He was very moved when Hannah described her father's death.

Now it was time to go in. They walked quietly back as they returned to the patients' wards. Anxious to hear more from Hannah, as they reached her ward, Hank asked,

"May I have the pleasure to your company tomorrow? I enjoyed listening to you about your family. I'd like to hear more if you would accept." Happily Hannah agreed, as she turned toward her room.

For the second night, as Hannah drifted off in sleep, she couldn't help but think of Hank. She recalled their entire day. Hannah knew tomorrow would be even better, if at all possible. As she thought about Hank, she had a good feeling. Hank was nice and could easily become someone special.

As Hannah's luck would go, she woke to rain. It rained for the next three days and the Indian summer weather turned bitter. Hannah saw little of Hank, leaving her to wonder if the day on the bench had been special. By the third day, Hank had drifted from her mind. Returning to the ward from occupational therapy that promptly changed. Standing by her bed was Hank. As Hannah approached him, he said,

"I've been thinking of you, if the other day was just that a day, or the beginning of something. I thought the best way to see is if we let it take its natural course, and add in slight human encouragement."

"Tonight is movie night. Would you go to the movies with me, Hannah?"

Hannah agreed, not with the joy she felt after their walk. Hank picked Hannah up at her ward and they walked to the movies in silence. Hannah and Hank watch "42nd Street." along with a few other patients and after they ate their snack together.

"I still have the remainder of your life story to hear. I'm eager to listen and anxious to hear the conclusion." Hannah agreed, but also reminded Hank,

"When I'm done I expect to hear about your life including all ancestors."

With Hannah's stress on ancestors they both laughed and Hank agreed.

The next day was deceiving. When Hannon looked out her window it resembled a beautiful spring day but as she approached the window she could feel the cold wind from outside. Hank picked up Hannah for their second a walk. Both were bundled up, but Hannah noticed some things missing on Hank. He did not have gloves, a hat or a scarf. Hannah knew what she must do do. In fact, Hannah already had plans to knit Hank a black sweater; so matching gloves, hat, and scarf would be perfect.

They found the same bench and sat close to each other for the sole purpose of maintaining warmth. Hank leaned into Hannah and said,

"Let me remind you where you left off the other day." Hannah listened to Hank's quick version of what she had said then as he paused she began. Hannah told Hank about life after her father's death. Her brothers were expected to pitch in and help Rose, Martha, and her. Almost all of her brothers were living at home, but gradually each drifted in their own direction in search of their lives. Although they might not have lived under the same roof, they were still a large part of their mother's financial success. Hannah appeared lost for a few seconds as she tried to decide the right approach when explaining her illness. She thought the best approach was the truth and tell Hank everything from beginning to now. Looking at Hank Hannah started,

"I guess I was sick for awhile before my mother realized she couldn't help me. My mother has always been the nurse-mother who could get anyone well. This time was different. One night she called my brother and they rushed me to St. Peter's Hospital. I was there for three weeks in an oxygen tent, and very ill. Because they had tried everything in their power to help me, it was decided I transfer here to Homer Folks. I've been here for almost a year and have no idea if or when I'll be discharged. I've given up asking. To be fair though, I do feel better, although I've had set backs. I do believe if I wasn't brought here I would have died."

Slowly, Hannah released a large sigh as if the weight of the world had just left her body. Hank took in all Hannah had shared and thought he had found his princess. As much as Hannah wanted Hank to share his story with her, she was tired and in need of a nap. Plus it was very cold and windy, which drained her more. Hank assured her he would begin the following day if she would allow him. Hannah agreed and they returned to their perspective wards. She wanted to hear Hank story but it was cold and she was exhausted.

Nurse Riley was keeping a close eye on Hannah. She knew Hannah and Hank were taking walks together and going to the movies. Nurse Riley also knew of the close relationship between Hannah and Carol, therefore she decided to speak with Hannah. She went to Hannah's bed, sat down and started a simple conversation. Hannah immediately was suspicious. Nurse Riley with her years of experience discreetly probed to find out exactly what Hannah knew about sex. In a motherly way expressed her growing concerns about the amount of time Hannah and Hank spent together Hannah said,

"Nurse Riley we have been taking walks, talking, and going to the movies."

Nurse Riley eased off Hannah's bed, turned to Hannah and said,

"I'm only trying to look out for you and I need you to be careful. Also, Hannah, if there is ever a time you need someone to talk with, please seek me out. You can talk to me about anything and it will remain between us."

Hannah could tell Nurse Riley was sincere but deep inside she laughed a little to herself wondering why all the toughness on the outside. Nurse Riley walked away and Hannah thought, maybe she would take Nurse Riley up on her offer.

Days passed before Hannah saw Hank again. Hank needed to admit he was just as scared of beginning a new relationship with anyone. In fact, he had never had a girlfriend in the true sense of the word. He dated and enjoyed being around women. Hannah was different which he knew from their first walk. The weather, he thought reminded him of Hannah and what was building between them. Each one's feelings varied as the weather did, leaving them both uncertain. Before he knew it, Hannah and Hank were outside for their walk. In surprise, Hannah handed Hank a brown bag and inside was a beautiful black knit scarf. Hank was at a loss for words, then said,

"The only other person who ever gave me a gift was my mother, which has been quite a while."

They spent the day walking with little conversation. Hannah and Hank just enjoyed the company of the other. Hank promised Hannah he would begin telling his life story during recreation time, that evening. Hank kept his word.

Hannah sat patiently listening to Hank speak of his family. She was startled when Hank revealed, he too was from Albany. Like Hannah, his maternal grandparents had come to this country from Ireland, but he never knew their names. His father's family immigrated from Germany. They were grocers before the depression. Throughout, Hannah noticed Hank would often talk of his mother more than other family members. Hannah let him ramble; she noticed it seemed good for him, something he hadn't really done before. Hank's father became a house painter after the depression, but he often went without work. He mentioned an older sister who usually took care of him. His mother was often ill with sick headaches. Hank was the third out of five and the favorite for his father to single out. Hank's father had died a couple of years ago. His older brother decided Buffalo would be better for his mother and younger sisters. Hank remained in Albany living with his older sister and her husband. When his mother moved away he was eighteen, and started to run wild. Hank never mentioned exactly what he meant by wild, but told her how he came down with tuberculosis. He picked up cigarette butts from the gutters and smoked them, not a pretty sight but that's how it was for him. Throughout listening to Hank, Hannah was moved with every word. Serious, Hannah asked Hank if he could do anything with his life, what would make him the happiest? Laughing Hank replied,

"Play golf!!"

SIXTEEN

For a change, Hannah was visiting Hank, rather than the other way around. That was until she approached his ward. As Hannah got closer, she could hear heart-wrenching sobs that immediately worried her. The cries were coming from Hank forcing Hannah to reach him as quickly as possible. Just as she turned toward his ward, Hannah came face to face with the ward nurse.

"Today is not a good day for Hank dear. It would probably be better if Hank had some time alone."

Shocked and confused Hannah replied,

"Why?" "What's wrong with Hank? Is he having a relapse?"

The ward nurse refused to answer Hannah's questions and Hannah knew she would not be permitted to see Hank.

Hannah turned around confused, and went back to her room. She thought about talking to Carol, but changed her mind knowing men were very private and no man would want to admit they'd been crying. Trying to figure out what would upset Hank so, Hannah prayed it was not his tuberculosis.

Days went by, and Hannah did not see Hank. He kept to his room. Staff members were becoming concerned because they knew how close Hannah and Hank were. Hank's despondency and withdrawal from everything, especially Hannah, forced them to summon Hannah; ask her if she would try and speak with Hank. Late in the day, quietly Hannah approached Hank's bed. Hank just lay there, on his back, with his eyes closed. Gently, she called, "Hank." Slowly Hank opened his eyes and said "hi." Hannah sat in a chair by his bed and smiled at him, waiting for Hank to initiate a conversation. He just stared at her, from and out of nowhere apologized for staying away. Cautiously, Hannah replied,

"Hank, do you want to tell me what's going on?"

Hank tried to be nonchalant,

"My mother died last week. She was fifty-six and had a stroke. No one told me until she was buried."

Hannah could hear his voice rise with each word he spoke.

"I am so really sorry Hank. How can I help you? What can I do?"

In his same calm tone he said to Hannah,

"I'll be all right in a couple of days."

With out realizing it, Hannah reached over and placed her hand on his. Hank a bit surprised, let her hand remain on his; he liked how it felt. As they sat in silence, Hannah turned to Hank,

"Hank, tell me about your mother, if you would."

"I'm not sure I can describe her in any other way than she was my mother and she loved me. Out of my family, she is the only person who really loved me, not only telling me but by showing me. And Hannah, you know what hurts and upsets me the most, I never told her just how much I loved her and now I'll never be given the opportunity. Not only did I neglect to say goodbye to her when I came here, now I'll never get the chance at all. I should have been told she was sick. I should have been the one to make the choice, whether to call her or not. I planned to visit her when I was discharged, but now I'll visit her resting place. I should have been a better son. I haven't seen her in over a year and now I never will. God, Hannah, I wish I could see her one more time, I'd give anything for that to happen."

As Hank spoke, he seemed to sink lower and lower in his bed. Hannah's heart ached for him. Hank had no family to console him. Hannah recalled when her father died; the entire family was a comfort for her. Thinking about it, she should have been more of a support for Rose. Hannah never had been one to comfort; she was always the one everyone looked after during a time of grief. Maybe instinctively or sheer luck, Hannah allowed Hank time to talk and get out what he needed to say in order for him to begin grieving. Hank continued talking for about another hour and eventually turned to Hannah,

"I do hope you can be patient while I try and deal with my mother's death. I think I need a few days alone in order to come to terms with everything that's happened. I need to search my soul to forgive myself for the son I became and not the son I should have been."

Hannah, with tears in her eyes, completely understood and told Hank to take as much time as he needed.

"Hank, I'm not going anywhere and you need to be alone during a time like this to think, remember, and no one can do it for you. You take all the time you need and I'll be where I always am waiting for you."

For the next few days, Hank often visited the chapel. Although he was lonely, sad, and depressed, that didn't mean he wasn't religious. Hank, having grown up an alter boy, knew for one to gain peace and release his mother from purgatory to return to Heaven, he needed to recite certain prayers. Deep down, Hank knew his mother was already by the Lord's side, but for Hank he needed to be positive. Therefore, he would recite the prayers daily, beg forgiveness for his sins, and pray to his mother for her love. Hank hadn't seen his mother in quite some time he loved her and wanted to be sure she knew it.

As Hank promised he began showing up to visit Hannah and the gang, but his mother's death weakened him physically as well as mentally. He had gone days with out eating and the doctors were beginning to show concern. He was angry because one of the doctors mentioned bronchoscopy. Hank yelled at Hannah,

"They are never going to do that to me again!"

Hannah tried to calm Hank down by reminding him that the bronchoscopy might be necessary to prevent a relapse, therefore postponing his "recovery". Without the strength to fight everyone, including Hannah, Hank gave in, agreeing to the procedure.

On the day of Hank's bronchoscopy, Hannah woke early in order to see Hank before his procedure. They chatted briefly until staff members on Hank's ward realized Hannah was there. To some, Hannah and Hank were spending too much time together and with Hannah by Hank's side so early irritated those staff members. Therefore, Hannah was told to return to her ward. As Hannah was leaving she turned to Hank,

"I'll say a prayer to St.Theresa, Hank. Don't worry you'll be fine."

Hank relaxed as Hannah left, admitting to himself, Hannah had released some of his anxiety. As he calmed, Hank said a couple of prayers of his own asking God for the strength and courage to get through the test.

The bronchoscopy went smoothly, surprising Hank. Later in that day Hank sent a message, via his friend Ed, to Hannah stating he would meet her in the recreation room that night. Hannah relieved to see the signs of Hank she had grown to like, slowly coming out of his shell. Precisely at seven, Hank entered the recreation room and headed directly to Hannah. They sat next to each other; almost close enough to touch, as Hank began accounting for his day. He told Hannah how calm he had been during the procedure. Not wanting to doubt Hank, Hannah wondered if he might be exaggerating the ease of the bronchoscopy. Hannah recalled the number of times she had suffered through it and couldn't equate it with calming, but rather frightening. It didn't matter, thought Hannah. Hank had gotten through it and she was seeing signs of Hank returning. With the test done and Hank was spending less time isolated, they could continue to see where their relationship was headed. Hank finally spoke up,

"Dr. Jones doesn't think there is much to worry about after reviewing the report of the bronchoscopy."

As each day passed, the routine at Homer Folks returned. The Hannah and Hank spent as much time together that was allowed. One place they did not share was the porch. Their wards had scheduled times and theirs never crossed. If it was a nice day, Hannah and Hank often went on walks, always on the "cure path". They would stroll, talk, and then rest on the same bench. Unknowingly they found plenty to talk about, especially Albany. They discovered Hannah was from the south end of Albany and Hank always lived in west Albany. Naturally they had gone to different high schools during different times. Hank had graduated four years ahead of Hannah. Hannah didn't know Hank was not into baseball due to his love of the Yankees, but was surprised to learn Hank had been All Albany in basketball. Hank got a kick out of hearing Hannah's explain her baseball days, playing with the neighborhood boys and her brother until her father decided little girls should not be playing sports. Often, the two would talk over the other as if competing to tell their best stories.

Hank again began telling Hannah about his life, which meant to Hannah, Hank was really feeling better, emotionally and psychologically. He shared his stories about his youth as an alter boy. Hannah thought he must have always had faith in God. He impressed her with his devotion to his religion. Hannah was now re-examining her own spirituality. Having always been a Catholic, Hannah knew she had to confess her sins before anything else. Hannah did go to confession and then started to go to Mass with Hank. The two, with other Homer Folks patients attended Catholic services every Sunday. After Mass, Hannah and Hank would take a walk on the grounds discussing the priest's sermon. Both were content and happy, but most of all, they seemed healthy.

Hank was becoming more aware of his feelings for Hannah. He obsessed over her health. Although Hank could become bossy with Hannah, he was always caring. Even though Hank might have had a difficult upbringing, one would never know by his manners. Always a gentleman, especially with Hannah, Hank would refer to Hannah as "his queen." One beautiful day Hank picked a bouquet of violets and hand delivered them to Hannah. Hannah, taken back with joy, wondered if the flowers were Hank's way of signaling a change in their relationship. Hannah wanted to respond and the only way she knew how was with her poetry. The poems Hannah wrote related to beautiful things that surrounded her. How could she write one for Hank that expressed her feelings about him? Hannah wasn't sure as to the meaning of the violets. Hannah had so many positive feelings that forced her to think about Hank constantly. For some patients Homer Folks became their defacto family. Also they were both aware of the policy of fraternizing with the opposite sex. What they didn't realize was the staff was aware of them but saw how positive they were for each other. The staff overlooked what they hoped was just a special relationship.

Secretly Hank and Hannah began holding hands, always mindful of staff members because even though it seemed little, it was still forbidden. Everyone at Homer Folks knew of the budding sweetheart's relationship. Most likely due to Hannah's character, many among the staff trusted Hannah and Hank to be discrete and respectful enough to not flaunt their feelings or cross the imaginary line. For Hannah and Hank, the smallest gesture of holding hands provided enough excitement and thrill for each, it made them giddy. The electricity between the two was immeasurable.

The two became teenagers. They would go to the movies, but only when the other would attend. And, they always sat together holding hands. One evening they decided to sit in the rear when Hank suddenly built up his nerve and slowly wrapped his arm around Hannah shoulders. Hannah, surprised, smiled to herself as she snuggled next to him. Hannah could not describe how she was feeling. Her emotions were very extreme. Sometimes she was anxious at the sight of Hank, other times she was nervous when he held her hand, but she was always happy. Hannah had experienced these feelings before and she knew they were natural, so why the tightness in her chest and flipping of her stomach with the thought of Hank, she wondered. A friend of Hannah's told her,

"You, my dear, are in love." Hannah just remained silent, wondering if she was right,

"Could I be in love?"

Hannah wished she had someone close she could confide her deepest secrets. Her friend Carol had been discharged the preceding month. Shocking everyone, Carole promptly got engaged to one of the doctors at Homer Folks. While Hannah was happy for Carol she missed her and wished she could be available for one of their girl talks. Hannah had friends at Homer Folks who she could confide in if needed, but since Carol left and Hannah spent most of her free time with Hank, she hadn't taken time to make another close friend.

Hannah received letters from her mother, often two or three a week, allowing Hannah to keep up with her family. She kept her mother's letters from Hank because, before her death, Hank's mother wrote him frequently. Hannah was successful until one day when they had been walking, a letter from Rose fell out of Hannah's sweater pocket landing at Hank's feet. Hannah immediately said

"I'm sorry,"

Hank handing Hannah her letter, sadly smiled and said,

"Please don't apologize for still having your mother with you."

Having Hank's arms around her for the first time overwhelmed Hannah with feelings she never knew existed.

It seemed to be a typical day for Hannah and Hank. It was beautiful out so they were walking while idly chatting when they reached their bench. The two relaxed until Hank asked Hannah,

"Tell me what you feel when I hold your hand?"

"Excitement," Hannah replied asking Hank the same question.

"I feel waves of emotions when I hold your hand, so much I don't want to let go." Hannah smiled as she watched Hank respond. Hank then wanted to know about the hug, did she like it? Hannah couldn't contain herself,

"Of course I liked it Hank. I've never felt a react to being hugged before. I wish we could hug all the time. I enjoy having your arms tightly around me."

And so their conversation went. What it boiled down to was they were both obsessed with each other. They didn't say they wanted more. More was not possible. So they relied upon holding hands and hugging. Another occasion when they were outside Hank had his arm around Hannah and she asked

"Why don't you kiss me?" Surprised Hank laughed and squeezing her hard.

"You are asking for trouble. If I were to kiss you, I would not be able to stop. I'd want all of you."

Hank hoped his answer would end the discussion he instigated; he neglected to be completely honest with his answer. Typical for Hannah, she persisted; forcing Hank to tell her the most important reason they could not kiss.

"Hannah you understand how the tuberculosis germ is spread, don't you?"

"Yes," said Hannah.

"Well if we kiss on the mouth we can spread the tuberculosis germs between the two of us."

"So," replied Hannah, "There are other places we can kiss, aren't there?"

How innocent and sheltered Hannah really was, Hank thought to himself. He needed to be even more protective of her now and he wasn't sure he had the strength within himself. As Hank travelled off in thought, Hannah without warning quickly kissed Hank's hand. Her actions not only startled him, but also thrilled Hank. As she turned her head to look at something, Hank leaned in and gently kissed her cheek. The two began laughing, knowing they had crossed over the imaginary line. From that day on, each time they were together, they would give the other a discreet kiss. Day by day their relationship was becoming more than they each imagined, more passionate than the day before.

Out of all the programs offered at Homer Folks, both Hannah and Hank loved recreational therapy. They went on picnics on the huge rock behind the barn. Hank and Hannah had become constant companions. Therefore, when a picture was taken as they embraced, no one seemed to notice. If an outsider, someone who didn't know what type of medical facility Homer Folks was, wandered upon Hank and Hannah, it could be thought of as a happy place. Not a medical sanitarium where death was a common occurrence. After the kissing episode they posed for the pictures with their arms around each other. One would not think it possible that they were very happy at the Homer Folks.

Along with recreational therapy, each enjoyed occupational therapy. Here they were working on handmade gifts for each other. Hannah was still hard at work knitting the sweater she started before Christmas. Hank was making a photo album for Hannah's pictures. Hank worked hard making a photo album for Hannah's pictures she accumulated during her time at Homer Folks. Hank paid special attention to the front and back covers by making them out of wood. On the front, he carefully burned Hannah's initials, HMW. Hannah would love his gift; Hank could hardly maintain his composure, until he could hand it to her.

When the gifts were completed, each wrapped theirs in newspaper, and then waited for a special occasion to exchange. The perfect time for a celebration was approaching, their year together. It was decided to exchange on that day. Hank opened Hannah's gift and was in awe of the sweater she knitted. Hank teased Hannah,

"Tell me where you bought this, I need one in every color." Hannah turning a bit red, smiled saying,

"With your hair it makes you look like a gangster, a handsome gangster though."

Anxious, Hannah's turn had come. She had no idea what Hank had made her, he'd been so secretive. As she opened her gift her eyes grew with surprise. She had never seen such a beautiful album. Hannah looked at Hank and wondered how he could have found the time to make an album so personal. There was only one thing she wanted,

"Hank when we are in occupational therapy next, would you burn your initials by mine?"

Even though the album was Hannah's, Hank agreed. When he finished the front of the album, it read HFS and HMW. Hannah knew it was perfect.

Hank had a second gift in mind but he wasn't sure he could pull it off. In order to give the second gift to Hannah, Hank wrote to his good friend Buzz. He asked Buzz to go to his sister's house and retrieve a little wooden box he had next to his bed. In the box there were three, old coins that had been given to him as a boy. Hank instructed Buzz,

"Could you sell them for me? Then, I need you to purchase a specific item without telling a soul." Buzz wrote back and assured Hank he would do exactly as asked and not to worry.

Hannah nervously wrote her mother sharing her news about Hank. She described how her days had changed with Hank around. Rose read Hannah's letter carefully, reading between the lines and determined Hannah was falling in love. Rose was also relieved in receiving a letter from Dr. Jones. While Dr. Jones normally wrote Hannah's health as guarded, Rose could tell her daughter's health was not as Hannah reported. Rose wrote Hannah back wanting to hear everything Hannah had to say in regards to Hank. In the meantime Rose knew she needed to visit as soon as possible.

Rose arranged for Edmund Jr. to drive her to Homer Folks. Harry, home on leave from the army, joined them, eager to see his sister. Hannah and Hank waited for the three to arrive in the visitor's center. She paced along the windows wishing Edmund Jr.'s car would appear. Hank was obviously nervous because he remained seated with his arms folded across his chest.

Hannah stopped pacing, turned to Hank, and said,

"They here. I can't believe they're here. Hank come here and look."

Hank slowly walked to where Hannah stood and looked out the window. He saw an elderly woman and two men. Hannah pointed out,

"Obviously the woman is my mother, Rose, and the man to her right is my oldest brother Edmund Jr., and to her left is my brother Harry."

Hannah was even more surprised to see Harry; she had not known he was home on leave.

After introductions were made, the five relaxed in a secluded corner of the visitor's center. Hank felt nervous as he listened to Hannah and her family talk. Occasionally, someone would ask Hank a question and although he was shy, Hank would answer whatever they needed to know. He knew Rose had concerns with Hannah, medically and personally, therefore, Hank wanted to be as helpful as possible. As Hank watched Hannah with her mother and brothers, he thought how much he already knew about this family. Hannah shared so many stories, he felt as if he could easily fit in. While Hank took in Hannah and her family, Rose was determined to meet the real Hank. She wanted to judge her self the type of man her beloved daughter had become smitten with, she didn't want Hannah's opinions, she wanted her own.

After an hour or so of talking, Harry decided to surprise Hannah. He had a box wrapped in brown paper. Hannah couldn't guess what her brother would give her until she ripped off the paper.

"Harry, a camera, a new camera with five rolls of film. How did you know? This is too much, I can't possibly accept this."

"Don't be silly. Mom told me you have grown to love photography and how can that be when you haven't anything to take photos?"

Hannah turned to Hank,

"Look Hank, I'll be able to take my own pictures now and put the most special ones in the album."

Hank nodded smiling at Hannah. Hannah got up and threw her arms around Harry, thanking him over and over.

"I promise to send you pictures with each letter I write from now on."

"You better, I'm going to hold you to that promise," smiled Harry.

As Hannah returned to her seat, next to Hank, Rose suddenly said,

"Do you two realize, you have the same aqua blue eyes?"

Hannah told Rose someone pointed it out and one day they stood side by side in front of a mirror to see. Everyone seemed a bit amazed by this.

The remainder of the visit seemed to fly by. Hank feeling more at ease, asked Harry his thought about the United States entering the war in Europe. The two discussed the war, while Hannah noticed Hank's expression changing. He seemed excited by the thought of the United Stated becoming part of Europe's war and Hannah felt a sense of dread.

Nearing their time to leave, Rose and Hannah walked to a private spot. Rose confided,

"Hank seems like a very nice gentleman. I can see how happy the two of you are and if he can make my baby girl happy, then I approve. I know I can speak for Edmund Jr. and Harry and they like Hank too. Hannah you must remember though, unless you take care of yourself and get rid of the tuberculosis, you will never truly be free to go on with your life. Hank must do the same. I want you both to promise your health comes first and then you can have the rest of your lives for love."

Hannah looked at her mother with tears in her eyes, hugged her, and then thanked Rose.

"I love you, mother."

Rose replied, "I love you too, Hannah."

Shortly after, Rose, Edmund Jr. and Harry left; they had a long, difficult drive ahead of them. Hannah turned to Hank, tears streaming down her cheeks, and said,

"I miss them already and it hurts."

Hank pulled Hannah in, hugging her and replied,

"I know, I know, but think of the afternoon we just shared. Remember Hannah, they are always in your heart and you'll be going home once you kick the tuberculosis."

The two stood there, embraced as the sun set.

That night Hank constantly talked about the possibility of war with the other men on the ward. While engrossed in conversation about the war, the reality of their situation was foremost. No one cured of tuberculosis was eligible to join the armed forces. They were all classified as 4F. Many of the men were upset because they could never serve their country. It was as if someone challenged their manhood because they contracted tuberculosis. One's pride was hurt and marked forever.

Hank's friend Buzz came for a visit. Hank introduced Buzz to Hannah. Hannah liked Buzz, but didn't like his manners, tough and crude, complete opposite to Hank. However, Hank and Buzz got along famously. They talked about golf and their friends. Hank was quite animated. Occasionally Hank tried to bring Hannah into the conversation but Hannah didn't fit. Hannah excused herself, and went to her locker, and got her camera. While she was away, Buzz gave Hank a package and change. Hannah came back asking to take Buzz and Hank's picture. She told Buzz,

"Just before I snap your picture, take the mask down."

After Buzz left, Hank hid the package in his room.

For the next week the weather was terrible; rain, wind, thunderstorms, hail, and anything else the weather gods could throw. On top of it, each day was very humid and hot. When heat got trapped in the brick buildings, it was like a furnace. Most patients spent their walking time outside.

July left and August came in and the weather broke. Granted it was still warm, but occasionally there was a lovely breeze. Hannah and Hank tried to spend as much time as possible outside. They walked along the "cure path" and around the buildings.

Lately Hank took to working in the garden, something different from his city life. He enjoyed letting Hannah know the vegetables they would have at dinner. Hank decided to work in the barn and was shown how to milk a cow. Hank daydreamed he would own a country house with Hannah someday. He made plans for them, but until he knew that both would be healthy, he would not share them with Hannah.

One morning Hank woke up knowing this was the day. Excited he couldn't wait to talk to Hannah. He had a full day events before he could see Hannah. There was a.m. care, doctor's rounds, porch rest, lunch, work, and rest, and then he could see Hannah on the path. As always, at four pm they met on the "cure path." Hannah could see excitement in Hank's eyes, but she didn't know the reason.

Intrigued, Hannah asked,

"What is it Hank? What's gotten into you today?"

Whatever Hank was up to, Hannah had a feeling it was going to be good. They walked past the bench hand-in-hand. Without warning, Hank pulled Hannah in the bushes, eagerly took her in his arms, and kissed her on the mouth, closed mouth. Hank stepped back to look at Hannah. Hannah was smiling at his unreadable grin. Before she could pull away, he kissed her again. His kisses were hungry and passionate. Then, he just held her, noticing how soft and wonderful she was. Hannah responded to Hanks kisses in the same manner they were given, passionate and full of hunger for more. Unable to think clearly, Hannah couldn't understand why Hank was acting so strangely. She felt as if her head was whirling with excitement and her body tingled in places she never knew existed. As they broke their embrace, Hannah began walking toward the path when she heard Hank,

"Hannah, stop, please come back. I have something for you."

Hannah couldn't resist as she turned and saw Hank down on one knee. Laughing, Hannah said,

"Hank what are you doing other than being silly?"

As Hannah went walked back to Hank, suddenly she realized something serious in Hank's eyes.

"Hannah Marie Wright, I love you with all my heart, would you do me the honor and marry me?"

For the first time Hannah was speechless. She never saw this coming at least not now and not here at Homer Folks. Slowly, Hannah bent down on both knees, faced Hank and replied,

"Yes, of course I'll marry you. I would be proud to be your wife. I love you too, I have for a long time."

Hank took the ring from the box and placed it on Hannah's finger. Hannah couldn't believe her eye. Hank had given her a perfect ring. The ring, set in gold, had a lovely size diamond and Hank had their initials engraved on the inside. Hannah couldn't stop herself from staring at the ring and thought how proud she will be wearing it forever. As quickly as they entered the bushes, they tried to return to the path without anyone noticing.

Unfortunately, Nurse Riley had seen Hank and Hannah enter into the bushed and return to the path. Knowing her patients as she did, Nurse Riley did see a change in Hank and Hannah's demurer. Nurse Riley decided to have a meeting with Hank and Hannah. Normally, Nurse Riley would have only met with Hannah, but she considered this situation serious, therefore both needed to attend. At first Nurse Riley's meeting with Hank and Hannah changed in tone and subject. She congratulated the happy couple and admired Hannah's ring. Following a few pleasantries, Nurse Riley addressed the matter at hand.

"You both know at Homer Folks we don't condone fraternization between male and female patients. You have disregarded this and built up a very close relationship. Granted some staff members looked the other way and even encouraged your friendship. From experience I know where this could lead, I shouldn't need to remind you and what happened to Carol. So, Hannah and Hank what are your intentions for the remainder of your stay?"

"Well, we plan to wait not only for our discharge, but until we're married," answered Hank.

PATRICIA SMITH JANSSEN

"You realize that could be awhile for both of you. Do you have any ideas until you're discharge?" Nurse Riley inquired.

Hannah decided to speak up, startling Hank with the direct approach she took.

"I intend to get married in the Church. Also I plan to be a virgin on my wedding night. Until we are discharged, Nurse Riley, I believe we are adults and will behave accordingly."

Nurse Riley, also surprised with Hannah's tone responded

"As far as Homer Folk's is concerned you may continue to see each other but some of your actions will need to change. From today on, there will be no holding hands, hugs, arms around each other, or kissing."

Hannah and Hank both agreed, not because they approved, but because they had no other choice.

Hannah and Hank still found plenty of time together, but were always careful to abide by the rules. In some ways they relaxed more because they spent time talking and enjoying each other without looking over their shoulders. Relived, Hank told Hannah now he was grateful for the curtailments, he wasn't sure how long he could have controlled himself. What they did do was talk. They so rather hold hands and sneak kisses. Hank always told Hannah about the house he would buy for her. Hank would go on about the six children they would have. He had the children's schooling decided and depending where they would live, Hank had a beautiful Catholic Church chosen.

Hank continued sharing his plans by describing the type of job he would get,

"I plan on becoming a salesman Hannah, it is a job that will provide us enough money to live comfortably." They discussed when they would marry.

"Hannah, I think we should wait until we have some money saved," said Hank. Hannah had different ideas,

"Hank I want us to get married as soon as we possible can." Both knew they could talk about the future all they wanted, it didn't change the obstacle they faced. Hannah thought she might be discharge before Hank since she had been a patient for two years. Hank had been a patient for just over a year.

Hannah and Hank decided to tell their relatives about their engagement immediately. Hannah wrote Rose telling how Hank had proposed, including all the details. Hannah also let her mother know how happy she was and how happy Hank made her feel. Hannah included in her letter the similarities Hannah saw in Hank that reminded her of her father. Lastly, Hannah shared with her mother the restrictions Homer Folks enforced concerning their engagement. She told Rose they were forbidden to hold hands and their time together was limited each day. When Rose read this part of Hannah's letter she relaxed. Even though she liked Hank, Hannah was her baby and she was concerned she would be taken advantage.

Hank, on the other hand, didn't know whom to write. He decided to write his older brother in Buffalo and his sister in Albany. Hank described Hannah, who she was, what she was like, and how much he loved her. He included she was from Albany also. Hank next wrote Buzz, especially since Buzz had gotten the ring for Hank.

Hank, not expecting replies to any of his letters was shocked to receive letters from both his brother and sister. This was the first mail Hank received since the death of his mother. His brother offered much advice. He stressed, marriage was a very serious commitment. He also cautioned Hank from marrying until he found a job that could support a family. Hank's sister was less than tactful than his brother. She reminded Hank, she was not in a position to help the newlyweds. She being married with two little ones could not be expected to house them if needed. Hank's sister seemed less than welcoming; she did wish them luck in the end. Hannah was surprised by Hank's sister's remark. Compared to Hannah's family that had always took care of each other no matter what! The circumstances, Hank's sister seemed so cold and distant. Hannah didn't mention her feelings to Hank, but she did not feel welcomed by Hank's family especially his sister.

Rose responded to Hannah's letter immediately. She was excited for both of them. Rose's letter was full of ideas and thoughts about the wedding. Hannah being her only daughter would be a beautiful bride and Rose couldn't wait to show off her daughter. The only concern Rose shared with Hannah was their health. Specifically, how would the two handle the discharge of one without the other? Although, they both had thought about this, neither Hank nor Hannah said anything to the other about it. Without realizing Rose's concern was about to be tested.

SEVENTEEN

S hortly after announcing their engagement and writing their families, Hank had a chest x-ray and a series of sputum tests. After the results were read, Hank's doctor notified him that his sputum had been negative for two months. Hank's chest x-ray showed no nodules and the cavities were healing nicely. The doctors wanted to perform one more bronchoscopy to ensure the sputum, deep in the lungs, was negative too. During this time Hank's job was upgraded, which meant he was responsible in helping to clear another path. Hank, who normally would have fought having the bronchoscopy, was eager to get it over with. Hank knew in his heart, his discharge was close especially after the bronchoscopy revealed the deep sputum was negative also. Hank, happy with the results, didn't know how to tell Hannah. He didn't want to leave Hannah, afraid of how she could react. Hannah was so sensitive; he didn't want her to become depressed, which could make her ill again. He decided he wouldn't tell Hannah until he absolutely needed to and until then act as normal as he could. Hank thought, he would plan on getting a job, working and saving money until Hannah was discharged.

Hannah knew Hank so well, and she knew something was wrong. At first she let it go, hoping he would tell her when he was ready. Hannah knew Hank's job had become more physical, which could mean a setback. Often a setback was common when they upgraded jobs. Hannah was also aware of Hank's bronchoscopy which Hank told her there was little change. This was the first time Hank lied to Hannah.

At last Hannah had pushed enough to convince Hank to talk. Hank told Hannah everything. He had been given clearance and would be ready for discharge in one month. Hannah was shocked; she never expected to hear this from Hank. Hannah looked at him, then immediately began to cry and rock back and forth. She knew he was going to leave her. Everything they shared had been a lie. Hank was in agony seeing Hannah react this way. When he finally got Hannah calm,

"Hannah, after I am discharged I'm going to Albany and stay with Buzz. There I will get a job in sales. That way I can request this area and I will be able to visit you often. I've already written to my brother and he has put me in touch with a gentleman looking for men to hire. I'll be selling business machines and with that I'll be provided with a company car. This way I can visit and save money for when we marry."

Hank looked into Hannah's eyes and though he saw doubt, he knew she believed him.

Only having a month before he was discharged, Hank had much to do between planning for his release and assuring Hannah everything will work out. In his brother's letter, he sent Hank the name and address of the man he needed to contact. Hank, excited wrote the man immediately, letting him know when he would be available.

Hannah did what Hank was afraid would happen, became depressed. She would become quiet and burst into tears with little provocation. Until now, Hannah and Hank had respected Nurse Riley's rules but Hank worried about Hannah more. Hannah was giving into the depression and each day she seemed worse. Hank thought if he could just reassure Hannah he loved her. Therefore, when they were out walking, Hank pulled Hannah into the bushes and kissed her, a kiss full of passion. While in his arms, Hank told Hannah how much he loved her. Hannah, opened up a little, told Hank how scared she was that he would find someone else. Hank tried to reassure Hannah he only loved her, but she had a fear he couldn't control. Hank continued to bombard Hannah with hugs and kisses whenever possible.

As soon as Hannah could, she tracked down Dr. Jones and asked, "Please tell my progress."

Dr. Jones had always been evasive with Hannah. After begging him to tell her the prognosis, Dr. Jones listened to Hannah's plea. Hannah made it clear she wanted to know when she would be discharged.

"Before I can answer your question Hannah, you will need to have a chest x-ray, sputum test, and a bronchoscopy. After we have the results of all we will sit down and determine what's next."

Dr. Jones came to discuss the results of Hannah's tests when she asked if Hank could be present, Dr. Jones agreed. Hank, Hannah, and Dr. Jones met in the doctor's office. Hannah eagerly waited to hear her prognosis. They were gathered in the doctor's office looking at a lighted box with Hannah's chest x-ray displayed. Dr. Jones had a large desk but he preferred sitting near the edge to be closer to the patient. It was his attempt to make them feel more at ease. Addressing his statements to Hannah, he began sharing what the tests revealed,

"Hannah your sputum series was negative but the sputum retrieved from the bronchoscopy tested positive."

Dr. Jones directed his attention to her chest x-ray. Using a pencil, he pointed to the various cavities within the right lung, some healing but not as much as they had hoped by now. Then, Dr. Jones pointed out a new nodule on her left lung. Dr. Jones concluded,

"It will be awhile before we can discharge you."

Hannah had known the outcome of the testing would probably not be in her favor. Therefore, Hannah channeled her mother's strength, turned to Dr. Jones, and asked him direct questions,

"How long before I'm well enough to be discharged?"

"It might be as long as a year or two, Hannah."

"Dr. Jones is this a guess or can you say for certain?"

"Honestly Hannah, I don't know."

Hannah dug deep to gain the strength to ask the next question,

"Dr. Jones are patients kept here until they die from tuberculosis?"

"I'm sorry to say, but yes that does happen," said Dr. Jones.

"Well I refuse to stay here until I die. There must be new or alternative treatments we can try."

Looking from Hank to Hannah, Dr. Jones simply replied,

"I'm sorry Hannah, there is nothing else we can do."

Dr. Jones had noticed since Hannah and Hank met, her spirits and health had improved. He, along with Hank, and other staff members were concerned for Hannah once Hank left.

Hannah's next question took Dr. Jones by surprise.

"What would happen if I decided to go home now?" inquired Hannah.

Not only did this surprise Dr. Jones, but Hank. Neither thought Hannah would ask this question specifically. Also neither had never given thought to this, therefore when Hannah asked, both were speechless. After the initial shock of her question wore off, Dr. Jones thought about it for a minute, he said to Hannah,

"I don't know what would happen. Most likely you would become sicker and eventually die."

Hannah, with her new found strength was not going to let anyone intimidate her, especially the staff at Homer folks. Hannah then suggested,

"What if I were to lead the same kind of routine I follow here? If I got plenty of rest, ate well, and took in fresh air, by following that schedule improve my chances?"

Taken back by Hannah's questions and the obvious thought she put into her argument, Dr. Jones simply stated,

"You know Hannah, if you could manage it might be possible. It could be difficult to accomplish in the city of Albany. There isn't much fresh air within the city. However I can't guarantee you a cure here and I could never promise on the outside. While you are determined to leave Homer Folks and whether you stay or go, your chances for a complete recovery are slim. Professionally I would have to advise you to remain here. Although it might be a limited life expectancy, the quality might outweigh the length. This is something you need to decide and discuss with your family."

"How long would I have Dr. Jones?"

"I would say two to three years, but recently there has been some ground breaking research, which may lead to medications being available soon."

"In the meantime, there is a tuberculosis clinic in Albany that I strongly recommend both of you have your disease monitored by them." Dr. Jones stated.

Hannah and Hank both thanked Dr. Jones returned to their building. The meeting with Dr. Jones gave each of them much to think about.

Hank walked Hannah to her ward, gently kissed her forehead, and headed for his ward. They each needed time to digest what Dr. Jones had told them. The following three days Hank and Hannah were inseparable, though they neglected to discuss what was bothering them. As they walked down the "cure path" they discussed their situation. Sitting on their bench, Hank listed the pros and cons if Hannah were to leave with him. Concerned Hannah might misinterpret what he meant, Hank stressed to Hannah how much time and thought he had devoted to their situation. He also assured Hannah how much he loved her and he couldn't possible show her how much if he couldn't take care of her. Hank thought the best choice was,

"Hannah, I believe for your sake, you should remain here, at Homer Folks, until I've secured a job and saved some money. If I can't take care of you I'm scared you'll have a setback, and I don't think I could ever forgive myself if that happened."

Hannah politely listened to Hank and agreed with everything he said, but she too had done some thinking and needed to share her thoughts with Hank.

"Hank, I agree with you and remaining here at Homer Folks is probably the sensible, responsible thing to do. You know I love you Hank and the last thing I want to do is have a setback or worse reinfect you. But, I can't seem to escape the words Dr. Jones said, where I only have two or three years. The last place I want to be or spend one extra second surrounded by is Homer Folks and it's patients. I believe we should spend each available minute together, not separated, waiting for you to find work and save money. We want to be married and build a life together, let's not waste anymore time."

Hank immediately took Hannah in his arms and hugged her. While there were medical risks involved for both, Hank wanted Hannah to leave when he did and told her as much,

"Hannah, I know we could be playing with fire, but I agree, on the day I leave, you will be by my side."

The next couple of days would be chaos. Hannah needed to inform the medical staff she was leaving Homer Folks against medical advice.

Next Hank needed to be assured he had a job when he reached Albany.

Last, both needed a place to live, somewhere with fresh air, Hank hoped.

Hannah and Hank informed Dr. Jones of their decision; Hannah would be leaving with Hank. All Dr. Jones could do was wish them well and repeated everything Hannah would require; plenty of rest, healthy food, milk and fresh country air if possible. Dr. Jones also reminded Hank and Hannah of the tuberculosis clinic and he would send their records so the clinic would have their histories. Finally, Dr. Jones turned to Hannah,

"You need to focus on resting and less on your discharge, because if you don't you'll relapse before you leave."

Hank spoke up,

"I'll handle all our discharge plans doc. Thank you for all you have done for both of us."

Hank and Dr. Jones shook hands as Hannah and Hank left Dr. Jones' office.

Hank noticed a letter arrived from Mr. Singer, the man he had written to about the job position. Mr. Singer, the owner, wrote Hank that he would be happy to interview Hank when he was in Albany. Hank would have liked to have assurance of a job but he was encouraged and was sure he could do well during the interview. To be safe though, Hank wrote his previous employer, at the newspaper, inquiring about a job when he returned to Albany. Hank knew deep down he had done everything possible in securing employment prior to his discharge; it was out of his hands now.

Hank had an idea that might help him secure a job after all. Hank wrote Buzz asking him to drive Hank to Albany to interview for the job with Mr. Singer. Hank offered to pay Buzz for his time and gas. Hank then checked with Dr. Jones to ensure he could have a two-day pass and Dr. Jones agreed. The last thing Hank had to do was make arrangements to set up a day to interview for the job with Mr. Singer.

With everything going on, Hannah decided she needed to write her mother. In need of a place to live, Hannah asked her mother if she and Hank could live with her. Hannah told her mother exactly what Dr. Jones said of her prognosis, she didn't want to worry her, but Hannah knew Rose had every right to know. Hannah let her mother know she and Hank would pay rent. Rose wrote Hannah immediately. She was happy Hannah was leaving Homer Folks; she always thought she was capable of taking care of her daughter. Rose also agreed with Hannah's decision to marry Hank. Rose did pass along some bad news. Until Hannah and Hank were married Hank would have to live elsewhere. Rose welcomed Hank to live with the family after the marriage was official.

When Hannah read Hank Rose's letter Hank was pleased Rose was excited to have Hannah home. He didn't know where he would live until he married Hannah. Hank decided to deal with his living situation over the two days he was in Albany.

Hank received a response from Buzz. Buzz would be at Homer Folks Thursday to pick Hank up. Buzz made arrangements with Mr. Singer to meet with Hank. Hannah was thankful for Buzz. Maybe she had been quick with her first impressions of Buzz, without Buzz's help, many of their plans would not be accomplished.

Thursday arrived with Buzz leaving Albany at six am, reaching Homer Folks at ten am. Hank was eager to go. He said his goodbye to Hannah, telling her to wish him luck. Hannah not only wished him, luck but said a prayer to St. Theresa. When Hank and Buzz were out of Oneonta, Hank offered to drive. Buzz gladly gave up the wheel because he was tired after such an early start.

After Hank and Buzz left, Hannah returned to her ward, delighted to see a letter from Carol on her bed. Carol wrote how happy she was to hear of Hannah and Hank's engagement. Carol stated she was not at all surprised, she had known from the beginning Hank was the perfect match for Hannah. Hannah was surprised when she next read, Carol was pregnant. Both of them thought Carol could never have a baby because of the abortion. Hannah wondered what else the doctors at Homer Folks were wrong about. Carol's letter continued with good news. Her husband, formally a tuberculosis doctor from Homer Folks, just took a position at a tuberculosis clinic in Albany. On top of that, he would also start private practice treating diseases of the pulmonary tract. Hannah couldn't believe what she was reading. She immediately wrote Carol filling her in on the latest, especially when Hank and she would be arriving in Albany.

Hank and Buzz finally arrived in Albany. Hank was tired but he needed to see his sister. Hank asked her if he could stay until Hannah and he were married, but as she stated in her letter, she didn't have the room. Hank assumed she wouldn't allow him to stay, but there was no harm in asking. He decided what was important was the job interview he needed to prepare for to ensure he got employed. The interview was set for Friday morning with Mr. Singer. His suit was clean and pressed, only he wished he could have gotten nicer clothes to impress Mr. Singer.

Hank's interview went well, so well Mr. Singer agreed to hire Hank. Hank would start in two weeks. Mr. Singer informed Hank of a month long training program, in which Hank's would be at the minimum level. After completion of the program Hank would receive a raise and a company car. Hank thanked Mr. Singer for the opportunity, promising Mr. Singer,

"You won't be sorry," as he left to go back to Buzz's.

It seemed the trip back to Homer Folks would never end. Hank was so excited to see Hannah and share his news with her. After what seemed like days Hank and Buzz reached Homer Folks. Hank tried to give Buzz money, but Buzz wouldn't take a dime. Buzz said to Hank and Hannah,

"We have been friends since grammar school, I will never take money from my oldest friend and I know he would never take money from me. We are here to help each other and that's what I did, helped my friends who were in need."

Both stood waving as Buzz got back in the car, heading back to Albany. When they no longer could see his car they headed inside to the recreation room.

As soon as they reached the recreation room, Hank told Hannah the good news,

"Mr. Singer hired me, I got the job."

Hannah, overjoyed, wanted to scream the good news as she jumped up and down. Hank, without thinking, grabbed Hannah, picked her up, and gave her a huge bear hug along with a passionate kiss. By this time the staff members ignored Hank's signs of affection, they were engaged and leaving shortly. So rather than try and stop them, many staff members shared in the joy.

Everything seemed to be falling in place for Hank and Hannah. Hank had gotten the job he wanted, they were going to be married, and Carol's husband was now their doctor. The only issue to be resolved was Hank's living arrangements. Hank knew where ever he lived it must be near Hannah so that he would be close enough to look after her. Hank knew between Rose and himself, Hannah's health was well taken care of with little to worry over. Hank's love for Hannah was so strong he was sure it was powerful enough to protect her.

With the ease of a phone call, their problem was solved. Buzz called and informrd Hank of an opening at the YMCA. He told Hank,

"It's about six blocks from Hannah's home and you would need to pay a weekly rent, but it's clean and safe."

Hank agreed and asked Buzz to take care of securing the room for him and when he got to Albany he would pay him back. Buzz agreed and all was set. Hannah felt she could relax for they had one week left.

On November 1, 1941 Hannah and Hank walked out of the Homer Folks, hand in hand, ready to begin a new chapter in their lives. Filled with anticipation, love, and anxiety, the two boarded a bus, destination, Albany.

EIGHTEEN

xactly four hours after leaving Oneonta, the bus Hannah
and Hank were on pulled into Albany. For both of them, it
had been quite awhile since they had been home; everything
seemed the same, yet much was different. Buzz was there to pick
them up and drive them to Hannah's house. Hannah couldn't hold
back her excitement, she was eager to go home.

Rose stood by the window, watching for Hannah and Hank. She
was so excited to see both of them, but especially Hannah. Rose had
met Hank and truly liked him; she worried if he would honestly be
able to take care of her baby girl. She had to give him credit, he did
obtain a place to live and a well paying job before leaving Homer
Folks, but something just nagged at her. After eating a delicious meal
with plenty of milk available for Hannah and Hank, both Rose and
Hank ordered Hannah to take a nap. Without argument, Hannah
slipped into her bedroom, crawled into her bed, and was asleep
before her head hit the pillow. It had been a long day and she could
feel it throughout her body.

While Hannah napped, Rose and Hank had a long conversation.
Both knew Hannah's health needed improvement, so they discussed
how they could achieve that task. During their talk, neither referred
to Hannah and her health in anyway other than her recovery.
Everything was spoken with a positive tone, neither would allow any
other way. For a couple of hours Hank informed Rose of his plans and
how he would take care of Hannah. Hank also discussed with Rose
his plans for their future and including Hannah's care. He told Rose,

"Hannah and I will marry after I complete the training for my job, even though Hannah would rather not wait."

Rose smiled knowing her impatient daughter, but also agreed with Hank's plans. She would need to remind Hank about posting their marriage announcement at the church.

Rose and Hank had a pleasant conversation and Rose thought to herself, how much Hank reminded her of Edmund. Not only did this make Rose wish Edmund was here to help her, but she felt good that Hannah was lucky to find someone who truly loved her. It was clear to Rose Hank was sincere, hard workingman, who had the best intentions for Hannah. During their conversation, Hank was sure of himself and the plans he had made to ensure Hannah's care and recovery.

It was late when Hank finally left Rose and Hannah. He was tired, both emotionally and physically drained. Hank knew he had been able to convince Rose of his intentions, but what if he could not care for Hannah as he said. He knew he should focus on the positives, but he never had the responsibility of taking care of another. Until now he had only himself to account for and look where that got him, placed in Homer Folks. Thinking about this upset Hank and as he reached the YMCA he was sure everything would be better in the morning.

Hank walked into the YMCA noticing a flutter of nerves spread through his body. He was greeted by a pleasant young man and paid a week's rent in advanced. Using the most of his money, Hank paid the fee. Hank was taken to his room and noticed how small it was in comparison to other places he lived. Thinking, it had the basic necessities; he could make it work for the next month.

Hannah woke early the following morning, overjoyed with being home. She thought no longer do I have Nurse Riley around telling me how to spend my day. As she dressed, Hannah looked forward to her mother's cooking rather than planned meals at Homer Folks. She also decided she could make her own schedule of when to sit on the porch or go for walks if she wished. Hannah finished washing and was dressed as she entered the kitchen noticing Rose had breakfast ready. As Hannah ate enjoying every mouthful, Rose showed Hannah the program Hannah was to follow to help her recovery.

"Hannah, while you were taking a nap yesterday, Hank and I had a long talk. He described the daily the routine at Homer Folks. Hank thought it would be beneficial to you if we designed a similar one for you." Rose told Hannah.

Hannah looked at her mother and said,

"I thought I would be able to follow my own routine, nothing quite as ridge as Homer Folks, but one I could follow at my own pace, on my own terms."

Rose replied,

"Hank told me this is what Dr. Jones suggested, following this I think, would speed up your recovery."

Hannah realized neither Rose nor Hank was being realistic about her recovery. They were hoping for a miracle and there was none to be had. Hannah made peace about her mortality. She asked God for one thing let her spend whatever time she had left with Hank.

To make Rose and Hank happy Hannah followed the routine. Rose followed the three-pronged approach for treating tuberculosis. Rose also set up a program dealing with the asepsis of contagious materials. She contacted her doctor when she learned of Hannah's return. Rose's doctor was quite definite in his explanation about the spread of tuberculosis.

Hank and Hannah arrived Friday afternoon, so Hank was able to spend the weekend with Hannah. Not only was Hank permitted to spend all his time with Hannah, but also Rose insisted he eat his meals with them. Rose knew Hank was susceptible to a relapse if he did not take care himself. To ensure Hannah got fresh air, Hank made it a point to go for a walk with Hannah on Saturday and Sunday. It was quite cold and a brisk breeze surrounded them as they walked to the nearby park until they found a bench to sit and rest. They only sat a couple of minutes because it was so cold; Hank decided it was in Hannah's best interest to walk back toward the house. As they walked, they walked with Hank's arm around Hannah, not only to protect her from the cold, but as a sign of affection. The two would occasionally stop, wrap themselves in each other's arms and kiss. It was apparent to everyone just how happy and in love the they were. Upon their return from their walk, Hank suggested to Rose,

"One of Hannah's bedroom windows should remain open a crack so she's sure to get fresh air, especially this time of year when everything is closed up tight."

Rose agreed with Hank,

"I never thought of getting fresh air in such a simple way, thanks Hank for your suggestion."

Right before Hank left Sunday evening, Rose brought up the marriage announcement that must be made in the church. The three decided the wedding announcement would be posted the following Sunday. Rose, Hank, and Hannah would attend Mass the next Sunday and their wedding announcement would be posted. Rose was very pleased and told the them as she excused herself so Hannah and Hank could say their goodbyes. Hank took Hannah in his arms and said,

"I think we made your mother very happy."

He leaned over and kissed Hannah goodnight. Hannah replied,

"You also made her daughter happy as well. You will be by tomorrow after work, right?"

"Of course I will and I'll tell you about my day."

And with that Hank gave Hannah another kiss as he headed out the door.

Hank was nervous as he showed up at his new job the following morning. Unsure of what time he started, to be safe Hank arrived at seven-thirty am. The night before, Rose sent him home with enough food to feed an army. As he waited for Mr. Singer, he ate the breakfast he made while he left the sandwich for lunch in his box.

About eight am Mr. Singer arrived, pleased to see Hank. Mr. Singer was aware of Hank's eagerness to begin his new job and this impressed Mr. Singer. Hank's day flew by. Most of the day, Hank and the others were in a classroom with various business machines learning how to take them apart and put them back together. Hank had a half an hour for lunch; Hank ate fast managing to get in a little walk before he returned for the remainder of his day. His day ended at six pm, and as Hank took the trolley to Hannah's, and he thought about his day. There was a lot of learning with his new job and Hank worried because he had been a weak student in high school. Interestingly though, what he learned on the first day was easy for Hank. Maybe working on the machines was going to be a snap, therefore giving Hank nothing to fear.

Hannah was eagerly waiting for Hank, wanting to know everything about his day. Hank enjoyed telling Hannah how well his day went and felt this was a good omen. Rose prepared a lavish meal for Hank in celebrating his new job. Hanks started to protest,

"Rose, I must stop you from making such a grand meals for me, it isn't necessary."

Rose told Hank,

"Don't be silly, today was an important day, you started your new job, therefore we must celebrate. Plus, I would do this for any member of the family, so don't think you're that important."

Rose smiled at Hank as she said the last part and soon the three were laughing. Although for Hank, Rose said a lot, as a member of the family he never felt so much love before. Later, as Hank made his way back to the YMCA, he realized the care package Rose sent with him was so much food and tonight she insisted on Hank taking a bottle of milk with him. He knew why, so that he remained healthy.

When Hank reached his room, he though it was beginning to look like a store with all the food Rose sent with him. To keep the milk cold, Hank set it on the windowsill. That night as he was drifting off to sleep, he thought, how grateful he was for Rose.

There was a phone for tenants' use at the YMCA and early one Saturday, Hank received a call. Nervous something might be wrong with Hannah, he was shocked to hear his sister, Maria, on the other end. She came right to the point stating she and their brother had been talking, they felt she should meet Hannah. Hank wasn't sure what they were up too, for two people who had little interest a couple of months ago, he wasn't sure this was such a good idea. Cautiously, Hank said he would arrange a time and also let them know the wedding date. Hank had always been the black sheep of the family, so this sudden interest surprised him. He still had some hesitation with introducing Hannah to his sister.

Later that day, Hank told Hannah about his sister's call. Hannah delighted, promptly asked her mother if they could have Hank's sister and family to dinner. Naturally, Rose agreed and immediately started planning the menu. They decided Hank would ask his sister to come to dinner the following Sunday. Recently Edmund Jr. had a phone installed for Rose, therefore at Rose's insistence Hank called Maria. Everything was set, Maria and her family would join Hank, Rose, and Hannah the following Sunday at Rose's house.

The week flew by for Hank. Work was very stimulating and he was learning the traits of good salesmanship. Hank followed the same routine as the previous week. Every night after work he would go see Hannah and Rose fed him. Hank was grateful as always. He would get his first paycheck on Friday. Hank determined with his money, he would pay his rent along with giving Rose money for all the food she provided. Unfortunately Hank was left with only a small amount to save. This didn't bother Hank, as much as he would have thought, because their plans were moving along slowly, and they were happy. Hank had relaxed a little with Hannah. He had asked Rose to begin taking Hannah's temperature in the morning and night. Hank was also pleased with the schedule Rose instituted for Hannah. Hannah seemed much more content and even started to knit again. Rose refused to let Hannah do anything around the house; therefore Hannah had a lot of free time. Hannah decided to use the time to catch up on her correspondence. She wrote to her friends at the Homer Folks. Hannah had also been thinking about Carol. Hannah wrote Carol informing her of Hannah's the address and phone number. Hannah also included her and Hanks wedding date, December 21, 1941, the Saturday before Christmas.

The following Sunday came quick with Maria and her husband, Jack, arriving for dinner as scheduled. Hannah thought they seemed very nice. Beside Maria and Jack, their two little girls came too. They were adorable and very friendly children. When they first arrived, Rose had everyone gather in the parlor. As they were talking, becoming acquainted, Rose and Jack realized they were second cousins. Rose and Jack were inseparable as they caught up with family gossip. Hannah thought this was a perfect time to talk with

Maria. Dinner consisted of a series of lively conversations. Hannah and Hank announced their wedding date. They wanted a small ceremony followed by a gathering at Rose's house. Rose enjoyed the control associated with such a major affair, she was grateful when Maria offered to help with the preparations for Hannah and Hank's wedding. Rose relaxed some knowing she would have help with the upcoming nuptials. As dinner finished, Hank helped Rose clear the table then offered to dry the dishes. Rose accepted Hank's help with appreciation. When everything was washed and put away, Maria and her family said their goodbyes and thanked Rose for a wonderful meal and company. Shortly after, Hank kisses Hannah goodnight, along with giving Rose a kiss on the cheek. Hank wanted to let Rose know how appreciative he was for all she had done to welcome his family without hesitation.

Thanksgiving came and all were grateful to have Hannah back home. Hannah had missed two Thanksgivings. Everyone in the family came including spouses and children. Hank was invited and brought flowers for Rose. Edmund Jr. brought the turkey and the wives each pitched in by preparing one of the side dishes. Rose allowed Hannah to help with the turkey. While Hannah had never expressed any interest in cooking, she realized since she was going to be Hank's wife, she should learn to cook. Hank entered the kitchen, looked at Hannah, and found he was bursting with pride and love. Regardless of what the doctors said, Hannah looked wonderful. She actually had gained some weight. Hank had met Harry and Edmund Jr., but he had not been introduced to the rest of the Wright family. As he was introduced to the other members of the group he thought how there were so many members of the Wright family. Harry was granted a leave so he could celebrate the holiday with his family. Little did anyone know, this would be their last family meal together. Thanksgiving reminded Hank of a Norman Rockwell painting. Hank quietly took in everyone talking at the table. Naturally, he sat next to Hannah and kept his leg pressed against her. After dinner everyone gathered in the parlor and continuing their conversation. Harry and Hank discussed at great length the world situation. Around ten pm the party began to break up. Hank left without spending any alone time with Hannah except for the long goodnight kiss they managed to slip by everyone. Hank was tired and Hannah knew Hank was scheduled to work on Friday.

Due to the weather, Hank did not see Hannah for two nights the following week. Hank made it to Rose's house on Friday December 7th. Hannah was happy to see Hank and let him know by immediately giving him a hug and kiss as he walked through the front door. When the three of them sat down for dinner the phone rang, three rings, and stopped. It immediately rang again and Rose answered it because she knew it was Harry on the other end. Three rings was their signal. Rose was able to say hello as Harry cut her off asking to speak to Hank. Hank got on the phone and for the next five minutes, Hank barely said a word. Hank listened to Harry and Rose and Hannah watched Hank knowing something was wrong. As soon as Hank hung up the receiver, Hannah begged Hank to tell them what was wrong. Slowly Hank looked at Rose then Hannah and repeated what Harry told him,

"Harry said he heard from a reliable source that the Japanese had bombed Pearl Harbor. Harry thinks the United States will be going to war within the next couple of days."

Hank looked at Rose continuing,

"Harry believes this will force the United States to enter the war. He said he wouldn't be surprised if we are in the war within the next couple of days."

"What about Harry? Will he be sent to fight?"

Hank felt sick having to be the one to answer Rose's question, but he relayed exactly what Harry said,

"He doesn't know what is going to happen. He does know he's being shipped out tomorrow for Great Britain."

Hank could see the tears in both Rose and Hannah's eyes. Hannah immediately turned the radio on, remembering how her father and the other men living with them would listen for hours during the depression. As soon as the station came into to tune, they heard Pearl Harbor had been bombed. There was little else said. Details relating to the bombing were not released by order of the President. The announcer stated the President was scheduled to speak to the nation the following day.

Hank was visibly shaken up by the news. He kept repeating, over and over,

"We're going to war."

As Hank paced the room, Hannah started to cry. She wasn't sure why she was crying other than she had a sick feeling in the pit of her stomach, what was about occur was not good. Rose worried about Hank, extended an invitation for him to spend the night, offering the couch. Hank graciously accepted, the YMCA did not have a radio, and he wanted to be able to hear the President's speech. Unsure of the future, no one was able to sleep well. Hannah and Hank stayed up listening to the radio. Hank found sleeping under the same roof with Hannah was torture. He desperately wanted to sneak up to her room, just hold her. December 21, their wedding day, seemed to take forever to arrive.

The next day President Franklin Delano Roosevelt announced the United States and Great Britain had declared war on Japan.

As a shock to everyone, by December 11th, Germany and Italy declared war on the United States. Hank wanted to enlist but due to the tuberculosis he was classified as 4F. Miserable, Hank felt he was only half a man.

Just as many feared, the United States was involved in another major war. Rose worried about Harry because he had been in the Army, therefore he could be sent anywhere the Army saw fit. Hannah's brothers Adam and Johnny decided to enlist as soon as they heard the President's speech, though they were not expected to report for duty until December 23. In the midst of all the excitement related to the war, Rose and Hannah were trying to plan a wedding.

Throughout all the external turmoil going on in the world, Hank finished the classroom training, graduating at the top of his group. As promised, Mr. Singer gave Hank a company car, a raise in his salary and a coveted territory with in the city of Albany. Hannah and Rose were so proud of him. Hank wanted to get an apartment immediately but Hannah thought they should wait. One day, just before their wedding, Hank stopped by Rose's. It was obvious he was excited about something and as soon as he saw Hannah he said,

"Hannah, I know you wanted to wait, but one of the men from work told me about a furnished flat on Barclay Street off Central Avenue. Please come with me and see it.

Hank invited Rose, because they wanted her input.

The three of them left in Hank's new car. Rose was thrilled just with the car ride, she never had been in a new car before. As they pulled up in front of fifty Barclay Street, everyone immediately got out of the car. The flat was located in a two family, white house that had a large enclosed front porch. The porch was enclosed with glass. When they entered, the three met an older woman; she owned the house. The available flat was upstairs and while she showed them around, Hannah became very excited. There was a large parlor decorated with rose flowered wallpaper, a green sofa, and a large brown chair. The dining room was empty. The kitchen was larger than either Rose or Hannah expected. In the kitchen was a formica table and four chairs. Besides the table and chairs it also had an old style refrigerator and stove. They followed the owner into the bedrooms. The first bedroom was empty, but second had a metal double bed and a dresser with a mirror. The bathroom consisted of a large tub, a sink and toilet. Hannah thought the flat was perfect. Rose was impressed and shared her thoughts. Hannah looked at Hank,

"How much?"

Hank gave her a hug and told her not to worry about the price, "We can afford it."

"Do you think we should take it?"

The only response Hannah needed to give Hank was a kiss and he turned to the owner,

"We'll take it."

Hank gave the landlady the first month's rent as Hannah and Rose returned to the car. As soon as Hank joined them, everyone began speaking at once. Rose was able to tell Hank and Hannah,

"Don't worry about a dining room table and chairs, there is a set in the attic. It just needs a little refinishing and it will be perfect."

Hannah thanked her mother and Hank smiled at Rose. Each expressed how delighted they were with the flat and how lucky

Hank was able to find out about it. The place was perfect for a newly married couple, except Rose thought how much she would miss the both of them. Hannah said to Rose and Hank,

"Just think, we found our own place one week before our wedding, it must be a sign of good things to come."

Rose and Hank agreed.

During the following week, Hannah and Rose did nothing but focus on the wedding. Rather than purchase an expensive gown, Hannah decided to wear her mother's wedding suit for her day. Hannah tried the suit on and after Rose tucked here and there, the suit fit like a glove, as if it had been made especially for Hannah. Rose and Hannah searched through Rose's trunk, the one from her acting days, looking for a pair of shoes and other trinkets Hannah could use on her wedding day. They found a little clutch and a beautiful bracelet Edmund had given Rose years ago. Hannah hugged her mother and said,

"Thank you mother for everything you have done. Thanks you for accepting Hank and thank you for being you. I love you."

Rose just held on to Hannah, smiling, and kissed her gently on the forehead

Each night, Hank would go directly to Rose's to spend time with Hannah and eat dinner. The two discussed every thing they wanted to do to their flat prior to moving in. Hank though, had been working on their home after he left Hannah's and before returning to the YMCA. He painted the rooms except the parlor because Hannah loved the wallpaper. Hank also retrieved the table and chairs from Rose's attic and brought them to the flat. Hank worked for hours each night with the intentions of having everything perfect for Hannah. During his lunch and breaks he would comb second hand shops finding lamps and end tables for the parlor, a bed for the first bedroom, and odds and ends he thought Hannah would want. Hank even managed to convince his sister, Maria, to make curtains. Hank thought it might be possible Maria was having a change of heart from the letter he received while at Homer Folks. As Hank walked through the flat one evening, he realized he was thankful they found a place with a porch. Although it was enclosed by glass, the windows could open allowing

Hannah to access fresh air. Hank decided for the last surprise, he had a phone installed for Hannah.

Rose and Hannah were in the attic looking around when Rose realized all of Martha's belongings were still there. She turned to Hannah and said,

"When Martha moved in with us she brought many items with her from her home and you may take any or all of it."

Hank and Hannah went to the attic to investigate they found a storehouse full of treasures perfect for someone starting out. There were pillows, sheets, blankets, dishes, Martha's sterling silver, pots, and baking pans. Hannah also found Martha's hope chest filled with fancy linens, Martha's wedding dress, and a bunch of clothes. Hannah wanted everything. She loved Martha, they were so close, and this was like a gift from her. Hank agreed to bring the items to the flat, while Hannah and Rose could unpack the trunks and boxes the following day.

It was Friday night before the wedding and Hannah was anxious and nervous. Hank's boss gave him the day off, so he helped where he could at Rose's then went to the flat. Everything was ready. Curtains were up, walls were painted, furniture in place, and now it was in move-in condition. Hank decided to go to the store for groceries. After he put the groceries away, he was tempted to spend the night. Hank thought he wanted the first night in the apartment to be with his wife, Hannah.

The wedding was held in a Cathedral with their wedding party numbering about twenty-five. Hank stood at the altar with his brother, Foster, who was his best man. Hank was shocked when Foster walked in the Church. Hank was touched to see his whole family; Foster, Maria, Annette, and Paula were there for him on his wedding day. He asked Buzz to be his best man, but when Foster showed up Buzz understood, and stepped aside, allowing Foster to stand as witness for his brother.

As the music began, everyone, especially Hank turned toward the aisle. Hank couldn't believe his eyes. Coming toward him with Edmund Jr. was the most beautiful women Hank ever saw, Hannah. Before Hank knew it Edmund Jr. was handing Hannah off to Hank.

Hank was in a daze; he wondered what he had done to get someone as smart, funny, and witty to fall in love with him. He made a promise to God that he would do everything in his power to ensure Hannah's recovery. Then, Hannah spoke to Hank, bringing him back to the ceremony. She whispered to him,

"I'm the luckiest woman alive."

The ceremony was brief and to the point. About fifteen minutes after Hannah entered his sight, they were now husband and wife. Neither one could believe they made it. After the ceremony everyone went back to Rose's for the reception.

The afternoon flew by. Everyone got along and it appeared everyone had a good time. Hank and Hannah enjoyed every minute of their day. They received beautiful gifts, thanking each person as they opened their gift. The only issue the two faced was their desire to be alone at their new home. They recited a count down for their ears only,

"Three hours till we're home, two hours till we're home, one hour till we're home."

After a long, taxing day Hank and Hannah were on their way home. As soon as the two were locked in the car, Hank took Hannah in his arms giving her a long passionate kiss with their first kiss involving their tongues. Hank decided open mouth kisses were fine because both their sputum tested negative. Hannah pulled away laughing.

"What was that?" Hannah said.

"That was just the beginning of many things I'll be showing tonight, which will give you pleasure, all of them," replied Hank.

Hannah thought and said,

"Can we do that again?" Hank answered, "Now?"

Not wanting to disappoint his bride Hank kissed her again. This time Hannah tentatively encircled his mouth with her tongue.

"I think I'm going to like tonight," said Hannah as she smiled sheepishly.

Continuing on their way home, Hank had to drive cautiously because it was snowing hard. When they reached their home, Hank led Hannah upstairs, and opened the door. Without a pause, Hank swept Hannah up in his arms, carrying her across the threshold. Hannah couldn't speak, not only from Hanks actions, but also at the sight of the flat. She had not seen any of the changes Hank had done.

Hannah wanted to walk around the flat and investigate more, but Hank had other plans. Hank picked Hannah up again, carrying her to the bedroom. Slowly Hank removed her clothes, gently, he kissed each part of her as she became more and more exposed. Before Hannah knew, she was lying naked, staring at Hank. Hastily Hank undressed, joining Hannah under the sheets. Hank tenderly cradled Hannah in his arms. She nestled close to Hank, closing her eyes and enjoyed everything Hank was doing. After kissing her cheek, Hank moved his hands so he could cup her tiny breasts. Expecting a response from Hannah, Hank looked into her beautiful face and saw she had fallen asleep. Laughing to himself, Hank gathered Hannah close in his arms thinking how lucky and blessed he was to have found someone as wonderful as Hannah. With these thoughts, Hank allowed himself to drift into a deep sleep.

The following morning, Hannah opened her eyes, and had no idea where she was at first. She looked around the room and next to her was Hank grinning.

"You're not planning on going back to sleep, are you? I've got many things planned for us today."

With that he turned Hannah toward him, and started kissing her. Hannah immediately tried to kiss Hank as they had the night before, using her tongue.

"Not so fast," said Hank, "You're going pay for last night."

The two kissed and explored one another's bodies with their hands and eyes. Hank was burning with desire and could tell Hannah was also. Hank touched Hannah where she had never been touched and he could tell how excited she was. Hannah twisted and pushed herself against Hank. Neither one could control themselves, reaching for a condom; Hank eased himself into his wife. Hannah gasped with pain at first, but as Hank slowly moved in and out of her, she could feel herself rise within. The faster Hank went, the more Hannah arched her back until she felt an explosion of sorts deep inside of her.

Panting Hannah had no idea what had just happened. Shortly after Hank stopped, shuddered, and collapsed. Over and over they told each other how much they love one another. Holding each other, the two kept repeating how much they loved the other. They had reached where they wanted to be, together without restrictions, married, and in love. They couldn't be happier.

NINETEEN

***

Hank and Hannah had been married four days and it was now Christmas. Rose asked Hank and Hannah to spend Christmas Eve and morning with her, but Hank insisted they spend their first Christmas as a married couple, in their new home. As with everything Christmas was especially magical for the newlywed couple. After work on Christmas Eve, Hank appeared with a straggly looking tree devoid of most of its needles. Hannah didn't seem to notice how the tree looked, in fact she loved it. They had taken a box of Martha's Christmas decorations from Rose's attic. That evening the two joyfully decorated their tree and flat. Hannah, was excited with their first Christmas, and took a picture of everything. Hank, was thrilled, but in another way. With a smile on his face, Hank suggested to Hannah,

"Let's christen the living room in front of the tree."

Spurred by passion that only newlyweds in love have, they lustfully christened the living room. Hank was full of desire for Hannah, so much so he wanted to christen all the rooms, but Hannah suggested they take their time. Rather, the two sang Christmas Carols, remembered past Christmases at the Homer Folks and then they shared their dreams for future Christmases. Hank and Hannah drifted off, in each other's arms, expressing how thankful they were for the other, and how each couldn't have asked for a better holiday. Christmas day, Hank and Hannah woke exchanged gifts, and later in the day went to Rose's for dinner.

After the holidays, Hank and Hannah established a routine. They got up at six-thirty in the morning; Hannah managed to cook eggs and bacon when available, along with juice, toast, and milk. It took some time for Hannah to learn how to cook. Even the simplest meals, Hank was always willing to lend a helping hand when she was in need. Hank's job was to wash and dry the dishes, especially in the evening when Hannah seemed tired.

After breakfast, Hank typically left for work around seven-thirty and returned home about six in the evening. During the day, Hannah kept herself occupied with lighthouse work. She took pride in keeping the flat clean. She did find some chores took a lot out of her; most of all was washing the clothes. To perform this chore, Hannah relied on the strength of her arms and hands. Due to the tuberculosis, Hannah lacked the strength to adequately complete the wash. Therefore during the afternoon, Hannah rested on the porch with the window open a crack to let in fresh air. Somehow, Hank found a chair similar to those at Homer Folks, which Hannah relaxed in on the porch. When she tired of sitting on the porch, often Hannah would lay down in bed for an hour long nap. Some evenings Hank would return from work finding Hannah sound asleep in bed. When this happened, Hank would leave Hannah to sleep and he would prepare their dinner.

Each Saturday, Hank would drive Rose and Hannah so they could shop. Rations were placed on certain foods because of the war and ration coupons were given at the beginning of the month. Everyone was expected to shop wise enough to make their coupons last. Hank realized the significance of the coupons, even though it limited what and how much they could buy, its purpose was to ensure the troops had enough supplies. Hank felt he was doing his civic duty by following the program and economizing.

Rose would spend a day with Hannah, helping Hannah with the household chores. Rose wasn't getting any younger, and this amazed both Hannah and Hank with how much she could help. Hannah wished her mother would be less critical, but Hannah was grateful for all of Rose's help. Hannah honestly could not be as thorough as Rose, especially with the floors and windows. Rose particularly enjoyed those two tasks. One day after Rose had been by the flat, Hank said to Hannah,

"We have the cleanest windows in the neighborhood. Thanks to your mother. "

Hannah smiled thinking how she prided herself in keeping a neat home. Rose, however, always suggested ways Hannah could clean more efficiently and although Hannah wished it didn't, Rose's comments bothered her.

Unaware how her comments hurt Hannah, Rose was becoming a stranger in her own home. Rose's home had been taken over by her daughter-in-laws and grandchildren while her sons were overseas fighting against the Germans. The boarders had left sometime ago, therefore she wasn't needed as much as she once been at her house. All but one of her sons' wives did the cleaning, laundry, ironing and caring for the children. The other daughter-in-law worked in a factory that made ammunition. Everything Rose did each day. Rose would not let them take over her kitchen. She insisted in preparing all the meals and if anyone tried to help, she would scoot them out of the kitchen. Therefore, when Rose would go to Hannah's at least there she felt useful, more so than at her own home.

Each night when Hank came home, Hannah would have dinner ready, on the table, so he could share with Hannah. She looked forward to hearing about his day, especially since she was so proud of Hank. To think, two months ago, Hank and Hannah were still at Homer Folks, recovering from their illnesses. Hank lacked any skills to gain employment, and because someone took a chance with Hank, he was gainfully employed and at the top of his field. Mr. Singer praised Hank frequently and especially after he made a large sale. Hank made two such sales recently and was patiently waiting for his commission check. When they finished dinner and Hank cleaned up the kitchen, the two would retire to the parlor and listen to the radio. Hannah loved music and shows, but they listened to the news and reports of the war. Hank still wished he could enlist, but on another level he was relieved to be able to remain home, caring for Hannah.

Hank not only cared for Hannah, but also constantly hovered over her. He felt it was necessary to watch over Hannah because he loved her so much. Every evening Hank would ask the same questions over dinner,

"Did you sit on the porch today and for how long? Were you able to go for a walk? And, what did you eat?"

Hannah, at times, would become so annoyed with Hank, she would make up answers.

"Yes I sat on the porch for two hours."

When she actually sat there for only an hour.

Even with their lovemaking he was controlling. He wasn't demanding with Hannah as to when they would make love. If she was tired they would wait until she was more rested. Hank also took care of contraception; he used condoms. Hank was especially aware of the consequence if Hannah became pregnant! He remembered the doctor at Homer Folks telling the two of them,

"If Hannah became pregnant, the pregnancy could affect her life expectancy."

Hank decided then, they would not have children, taking care Hannah was enough.

Hannah was beginning to lose her patience with Hank's controlling behavior. One night, two months after being married, Hannah could no longer take Hank's questions. When he asked the last question Hannah said,

"Honest Hank, you act as if I'm a child, unable to determine what is good for me. You can't possible think I want to die? I plan on being around for a while and I know what I need to make that happen. Please let me do what I need to without the third-degree each evening. I already had a Nurse Riley, I don't need another."

During dinner, after Hannah had spoken her mind, neither said much to the other. As they listened to the radio, Hannah didn't ask Hank questions as she often did and Hank refrained from making comments related to the news. Unable to put up with the silence between the two, Hannah moved in close to Hank, laying her head on his chest. Quietly, she said,

"I love you."

"Even if I'm bossy?"

"Yes even when you are bossy."

Smiling as she said it.

They had celebrated a lot of first and this was their first disagreement. Having celebrated many of their firsts, they decided they needed to do so with their first argument. Hank and Hannah walked hand in hand into their bedroom.

Winter was especially nasty with storm after storm and very cold days and nights. Before anyone realized spring had snuck upon them and it was beautiful. Hannah was excited to see a robin and crocuses beginning to sprout through the ground. Hannah appeared to have more energy compared to a month ago. Hank also noticed a healthy, rosy glow to Hannah's skin. Deep down he hoped the doctors at Homer Folks had been wrong and Hannah was not as sick as they said. Hank did notice difficulty Hannah had walking up the stairs, which often lead to her having labored breathing. Hank decided to monitor this, and wait saying anything to Hannah or Rose. He didn't want either to worry.

Hank came home from work one day, and told Hannah about starting a vegetable garden down the street. Hannah looked at him confused, as Hank continued to explain,

"There is a vacant field at the end of the street that has been designated for people to grow vegetables. President Roosevelt started a program called Victory Gardens where people could use the vacant land to grow vegetables so that more would be available to send the troops. What we grow we keep and eat rather than buying vegetables."

Hank was so excited; he had already roped off a corner of the lot for the two to garden. Hank reminded Hannah all he had learned while at Homer Folks when he worked on the farm. Before Hannah knew Hank had planted a couple of vegetable plants and now the two were busy debating over seed catalogs. On weekends, Hank, Hannah, and Rose would drive out to the country to various feed stores. Although Hank consulted with Hannah, he ultimately made the final decisions concerning the garden. Hannah enjoyed watching Hank tend to his garden and she particularly looked forward to their evening strolls to check the garden. Hank had even built a bench so Hannah could relax and watch him as he tended the garden. Hannah marveled how the entire neighborhood seemed to be involved with the garden. At first she was concerned Hank would be the only one with any interest but she could only smile as she watched everyone working. Hannah wanted to help with the garden, so Hank would have her weed as long as she didn't seem tired. Having learned his lesson in assuming Hannah's feelings concerning her health, he tried a different tactic when he felt she was too tired to work, rather than say,

"You look tired I think we should go home."

He tried,

"Gee, I'm tired, I think we should go home".

Hannah knew exactly what Hank was up to, but she was grateful to let the decision be hers. In all honesty, Hank was tired and was well aware he could have a relapse. This haunted Hank because he worried what would happen to Hannah if he became ill again.

After three months of working for Mr. Singer, Hank applied for health insurance. Unfortunately due to his pre-existing condition, he was denied. Hank, upset, wondered how long would he have to live with the stigma of tuberculosis hanging over his head. It was just one of many disappointments he was forced to accept.

Hank thought since it was six months from their discharge from Homer Folks, both he and Hannah needed to go to the tuberculosis clinic for a check up. Upon mentioning this to Hannah, she immediately became anxious stating, "what if."

"Hank what if my sputum is positive for tuberculosis? What if my lungs have more cavities or the ones I have are worse?"

Hank tried to reassure her, insisting, the two would face things together as they happen. With out admitting to Hannah, Hank was concerned also. He was worried about Hannah's health and his own.

Shortly following their discussion, Hank and Hannah visited the tuberculosis clinic. When they arrived, there were many people waiting. Hank was able to find two chairs located a distance from the others because he worried clients could be carrying active tuberculosis germs. When it was finally their turn, both had chest x-rays and provided samples of their sputum. Next, they were taken to the doctor's office to hear their results. Prior to the visit, and as

Dr. Jones, from Homer Folks said, their records had been sent to the clinic. Therefore the doctor at the clinic was able to familiarize himself with their histories. When the doctor entered his office, he asked Hank and Hannah if they wanted to be seen together. Both insisted upon it, knowing they needed one another for support.

With Hank's x-ray hanging from the light box, the doctor addressed Hank's condition first. He was quick. Overall the x-ray showed continued healing of the cavities. The doctor did tell Hank,

"There is a lot of scar tissue on your left lung. In the future, you may have some difficulty with it. Also Hank, your sputum is negative."

Hank was relieved but anxious to hear the outcomes of Hannah's tests.

Turning to Hannah the doctor began,

"Your x-ray does not show any changes since you left Homer Folks. On the other hand Hannah, your sputum was also negative."

Hannah was satisfied but she wished there had been some healing. The Doctor asked Hannah how she takes care of herself during the day. Hannah replied,

"I rest on the porch with fresh air and I follow that with a nap."

Appearing satisfied with Hannah's answer, he suggested Hannah return once a month so they could monitor her sputum. He did let them know if Hannah's sputum tested positive, he would have no choice but to isolate her.

Both were happy and relieved with their results, Hank's had mixed feelings about Hannah's. He knew some how he would have to do more in aiding her recovery.

As they drove home, each was lost in their own thoughts. Hank was convinced his plan would help Hannah get better. Hank was motivated by love and willpower, with no room for failure. Hannah, on the other hand, saw things in a more practical way. In her mind, this doctor just reiterated what Dr. Jones said in reference to her life expectancy. Hannah decided she was going to focus and live for the day.

Hannah had something else on her mind, their choice of birth control. Hannah went to confession frequently, she never was able to ask the priest. Deep down she knew the Church forbade using condoms, but she was at a loss as to what they should use. For a brief moment, she thought about asking her mother, but quickly dismissed that option. How could she ever have thought about going to Rose with such a personal question. She had already brought up the subject with Hank and he reassured her,

"Because of your health issues I believe using condoms would never be an issue."

Hannah wanted to believe Hank, but she honestly didn't think the Church would agree. Hank also had his doubts, but he would rather burn in hell than have Hannah become pregnant and possibly die.

A month passed and one evening after dinner, Hannah brought up the issue of condoms again. Only during this conversation, Hannah insisted they see a priest and find out where the Church stood. She was obsessed about following the Church's rules, but Hank refused. He said to Hannah,

"I don't want to talk to a priest about our sex life."

When honestly he knew what Hannah would hear and he was not going to give up that part of their relationship. Hannah was adamant and would not let this rest. Hank finally gave in and they made appointment with their parish priest. Hank thought if they spoke to the younger priest, he might be more compassionate to their situation. Both were nervous when they sat in the office of the rectory. It was decided Hank would explain their situation rather than Hannah.

They received a warm welcome from the priest as he inquired as to how he might help them. Hank quickly, with embarrassment, explained the situation he and Hannah faced. Hank was sure to include what Dr. Jones had told them in regards to Hannah becoming pregnant. Realizing Hank and Hannah had a unique position, the Father started by saying,

"I realize the predicament you are faced with and I'm truly sorry. However, the Church is quite strict on this matter. According to the Church, sex must be for propagating the faith, not for pleasure. I know this is difficult to accept, but you must rely on your faith to keep you strong." Hank was speechless. How could this man deny them something so natural? Hank inquired,

"Is there nothing we can do?"

"Well the one thing the Church permits is the rhythm method. My advice would be to visit an obstetrician and have him explain the proper way to follow this method."

Hannah called Carol the following day to get the name of her doctor. Unfortunately, Carol assumed Hannah needed the doctor's information because she was pregnant. Hannah laughed as she explained what Dr. Jones had told her. Carol apologized but Hannah cut her off,

"Don't be silly Carol, I've come to accept this, believe me there's no reason to apologize."

Carol said,

"Well then you want to know about birth control."

"Yes," Hannah admitted.

Carol gave Hannah the name of her doctor and wished Hannah good luck. Carol again said she was sorry Hannah could not have children. Carol absolutely loved her baby.

As soon as Hannah hung up with Carol she immediately called the doctor's office, making an appointment. Hank insisted he be included at the appointment. It wasn't a lack of trust in Hannah, he was being over protective.

After her examination, Hank was called into the doctor's office with Hannah. The doctor began discussing birth control.

"Hannah you must take your temperature every morning. If it is elevated, then you must abstain from sex."

The doctor continued,

"Now you both must understand, the rhythm method is not fool proof, there is a risk of pregnancy compared to using condoms but it is the only form of birth control sanctioned by the Church. It's important to improve its success by following the schedule of your temperature very closely. Do either of you have any questions?"

Neither Hank nor Hannah could think of a question, they were both still trying to digest everything they had been told.

That afternoon, Hannah made a chart exactly how the doctor suggested. She also put a thermometer on her nightstand so she could take her temperature as soon as she woke in the mornings. When her temperature was higher than normal she knew they would have to abstain from sex. After about a month of charting her temperature, she determined she and Hank could only have sex two weeks out of the month, the week before and after her period. Hannah became concerned, that would not be enough sex for Hank.

Hannah's fears were justified because Hank was becoming more and more frustrated with the rhythm method. He did admit without the use of condoms, sex was more fulfilling, but the infrequency was playing on Hank's nerves. One evening while listening to the radio, Hank and Hannah were necking on the couch like teenagers. Hank turned to Hannah, very aroused, and said,

"I have an idea that will allow us to make love right now."

Hannah loved being with Hank so she eagerly agreed. Hank began undressing her and kissed her on all the places on her body that aroused Hannah. When Hannah stood in front of Hank naked, he quickly removed his clothes, both eager to be intertwined. After they each explored the other's bodies with their mouths, Hank pulled Hannah on top of him, and they made love. As Hank began penetrating Hannah, she started protesting, but Hank assured Hannah everything would work out fine. Hannah decided to trust Hank and she let herself enjoy what was happening and what she was feeling. She finally arched her back, held her breath, and shuttered. Completely satisfied, she laid on top of Hank breathing heavy.

"Were not done yet." Hank said between heavy breathing.

Hank pushed Hannah over and pulled out of her. Hannah then felt his hard hot member press on her abdomen. Within seconds, Hank let out a big sigh as she felt something warm and sticky oozing over her stomach. Quietly he asked her if she liked it. Hannah replied,

"Couldn't you tell? Are we okay because you did not come inside of me? Out of curiosity, how do you know so much about sex?" Hannah asked.

Hank gave her a hug, ignoring her questions. However Hank did tell Hannah another way for them both experience pleasure and the next time they were feeling frisky, he would show her. Hannah thought to herself how she never expected to enjoy making love as much as she did with Hank.

Hank continued to succeed at work, professionally and personally. He found himself making friends with the other salesmen. Many of the men who worked there were 4F, which meant they were denied joining the military. Since Buzz had enlisted, Hank was in need of male companionship. Therefore, there was one co-worker who Hank liked. One day after work, Hank suggested too Hannah that they have Bob and his wife, Eliza, for dinner. This made Hannah nervous because other than family members, they had not entertained. Hannah decided to ask Rose for help. Her mother was more than happy to aid Hannah with her first dinner party. When the day arrived for Bob and Eliza to come for dinner, Rose was at Hannah's early and helped with the cooking. As everything was ready at three, Rose left Hannah with specific instructions relating how to have the food ready for dinner. Hannah was extremely thankful for all her mother's help and told her so as she hugged Rose good-bye. Part of Hannah wished her mother could stay but she knew better.

Bob and Eliza were prompt and Hannah liked them immediately. Eliza was not only friendly, but insisted on helping Hannah with dinner. After they finished eating, the four moved to the parlor and Hank suggested they play cards. Bob asked if they would enjoy playing bridge and both were happy to play. Hank was thankful he had taught Hannah to play bridge and she reached the point where she could hold her own during a game. As with many things, Hank thought himself as an expert at the game. After about an hour of playing Hank noticed Hannah beginning to fade. She wasn't talkative and her eyes appeared heavy. Therefore, Hank discreetly came up with an excuse to end the evening early. Hannah was disappointed but she knew Hank was right and looking out for her best interests. From that evening on, Hannah and Hank socialized frequently with Bob and Eliza. The four were becoming fast friends.

Besides Bob and Eliza, Hannah and Hank had been to Carol's for dinner a couple of times. Hank always felt uncomfortable when they were at Carol's house. In a way he felt inferior around Carol's husband because he was a doctor.

Between Carol's and Bob and Eliza's homes, Hannah began to ache with the desire to have a baby. Carol's daughter was just over a year old and Bob and Eliza had three children, the youngest a two month old little girl. Hannah was crazy about the baby. Whenever they were invited to Bob and Eliza's house, Hannah would talk about their baby all day.

Hannah read an article describing adoption, which gave her an idea. When Hank got home from work he noticed Hannah had prepared his favorite dishes. Following dinner they made passionate love. As they lay in each other's arms Hannah brought up her idea of adopting since she couldn't have children. Hank's face turned varying shades of red as he became angrier and angrier.

"Absolutely not! There is no way on god's earth I will raise someone else's kid."

Hannah was shocked by Hank's reaction and rather question him about it, she decided to drop the idea completely.

Not only was Hank upset by the topic of adopting, Hannah could sense something else was bothering him.

"Hannah is that why you made my favorite dinner and then trick me with sex?"

Meekly Hannah replied,

"Yes and don't refer to our love making as sex."

"Don't ever try and trick me again," Hank warned Hannah.

It seemed to take forever for Hank to cool down. He couldn't remember ever being so angry with Hannah before tonight. However, Hank loved Hannah so much it was impossible for him to remain angry with her for very long. Hank pulled her to him and they slowly made love. When they were finished, catching their breath Hank said,

"Now that was making love, my love."

TWENTY

Without either realizing what date was approaching, their first year wedding anniversary snuck up on them. Hannah and Hank agreed, they had a wonderful first year of marriage and they both were thankful to have found the other. They believed they were more in love with each other. Both, Hank and Hannah, thought they should celebrate the year they spent as a married couple, but what should they do? Hannah thought they could go out for the evening, but without saying anything to Hannah, Hank had another idea. He secretly made arrangements to go on the honeymoon they never had. Hank knew not only would Hannah be surprised, she would also be thrilled to go away.

December twenty-first arrived and each was excited. They celebrated by making love before they got out of bed. Rose called around ten wishing them, happy anniversary, while Hank and Hannah were still in bed. Having sensed she interrupted something. Rose told them she would call back later, abruptly hanging up. Hank and Hannah became hysterical as soon as they realized Rose figured out what the two were up to when she called. Finally deciding it was time to get up, they decided to take a shower together. They took turns lathering each other's body. Hannah enjoyed this, especially feeling Hanks hands, covered with suds, washing every inch of her body. Hank felt the same and the two remained in the bath until there was no more hot water. After drying each other and dressing for the day, they headed for the kitchen to prepare breakfast.

When they finished breakfast they exchanged gifts. Hank left Hannah's surprise until the end. Hank handed Hannah a long rectangular box, wrapped in golden paper with a beautiful bow centered perfectly. As soon as Hannah opened it, she said,

"Oh Hank what a beautiful bracelet, I absolutely love it."

Hank was thrilled with the gift Hannah gave him. Hannah saved from her weekly house money for months. Edmund Jr. took her to an office supply shop where she was able to get Hank a brief case. Hank was actually excited by Hannah's card, although he loved his present. The card read,

"Many nights of me giving you pleasure, love Hannah."

When Hank read the card he laughed out loud. Shortly after, Hank reminded Hannah how she responded to the evening he showed her exactly how to pleasure him. He said to her,

"Don't you remember what you said, both of us will end up in hell for what we do."

Next Hank gave Hannah her card and written inside Hank wrote,

"Our honeymoon trip, destination to be announced at a latter date, be packed and ready to leave, date February 14th."

Hannah was shocked. She never dreamt they would actually have their honeymoon. As suddenly as she was excited, her excitement faded, and Hannah said,

"Hank can we afford such a trip?"

Hank assured her by reminding Hannah of the big sale he made.

"That's all we will need is the commission money, so don't worry about anything."

The remainder of the day flew by. Later that evening, Hank and Hannah went out to a nice restaurant to celebrate their anniversary. After dinner Hank surprised Hannah by taking her dancing. For Hannah it had been a long day and by the time they returned home it was obvious Hannah was exhausted. As they lay in bed, holding each other, Hannah said to Hank,

"Thank you, my love, for such a wonderful day and an amazing first year of marriage. I love you with all my heart."

Gently she kissed him on the lips. They both agreed they had had a magical first year as husband and wife.

While Hannah and Hank were celebrating their anniversary, Rose was concerned for her sons serving overseas in the Army. Ever so often Rose would receive a letter from one of her sons, and Rose seemed at ease after reading their letters in which they tried to assure her that each was fine. Rose seemed relaxed after reading one of their letters until she received a telegram one day. Rose knew the telegram was not delivering good news and as she read it, her heart sank, Harry was missing in action. Rose thought at first, this wasn't the worse news, Harry could still be alive. Then Rose remembered hearing about the Nazi's and how vicious they could be, especially to prisoners. Without any options, Rose knew all she could do was pray for Harry's safe return home.

Like Rose, Hannah was devastated with the news of Harry. Hannah drifted into a depression, where she rarely slept or ate. She refused to follow her daily routine, and Hank was worried. Hank became desperate, to the point where he called Carol's husband, their doctor. Carol and her husband came to the flat and he pulled Hannah on to the porch to talk to her in private. He spoke to Hannah sternly, reminding her of the consequences if she didn't begin taking care of her self. Hannah listened; knowing what Carol's husband said was true. She also knew she was not ready to die; she loved Hank with all her heart and soul. She needed to find another way to grieve. Upon leaving Carol's husband reassured Hank,

"Hannah will come to her senses, just give her space and time to process the unknown about Harry, and be patient."

The doctor was right because within a few days, though she was still sad and worried Hannah returned to the daily routine.

February fourteenth was days away and Hannah decided to pack for their trip. Hannah packed the nicest clothes she owned, along with a beautiful nightgown and matching robe Rose had given her for Christmas. Hannah saved her mother's gift especially for this occasion. Hank was holding their destination close to the chest; he only gave her one hint,

"We will be going to a variety of fancy places."

It drove Hannah crazy, yet her excitement overwhelmed her.

As they headed south, Hannah still had no idea where Hank was taking her. She tried to trick hints out of him, but it was impossible. At last, after four hours, Hannah could see the skyline.

"Hank, we're going to New York City?"

Hannah asked giddy with excitement. Even though she had never been there, Hannah felt as if she had though because of the stories her mother and father shared. Hannah leaned over kissing Hank on the cheek, over and over. As they came closer, Hannah's head continuously turned to the left and then the right, trying to see everything. Hannah could not remove the smile plastered on her face, she always wanted to visit the City and now they were there.

Hank drove to the center of Manhattan, Time Square. They pulled up to a large impressive hotel and as they exited their car, a bellhop saw to their luggage and another parked their car. Hank registered them as Mr. and Mrs. Hank Schmidt, and Hannah realized this was the first time since their wedding, had they been referred to as Mr. and Mrs. The bellhop directed the couple to the elevator and their room, pushing their luggage with them. As soon as Hannah saw their room, not only was she impressed, she felt like a queen. Hank tipped the bellhop and Hannah went over to Hank, giving him a long kiss and hug to show him how happy she was. Hank was as excited as Hannah, but he insisted she rest for an hour. Disappointed, Hannah agreed. While Hannah rested, Hank returned to the lobby and met with the concierge. By the time Hank returned to the room, He had made dinner reservations and brought tickets for a play. As he entered the room, Hannah was up, looking out the window, and getting anxious to walk around Time Square. Knowing he could never keep her in to rest some more, Hank agreed and they walked around Time Square arm and arm. They looked at various store windows and restaurants until they reached the theater district. Hannah thought, how her mother was drawn to such a place. Hannah absolutely loved the sights and sounds, so much she impulsively said to Hank,

"Let's move here. Wouldn't it be wonderful?"

She was overcome with New York City. Hank laughed at his wife and loved seeing the excitement in her face. After an hour or so, they returned to their room to dress for dinner. Hank was so stunned as

Hannah appeared, dressed and ready to go, Hank sat overwhelmed by how beautiful Hannah was. Again he wondered to himself, how he got so lucky, she could have had anyone, and she picked him. Proudly Hank walked into the restaurant with Hannah's arm intertwined in his. Hannah was in awe with the restaurant, thinking how expensive everything must be. As she thought that, Hank, as if reading her mind, said,

"Order what ever you like, I forbid you to look at the prices." Although difficult, Hannah ordered what she wanted and they thoroughly enjoyed every bite. After dinner, they walked hand in hand to the theater. Hannah couldn't put into words how much she enjoyed the performance. When they returned to their room, they hungrily made love and fell in to satiated sleep.

Upon returning to Albany, Hank was as busy as ever at work. Hannah threw herself into her curative routine. She noticed feeling very tired and queasy during the day. She made sure she sat on the porch daily and always ate something, especially at dinner. She didn't want Hank to know how she felt. Eventually though, Hank realized what Hannah was doing and became concerned. At Hank's insistence, they went to the tuberculosis clinic. As usual, before they took a chest x-ray, the technician asked Hannah if she was pregnant and the date of her last period. Hannah couldn't remember, she thought it was two months ago, but she wasn't sure. Due to her condition it wasn't unusual for her to skip a period. Hannah wasn't concerned, they had been following the correct way with the rhythm method of birth control. The doctor at the clinic refused to perform a chest x-ray until Hannah saw an obstetrician. The doctor suggested Dr. Kiernan. Hank was upset because they refused to do the chest x-ray and like Hannah he was confident she couldn't be pregnant.

Hannah made an appointment with Dr.Kiernan insisting she could go by herself. Dr.Kiernan performed a complete physical, including an internal. After the exam, Dr. Kiernan had Hannah come into his office. Sensing Hannah to be sensitive, Dr. Kiernan gently discussed his finding from her exam. To Hannah's shock, Dr. Kiernan told Hannah he guessed she was two months pregnant. Dr. Kiernan told Hannah he was also Catholic, so he knew the dilemma she and her husband were in. Hannah was given two options, first go ahead with the pregnancy, which included the potential of shortening her life, or the second, terminating the pregnancy. Dr. Kiernan suggested Hannah talk to her husband before making any decisions.

Hannah couldn't believe what she was hearing, how could this be, they had been so careful. She knew Hank would be out of his mind, she didn't know what to do. On her way home, Hannah realized she needed to decide for herself before talking to Hank. Hannah had no idea what to do and how long it would take for her to make up her mind. Hannah did decide to tell Hank it would take a few days to get the results of the pregnancy test, allowing her time to think. Hank came home that night, eager to hear how the doctor's appointment went. Hannah told him,

"The doctor did the pregnancy test and he won't know the results for a couple of days."

This was Hannah's first lie to Hank and she felt awful.

Over the following three days, Hannah did nothing but think about being pregnant. She knew she really wanted this baby, it represented their love. Having the baby could cost her precious time with Hank. Hannah knew if she had this baby she would never live long enough to see the baby grow up. Hannah did not know what to do.

Seeking guidance, Hannah went to see the parish priest. She told him her dilemma and wanted to know the position of the Church. The priest was quite frank, he told Hannah,

"If by having this baby means your immediate death, then an abortion could be considered."

Hannah knew this wasn't her case, she wouldn't die. Accordingly the priest said,

"The doctor told you your life might certainly be shortened. That is not the same in the eyes of the Church."

That was all Hannah needed to hear to confirm her decision.

Later that evening, Hank arrived home, asked Hannah if the doctor called hoping he would hear what he wanted. Hannah replied,

"Yes, Hank, he called."

Agreeing to discuss what the doctor said after dinner, Hank knew Hannah was pregnant. Just as planned, after dinner Hank and Hannah moved to the couch. Hannah took Hank's hand into hers and told him,

"I'm, two to three months pregnant."

Hannah knew by Hank's expression, he was angry. Besides anger, Hank was scared to death and wanted to know how this happened, they had been so careful. Hank turned to Hannah and asked,

"How did this happen, Hannah?"

Repeating what Dr. Kiernan had told her, Hannah said,

"Dr. Kiernan told me the rhythm method is not fool proof, there was always a chance I could get pregnant."

Hannah then told Hank their options and all he could do was sit back and let this all process, then he said,

"We don't have an option, you'll have an abortion Hannah."

Although Hannah knew Hank would react as he did, she nervously shook inside because she had never gone against him, until now. Hannah decided to share her conversation she and the priest had in regards to the Church's stand on abortion. As Hannah spoke, Hank suddenly realized Hannah had known about the pregnancy since her doctor's appointment.

"You've known about the pregnancy since you saw the doctor, haven't you?"

Hannah saw the hurt in Hank's eyes. "Yes," was all she could reply.

Hank realized he needed time to think not only about the baby, but Hannah's deception. Feeling as if he was drowning, he told Hannah he needed to go for a walk alone. As he walked around the neighborhood, he thought about the position they were in. They both were very devout and if the priest said the Church would approve abortion, then he would insist upon it. In Hank's eyes Hannah was much more precious than any baby. When he returned, Hannah made a suggestion,

"Why don't I make another appointment with Dr. Kiernan, then both of us could go and listen to what he has to say."

Hank agreed and the two decided to go to bed.

As they lay in bed, Hannah could sense Hank was no longer as angry as he had been earlier. Hannah moved close to him, putting both arms around him. Hannah loved Hank so much; all she wanted was for him to be happy.

During their visit with Dr. Kiernan, Hank was told the same thing as Hannah. Dr. Kiernan had information he did not have when he saw Hannah previously. He informed them,

"Since I saw Hannah, I have done some research relating to her condition. There are those who believe in an obscure school of thought that basically think once pregnant the uterus enlarges therefore pressing against the lungs. Those who believe in this, argue with the uterus pushing on the lung it allows the lung to rest providing time for the lung to heal. In all honesty, not many within the medical community believe this to be true and I certainly don't want to provide you with false information, but I can see how it could be beneficial for the lungs. In any event, the two of you must make a decision soon if we are going to perform a therapeutic abortion. Let's make a follow up appointment for one week. I apologize I can't tell you everything will be fine if you decide to have the baby. I wish I could make your decision easier. I suggest you turn to your faith and use that as a starting point and I'll see you both in a week."

Each time they tried to discuss their situation, it would lead nowhere. Hank brought up the abortion and Hannah finally told Hank,

"I don't want an abortion, Hank, I want our child, I want this baby. Just think Hank he or she would be proof of our love for each other. Besides everything, Hank, you would be a wonderful father."

Hank tried to reason with Hannah by saying,

"Hannah, think about this, you always become tired easily and a baby would add to that. Plus how could you manage your schedule for recovery along with a baby's demanding needs. Not only would you have to respond to the daily needs of the baby, but think about at night when it's fussy and refuses to fall back to asleep. Do you honestly think you could handle a baby and your recovery?"

Everything Hank said scared Hannah, but she was determined, knowing she could cope. She only wished Hank knew she could handle both.

"Hank, I never said having this baby would be easy, but I know we can manage."

Two days passed before either broached the subject again. It was Hank who turned to Hannah and said,

"Well, I guess we have made our choice, we will be having a baby."

As he said that to Hannah, he hugged her so much that her feet left the ground. Then he gave Hannah a lovingly, long kiss that sent butterflies through her stomach. Hank continued,

"I'll be taking care of you to ensure both mother-to-be and baby are healthy."

During their following doctor's appointment, Hank told him their decision. Dr. Kiernan reassured them,

"I will do everything I can to make sure the health of both mother and baby remain in excellent conditions. May I also suggest, refrain from telling anyone immediately. There is always the risk of a miscarriage, especially with in the first three months. Therefore your due date will be around the twentieth of September."

The more Hank heard from Dr. Kiernan, the more excited he was getting. He imagined Hannah having a little girl that looked just as beautiful as her mother. Hannah though, wanted a boy. A baby boy would take after his father and please Hank as he grew. While they each choose what sex the baby was, they shared a common bond, both were excited to welcome a new member of their family.

Once Dr. Kiernan assured Hannah she was at least three months pregnant, she and Hank immediately told Rose. Hannah couldn't believe the reaction she received from her mother. Rose didn't seem surprised or happy that Hannah and Hank were expecting. Hannah had been wrong, she completely misunderstood Rose's reaction. Rose turned to Hank and Hannah and said,

"I guessed you were pregnant about a month ago. I was waiting to see how long it would take you to figure it out."

After Rose congratulated Hannah and Hank they knew they needed to discuss what implications went along with the pregnancy. Rose wanted to know how the pregnancy would affect Hannah's health. Hank and Hannah shared everything Dr. Kiernan had told them, including how the pregnancy could help Hannah. Rose seemed somewhat at ease once she knew about Dr. Kiernan and his plans. Then Rose offered to help in any way she could. She immediately insisted she would increase her visits from once a week to three or four times. Hank was overwhelmed with relief in knowing Rose would be there for Hannah so often. Rose's assistance would be essential for Hannah to get through the pregnancy relatively healthy.

The number of milestones they would experience with the pregnancy surprised Hannah. During her first three months, Hannah had not gained weight. Dr. Kiernan insisted Hannah eat as much as possible. He wanted Hannah to gain at least thirty pounds.

At Hannah's next visit to Dr. Kiernan, she couldn't believe what she experienced; Dr. Kiernan heard the baby's heartbeat. If anything made Hannah feel pregnant, this was it. As soon as Hank came home that evening, Hannah told him about the baby's heartbeat. She was so thrilled, yet Hank was worried. He knew he wanted the baby, but he also knew he wanted Hannah more. He tried to seem happy about the heartbeat, but he knew this meant the baby was real. He hated feeling like he did, he wanted to be as pleased as Hannah, but he didn't have it in him yet. All he knew was there was no turning back; they were going to be parents. Hank had to admit, he enjoyed watching Hannah each time she had news or something to share. Her expressions were unforgettable and at times so amazing. They both noticed as Hannah began to gain weight. Then overnight, Hank noticed how her belly began to enlarge. Hannah walked around with a glow to her face.

Rose arrived one morning and Hannah complained about a constant feeling of gas. She also told her mother she felt fluttering in her lower stomach. She stressed how it had been going on for a couple of days and wondered if she should call the doctor. Rose smiled at her daughter, gave her a hug, and said,

"Hannah, my love, there is no need to call the doctor. What you are feeling is normal. The baby is moving and kicking you to let you know he or she is in there waiting to make its appearance." Hannah laughed and was surprised by what she was feeling. She couldn't wait to tell Hank and have him feel what she felt. It wasn't much longer, Hank arrived home from work, and Hannah asked him to join her on the couch. He did as asked and without saying anything, Hannah took his hand and placed it on her belly. Within seconds Hank started laughing. He couldn't believe what he was feeling. He felt his baby moving. Hank didn't want to move his hand. They sat there for at least an hour when Hank said,

"We need to feed the two of you."

After dinner Hank and Hannah laid down in bed, Hank cuddling and returning his hand to her belly. The two fell asleep each with a smile on their faces.

Hannah felt the months fly by. After the initial nausea and fatigue, she felt great. Hannah took this as a sign from God, that everything would be fine. Hank still nagged Hannah about resting, eating, and getting enough fresh air. On weekends, Hank would take Hannah to the country for walks. Hank still worried, as time went by, he allowed himself to feel some pride in helping make their baby.

On September first, following dinner, Hannah told Hank she was feeling pain in her lower abdomen. Hannah described the pain as not the worst she had ever felt, but it continued to get stronger. Hank immediately wanted to call the doctor. Hannah wasn't sure, there were still a couple of weeks until her due date, and maybe the pain would subside. By nine pm Hannah agreed to call Dr. Kiernan. Dr. Kiernan insisted Hank take Hannah to Brady Maternity Hospital immediately, and he would meet them there.

Normally, Dr. Kiernan would allow the resident to examine a patient and wait until he was called but with Hannah he wanted to do the examination.

Dr. Kiernan met them at the hospital, examined Hannah, and found she was in labor. He went out to speak to Hank. Dr. Kiernan met Hank in the waiting room, told him Hannah was in labor, and not to expect anything to happen soon. He explained to Hank,

"Since it is early with Hannah's labor and because it's her first baby, she will probably take awhile to give birth. I'll be staying in the hospital so I can check on her frequently. As soon as I have news, I'll be out to see you."

Hank didn't know what to do. He paced, read, drank coffee, and finally sat down when hours later Dr. Kiernan came out. This time Hank could tell he looked tired, but he was smiling. He told Hank,

"Everything is going smoothly, Hannah is progressing nicely, and I believe there should be a baby within an hour or so."

By this time, Rose was there along with Hank's sister, Maria. They all were excited, but none as much as Hank.

Forty-five minutes later the doctor came out dressed in scrubs and a mask. It seemed to Hank that Dr. Kiernan had tears in his eyes, but he was smiling.

"Congratulations you have a healthy baby girl and a very brave wife".

"Is Hannah okay doctor?"

"She's better than okay," Dr. Kiernan said.

"It's a shame she can't have more children, she's made to have children. Hank go to the nursery, and see your daughter, and then you may see Hannah."

Rose, Maria, and Hank went to the nursery. Hank motioned to the nurse and she brought a small bundle to the window. She removed the baby's blanket and Hank had his first glimpse of his daughter. He couldn't help smiling with pride. His little girl was crying, her face scrunched up, with an expression saying she was angry at the world. Rose was amazed at the baby's size. The little bundle was short fifteen inches and pudgy six pounds and fourteen ounces.

Hank went back to the waiting room to see Hannah. It seemed like an eternity for the nurse to come and escort him to Hannah's room. Hank couldn't get over the sight of Hannah; she was radiant, absolutely glowing. Hannah was so excited to see Hank; she was pleased he had seen the baby. She asked him what he thought of their daughter.

"She's absolutely beautiful but where is her hair? Her eyes were shut, so I couldn't see the color. Are you okay?"

Hannah assured him she was fine. They spent their time talking about the baby. When Hank left he leaned over Hannah and said,

"You did a good job, mom." Hannah beamed.

TWENTY-ONE

E ach night after work, Hank would go by and see his two girls. They hadn't come up with a name for their baby girl until Hank mentioned naming her after his mother, Maria. Hannah loved the name and knew naming their baby after his mother would make Hank happy. Then, when Hank arrived the following evening everything changed. Hank told Hannah,

"I don't think we should name our baby Maria, not because I don't want to, but there are too many Maria's already on my side of the family. Not only is my sister named after my mother, her oldest daughter is also named Maria. I want our daughter to have a name all her own."

Hannah knew Hank was disappointed, she understood and agreed with Hank. Hank decided Hannah should pick a name this time. After some thought, Hannah said,

"Matilda Rose, Matilda was the name of my grandmother and Rose you know is my mother's name."

Hank immediately thought Matilda was too old fashion for such a beautiful little girl. Hannah had an alternative to Matilda,

"We will call her Mandy, rather than Matilda."

Hank agreed and their baby finally had a name, Matilda (Mandy) Rose Schmidt.

Rose felt honored they chose to name their daughter after her mother and herself. Her mother had immigrated from Ireland and had a difficult life. Rose had loved her dearly and Hank and Hannah had given her the best gift ever, even if they hadn't realized what they had given her.

Hannah and Mandy came home from the hospital a couple days later, to a surprise. Prior to Mandy's birth Hannah was reluctant to prepare the baby's room, she felt it was bad luck to get the room ready. Hannah thought Mandy would sleep in their room, in a bassinet, until she had the nursery ready. Hannah felt it was something they could take their time and complete together.

While Hannah was recovering in the hospital, Rose and Hank had different plans. Hank painted the nursery pale pink. He found a second hand crib and a dresser for the baby's room. Rose clean each, then made special sheets for the crib. Edmund Jr. gave a little table perfect for holding diapers, powder and lotions. As soon as Hannah saw the room, she let out a squeal of delight. The first thing Hannah noticed was Rose's was the rocking chair. It reminded her how Rose rocked each of her children in the same chair. Hannah turned to Hank and Rose, hugged them both, and said,

"Thanking you both so much, I absolutely love it."

Hannah believed they had everything they could possibly need to begin their life with Mandy. That was until Hank told her there was one more surprise, making Hannah close her eyes, Hank and Rose lead her to the back of the house. On the count of three, Hannah was told to open her eyes. When she did, she was speechless. In front of her was a washing machine, with a clothesline attached to the house, at the window, and a large tree in the back yard. Hannah couldn't believe her eyes and she thought, no longer will I need to use that old washboard. Immediately she hugged Hank, thanking him over and over. Then turning to her mother she said,

"Can you believe it mother, I have a washing machine."

Due to Hanks insistence, Mandy's christening would wait until Hannah was physically stronger. Maria had given Hannah and Hank a christening gown that was worn by Hank and each of his siblings. Maria told Hannah, each of her children had been baptized in the same gown. Hannah felt it was only right Hank's daughter should wear the same christening gown. As Mandy turned three weeks old, Hannah was strong enough to proceed with Mandy's christening. Mandy, dressed in her father's family christening gown, was adorable. Hannah insisted Hank take a picture of mother and daughter. During the ceremony, Mandy was so good she surprised everyone. When the priest poured holy water over Mandy's baldhead, she didn't make a sound. It was evident to all in attendance how proud Hank and Hannah were of their little angel.

Following the christening, Rose held a large party at her house. There were many people who came to share in the christening, not only were they there to celebrate Mandy, but to Hannah's amazement many brought gifts. Hannah found her sister-in-law's gift to be the most heart felt. As Maria handed over a large box to Hannah, she said,

"Hannah, I'm finished having children, therefore I couldn't think of anyone else who would appreciate the baby clothes my children once wore."

Hannah thanked Maria, gave her a hug and said,

"I'll be proud to have Mandy wear these clothes, I can't thank you enough."

Hannah truly was taken back by Maria's generosity. As Hannah and Hank took in the gifts, Hannah thought Mandy was set for some time. She received clothes, receiving blankets, dishes, bottles, a cross and chain, and someone gave her a pressed four-leaf clover. Hannah prayed her baby would never need luck; she wanted Mandy's life to be filled with good positive happenings. If Hannah had any say that's exactly what Mandy had to look forward to.

Everyone was enjoying the party when the doorbell rang. Rose opened the door and to her surprise there stood a young man with a telegram. Rose had been preparing herself for the worst since she received the first telegram stating Harry was missing in action. Rose slowly opened the telegram while Hannah prayed Mandy's four-leaf clover would bring luck. Once opened, Rose read the telegram aloud,

"This is to notify you, your son Sergeant Harry Wright was injured in the line of duty. Sergeant Wright is currently recovering at an Army hospital. As soon as he is well enough, he will be returned stateside. Sergeant Wright will notify you of his return."

Everyone cheered for joy. Rose performed the sign of the cross and thanked God for sparing her youngest boy. Questions began flying across the room because the telegram lacked any answers. Someone wanted to know which hospital Harry was in? Another, asked how seriously wounded was Harry? How long before Harry would be shipped home? And lastly where would Harry be shipped? No mater who asked the questions or how many questions people had, everyone could agree, it was a miracle Harry was alive and sometime in the future he would be home where he belonged. The party had been for Hank, Hannah, and Mandy, there was more to celebrate now, Harry was alive and coming home. The excitement could not be contained and it was apparent on the faces of all the guests.

It seemed Mandy ruled the household for the first six weeks she was home. Hank and Hannah were forced to follow her schedule. Hannah read a number of baby books during her pregnancy and each said the same thing. A newborn typically followed a four-hour schedule of eating, sleeping, and changing. Mandy's schedule was quite different. Her daily routine was, Mandy ate and slept four to six hours during a stretch. Her nighttime routine was very different. At night her stretch would last two to three hours, then Mandy would wake everyone with crying, usually wanting to be fed. For the new parents, it became so exhausting, they took turns each night. If Hank got up with Mandy on Monday night, then Hannah would tend to Mandy Tuesday night. This worried Hannah, Hank always appeared tired. Hannah would try to convince Hank to let her get up with Mandy,

"Please Hank let me get up with Mandy every night. You must go to work and I'm able to nap when Mandy does."

Hank refused, he told Hannah,

"I love Mandy, but I don't get to spend the amount of time with her as you do. By getting up with her, I get to form a bond with Mandy I might not otherwise be able to form because I work so much."

Hannah understood, but she still thought he needed more sleep. In all honesty, Hank only spoke half-truth. Yes, he wanted to bond with Mandy, however more importantly, Hannah needed as much rest as possible. Hannah was and always will be the most important person in Hank's life.

One night Mandy was up around three am and it was Hank's night to care for her. As Hank was trying to get Mandy asleep, Hank took the time to have a chat with his daughter. Very quietly, Hank said to his daughter,

"I love you Mandy, but if your needs shorten your mother's life by a single day, I don't think I would ever be able to forgive you."

Mandy looked at her father with an expression that seemed to understand what her father said. What Hank said sounded uncaring; it wasn't by any means as far as Hank was concerned. This was something he needed to say because his love for Hannah was irreplaceable in his mind. He was doing what he always did, looking out for his wife.

By Mandy's third month, she was sleeping through the night. What a great relief for both mother and father. The more Mandy slept, the better Hank and Hannah felt, both emotionally and physically. Hank began looking like his old self, which meant Hannah didn't have to worry about him.

Hannah decided she would not rely on baby books and threw them out. She knew her common sense and help from her mother would be enough guidance to take care of the baby she loved and adored.

Hannah noticed Mandy smiling and talking more baby talk. Hannah spoke back to Mandy whenever she started babbling. Besides smiling, Mandy would make other faces, most likely related to gas, but they still entertained Hank and Hannah. The two would play with Mandy for hours during the evening, imitating sounds Mandy did and making faces like Mandy's.

Not long after sleeping through the night Mandy celebrated another milestone, eating cereal and milk. The only thing that concerned Hannah was Mandy never seemed to be full. Hannah thought her daughter was a fat baby with too many roles on her thighs. Hank thought it was funny how his daughter ate and he tried to reassure Hannah,

"It's just baby fat. As Mandy grows you'll see it disappear." Hank's words did not help. Hannah called Rose and told her,

"Mandy's eating too much and she's getting fat."

Rose's response was similar to Hank's,

"Hannah, as long as Mandy is content, sleeping through the night, and happy, let her have whatever she wants. Mandy has baby fat and it will disappear once she starts growing and moving around."

Not hearing what she needed, Hannah brought Mandy to the doctor. It seemed as if everyone had the same thought because the pediatrician told Hannah,

"Mandy is a very healthy baby who enjoys eating. There is nothing wrong with Mandy or how you are caring for her. Let her eat what she wants and as soon as she starts to crawl and walk you will notice a big change with Mandy. Now I've given Mandy the BCG inoculation to protect her from tuberculosis."

Hannah was thankful because that was a constant concern of Hannah's, Mandy catching tuberculosis from her.

Each month Hank and Hannah would go to the tuberculosis clinic; it was becoming part of their routine. During this visit, it seemed as if it was going to be like all the previous. They both had negative chest x-rays and their sputum was negative, although Hannah had a different results when the doctor began discussing her lungs. This time Hannah's x-ray showed increased healing within the cavities of her right lung and there weren't any nodules. Hannah almost couldn't contain her happiness. Once outside Hank hugged her and said,

"We're doing it, we're beating the tuberculosis."

Hannah was so excited she had been given good news relating to her health. Thinking to herself, she thought maybe if she continued to heal she could have another baby. Hannah didn't dare mention it to Hank, she knew exactly how he would react and he definitely wouldn't agree with what Hannah desired.

As Mandy turned five months old, a little bit of peach fuzz appeared on her head. The little bit of hair was practically white and her eyes were an aqua blue, just like her parent's eyes. Hank thought now she looks like a normal baby rather than a bald headed baby. With the temper Mandy possessed, each time she became angry her whole head would turn bright red, especially her face and scalp.

Hannah enjoyed placing Mandy on the floor; Mandy would raise her head looking around. Mandy would laugh, and make herself turn over lying on her back. One day, shortly after Hannah laid Mandy on the floor, Mandy managed to use her arms, raising her upper body off the floor. By the time she was six months; she was able to sit up on her own. One of the most significant milestones for Hannah and Hank was Mandy's ability to recognize her parents, which she did at a couple of months. She was also making choices such as only wanting to be held by Hannah. Hannah could see this hurt Hank and she tried to explain to him why Mandy was in this phase,

"Hank you need to realize Mandy is with me the entire day. By the time you get home, she is nearing her bedtime, so tired and cranky. If the situation was reversed and I was going to work each day and you stayed home taking care of Mandy, she would want you. You need to trust me when I say this is a phase and it won't last long."

Hank didn't like it, but he accepted Hannah's reasoning.

As March came in, Hannah noticed her body was getting extremely tired and walking up the stairs caused shortness of breath. If she was carrying Mandy, Hannah had greater difficulty breathing. Because it was spring Hannah took Mandy for walks. She would be sure to bundle Mandy up along with herself. Hannah tried everything to hide her symptoms from Hank, but he figured it out. Not only had he figured out Hannah's relapse, He had made an appointment for her at the tuberculosis clinic. Together, Hank and Hannah arrived at the clinic. Hannah had a chest x-ray then the doctor examined her. When he finished, Hank and Hannah waited for the doctor in his office. Shortly he joined them, sharing Hannah's results,

"First, let me ease your minds, Hannah is not having a relapse. Her lungs are healing nicely. There is an issue though, in Hannah's right lung, the lower lobe is not expanding fully. This is caused by the amount of scar tissue that has built up there. This explains Hannah's difficulty breathing. There is nothing that can be done now; possibly in the future as Hannah becomes stronger she could have an operation to remove the scar tissue. I must advise you both this is a very dangerous operation, therefore until Hannah is much stronger, no one would attempt it."

Before Hannah and Hank left, the doctor told Hannah to begin doing deep breathing exercises she had learned at Homer Folks and to do them preferably outside.

Hannah was almost giddy with relief. Her biggest fear was a relapse so strong her only choice would be readmission to Homer Folks. Besides that Hannah's fears had been suppressed, Hank's were also. The relief he felt as he heard the doctor speak almost took his breath away. Hank often worried what he would if anything happened to Hannah. He knew he wouldn't want to continue living, but what would happen to Mandy?

It was August, Mandy was nine months old and she had begun walking, talking, and had three teeth. Hannah was given a baby book and recorded all pertinent information on Mandy. She especially enjoyed rereading the passages she filled in making little notations. Hannah bragged thinking Mandy was very advanced for her age. One thing Hannah did know, Mandy was so active there was barely a day Mandy didn't ware out her mother.

When Mandy napped Hannah focused on her breathing exercises. Hannah told Hank that she noticed a difference, but in reality there wasn't any change.

Christmas was approaching and the excitement in the Schmidt household was overflowing. Last year, Mandy was too young to notice anything, but this year things were different. Hank wired the tree to the wall, so Mandy couldn't pull it over. Hannah thought leaving the lower branches bare of ornaments was wise. Hank and Hannah only trimmed the upper portion of the tree.

Mandy had a playpen, but she wailed so when lowered into it Hannah, decided to let her roam free through most of the flat. Naturally Hank had baby proofed the flat before Mandy came home from the hospital.

This Christmas was special, for the entire Wright family, Harry was home. He had spent the last year in a VA hospital and three months in rehabilitation. Harry was given a medical discharge due to the injury to his legs. Both legs were severely fractured and had healed crooked. Besides his legs he was in so much pain, especially when walking, he walked with a limp. Harry kept telling everyone he could deal with the pain, he was grateful to be alive. He had lost a lot of his friends and that bothered him a great deal. Harry was thankful for one thing, his niece, Mandy. He absolutely fell in love with her and she took to Harry without hesitation.

Hannah noted how her mother aged over the past year. Rose was sixty-five and beginning to slow down. Although she still would come to Hannah's at least three times a week, Hannah tried to convince her to stay at home. Rose was adamant, she would not stop helping Hannah, Rose worried about her little girl, now she had two to focus on.

When New Year's arrived, the three members of the Schmidt family were down and out. Mandy was sick with a cold, her nose ran, she coughed, and felt feverish. At first Hannah though Mandy was cutting a new tooth until a few days passed and Mandy wasn't getting better. With no signs of improvement, Hank and Hannah brought Mandy to the doctor. Mandy had never been sick and the new parents hadn't experienced a sick child. The doctor examined Mandy and told the anxious parents,

"Mandy has a bad cold. Go to the pharmacy and pick up "Save The Baby" salve.

In about a week Mandy should be better. Call me if she begins to run a high fever."

A week later Mandy was better and returned to the happy little girl she was before her cold. Unfortunately, Hannah was overwhelmed with fatigue, which wasn't getting better with rest. Hannah didn't know how long she could manage.

TWENTY-TWO

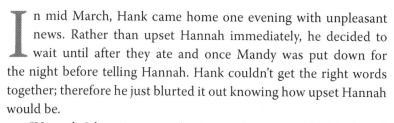

In mid March, Hank came home one evening with unpleasant news. Rather than upset Hannah immediately, he decided to wait until after they ate and once Mandy was put down for the night before telling Hannah. Hank couldn't get the right words together; therefore he just blurted it out knowing how upset Hannah would be.

"Hannah I have to go on business trip next week," Hank said carefully.

"Where are you going?" inquired Hannah.

"Binghamton," Hank replied, hearing the concern in Hannah's voice.

Hannah asked, "How long?"

Hank replied, "Five days."

As far as Hannah was concerned, Hank might as well be gone five weeks.

"How will I get by without you, you take care of everything, including me?"

Hannah leaned in against Hank resting her head on his chest. They had never been apart, even when Hannah was in the hospital during Mandy's birth, Hank visited daily. Hannah's anxiety was increasing, which in turn made her scared to be alone. Hannah noticed pain in her chest, similar to a vice being tightened the more she thought about his trip.

Hank tried to reassure Hannah he would make arrangements so that she would not be alone. Hank and Hannah discussed whom she could call if she needed help. Hannah acted almost child like, saying,

"I don't know Hank."

Trying to keep his patience with Hannah, he reminded her,

"You can call your mother, Harry, or even Eliza, Bob's wife."

Hannah felt silly, acting like a child with her fears, which were unfounded. She knew how important this trip was for Hank. Hannah knew she needed to act like a supportive wife for her husband.

Hannah thought about it and with Mandy over her cold, she could handle a few days without Hank. Hannah did have a scratchy throat, and if Hank knew, he certainly would not go on the business trip.

Before either knew, the last day arrived before Hank would be leaving on his five-day business trip. Hank had prepared everything; he paid the bills, and called Rose. He needed reassurance she would be available should Hannah need her. Of course Rose would be available. Along with contacting Rose, Hank made sure there was plenty of food, he stocked the pantry and refrigerator. He put together a list of instructions for Hannah, which was when she reached her breaking point. Hannah thought to herself, if I get one more list or order, I'm going to scream. The night before Hank was to leave he arranged a special evening for the two of them. Harry came over to babysit Mandy. Hank and Hannah went out for a wonderful dinner and evening of dancing. When they reached home, both thanked Harry and Hannah checked on Mandy. Hank and Hannah retired to their bedroom made love and quickly fell asleep. Hannah was still fighting fatigue.

The following morning, Hank packed, and was ready to leave. He kissed and hugged Hannah then he gave Mandy a kiss on the top of her forehead, reminding Mandy to be a good girl for her mother. As he drove toward Binghamton, Hank had an overwhelming feeling of dread. Hank couldn't get this feeling out of his head, it warned him he should have stayed home with Hannah. Hank was so tempted to turn around, but he knew Hannah would be fine. Something deep inside his soul told him different. As soon as he got to the hotel, he immediately called Hannah. Hank needed to know she was okay.

Hank felt nothing but relief as soon as he heard Hannah's voice with her insisting everything was fine.

Hanks conference was structured similar to his first month working for Mr. Singer. The first day passed smoothly.

Hank called around seven pm, he didn't want to wake Mandy and he knew Hannah didn't put their daughter to sleep until seven-thirty. Hannah monopolized the conversation; she was excited and full of things to tell him. She felt he had been gone for weeks rather than one day. After Hannah filled in Hank on her day with Mandy and Rose, he wanted to tell her about his day. He described the meetings and how he wished he would be leaving the following day. Before hanging up Hank said,

"I love you Hannah and give Mandy a kiss from her father. I miss you so much, behave your self."

Hannah returned Hank's sentiment, wishing he was home.

By the second of Hank's trip day Hannah started to feel sick. She had a cough, her nose was stuffy, and she had a terrible headache. During the day she rested on the sofa watching Mandy play. Besides Hannah not feeling well, Mandy was in the process of cutting a molar, which made her cranky. Early in the day Hannah thought night would never come. That evening Hank called and Hannah tried to hide how she sounded. She wanted to be as excited as she had been the prior night, but she was having a difficult time pretending. She told Hank Mandy's new a tooth was causing Mandy to be whiney and difficult. Hank asked if something else was wrong and Hannah tried to assure him other than Mandy all was well. He then directly asked about Hannah's health, stating she sounded as if she was getting a cold. Hannah, finally told him,

"Yes, I have a little cold, but it's nothing to worry about."

Hank suggested to Hannah,

"Why don't you call Rose, explain the situation with Mandy and you, and ask her to spend the night."

Hannah agreed with Hank, thinking calling her mother would be wise, especially since Hannah felt worse.

"Hannah, are you all right? If I left now I could be home in four hours," Hank said.

"No it's just a cold, don't worry."

Still uneasy about Hannah, Hank told her,

"I miss you and love you very much. Please call Rose and get a good night's sleep. Good bye my love."

Concerned after hanging up, Hank seriously considered going home. Worrying about Hannah, Hank spent the night tossing and turning. Hank decided, if Hannah wasn't better by their next conversation, he would go home.

When she hung up with Hank, Hannah called Rose, told her she was sick, and asked if she would spend the night. Rose arrived at Hannah's so quickly, it amazed Hannah. Edmund Jr. drove his mother to Hannah's. He insisted he come in to assess Hannah's the situation. He agreed with Hannah, she had a bad cold and with their mother's care, Hannah would be fine. Edmund Jr. left his mother with strict instructions though. If Hannah got worse or if either needed him for anything they were to call immediately.

Hannah woke the next day feeling worse than the night before. She knew she was getting sicker. Between her deep cough and the rust colored sputum, Hannah was scared. Rose was relieved Hannah's sputum was void of blood, which was a positive sign. Rose took Hannah's temperature, although it wasn't necessary. Rose could tell by looking at her daughter, she was running a high temperature, it was apparent through Hannah's coloring and the glassiness of her eyes. Hannah knowing she couldn't help with Mandy insisted her mother call Harry to help out. Hannah turned to Rose practically pleading,

"Mom, please call Harry to help, now."

Each time the phone rang; Hannah would answer it as normal sounding as possible. At last, the phone rang and it was Hank. He wanted to know how Hannah was feeling. Hannah did not want to ruin Hank's business trip, so she refused to mention her fever or the color of her sputum. He quizzed her about her symptoms. Hank asked to speak to Rose. Once Rose got on the line with Hank, he wanted to know honestly, how Hannah was. Rose let Hank know what she had been doing for her daughter. Trying to reassure Hank, Rose said,

"She has a chest cold similar to those she had as a child, it's nothing serious, if anything it's an inconvenience."

Somehow speaking with Rose brought Hank some comfort. Hannah returned to the phone, trying to tell from the tone of Hank's voice if he was satisfied with Rose's explanation. Since he did not bring up her illness immediately, Hannah was sure he accepted Rose's explanation. They each told the other how much they loved the other, as they were getting ready to say goodnight. Before Hannah hung up she heard Hank plead,

"Please get better."

"I will, I promise my love," replied Hannah as she hung up.

Hannah smiled to herself and thought how lucky she was to have Hank.

Throughout the night, Rose constantly checked on Hannah. She tried to keep Hannah's temperature down with aspirin, however when the aspirin failed, Rose tried ice packs on Hannah's head. Rose noticed Hannah was not sleeping though during the night, she seemed to be in out of sleep. When morning arrived Harry said to Rose,

"Hannah is very ill, she has more than a chest cold. Please mother, we need to call the doctor."

Rose refused; she insisted she could do just as much for Hannah as the doctor.

As the day progressed though, Hannah was still running a high fever, her cough was torturous to hear and the sputum was still thick and still rusty.

With all the commotion around her Mandy was as good as gold. She must have sensed something was wrong, because she would cry with her arms outstretched for her mother. Harry carried Mandy into the bedroom so she could see Hannah and it seemed to placate her.

Hannah was only getting worse; she would slip between sleep and delirium. Hannah often called for Hank not realizing he was away. Rose finally admitted she could not help Hannah and as she picked the phone up to call Edmund Jr. to get Hannah to the hospital, Hank walked through the door. He took one look at Hannah and yelled,

"Called for an ambulance now."

Hank was beside himself with anger. He looked at Rose, wondered why Hannah wasn't in the hospital. How could Rose have let this go so far and why didn't she call me?

The ambulance arrived quickly. Harry stayed at the flat with Mandy, while Rose and Hank rode with Hannah to the hospital. Before Hank left, he asked Harry,

"Call our family doctor, Dr. Britt, and let him know Hannah's on her way to the hospital."

Hank yelled thanks as he ran to the ambulance.

During the ride to the hospital, Hannah woke and was coherent. She held Hank's hand and smiled because she was thankful he was home. Hank kept repeating to Hannah,

"You're going to be all right, I promise."

Hannah was frightened to be going to the hospital. She kept remembering her stay before that resulted in her going to Homer Folks. The ambulance ride took forever. At last, they were at St. Peter's Hospital.

TWENTY-THREE

r. Britt arrived five minutes after Hannah, Hank, and Rose. As he examined Hannah, he listened to her lungs and noticed the color of the sputum she coughed up. When he finished the examination, Dr. Britt asked Hank to join him in the hall. Dr. Britt told Hank,

"Hannah has pneumonia and I think it's best she be hospitalized."

As they stood in the hall, two orderlies wheeled Hannah to a room where she was immediately placed in an oxygen tent. An intravenous was started so Hannah could receive fluids. Dr. Britt knew how committed Hank was toward Hannah's health, which is why he decided, for Hank's sake, not to tell Hank everything relating to Hannah. For instance, Dr. Britt was concerned Hannah was running a temperature of 103, her pulse was fast at 150 and her blood pressure was low, 88/50. Along with her poor vital signs, Hannah's lips had a bluish tint and it was obvious she was having difficulty breathing. Together these were indications of a critically ill person. Once Hannah was settled in her bed, her whole body seemed to relax.

Hank asked Rose to take Mandy home with her because he was not leaving Hannah's side. Typically the nurses would have given Hank a hard time spending the night, but Dr. Britt had written an order in Hannah's chart that permitted Hank to stay.

Throughout that night, Hannah drifted in and out of consciousness. When she was aware of her surroundings she would try talking with Hank. Hank tried to keep her from talking much because it just made her breathing more difficult.

When he thought Hannah was sleeping, he quickly called his sister, Maria,

"Maria, Hannah is in the hospital very sick with pneumonia. Would you please take care of Mandy?"

Maria was hesitant at first, because she had thee children of her own. The youngest was just a year older than Mandy, however when Maria heard the worry in Hank's voice she agreed. Hank told her Rose had Mandy for the night, if she could pick up Mandy the next day he would be very appreciative.

Hank then called Rose, he let her know Maria would be by the following day to pick up. Mandy. At first Rose began to insist, she could take care of Mandy, but Hank reminded her,

"Rose you know you will want to be with Hannah and by looking after Mandy that would be impossible. Let my sister take care of Mandy, she has three of her own so it won't be difficult for her."

When Hank left for Hannah's room, Rose gathered a few items of Mandy's, and headed home with Harry. Maria stopped by Rose's a short time later and picked up Mandy.

Rose was exhausted and blaming herself for Hannah's illness. Deep down she realized she should have listened to Harry and taken Hannah to the hospital days ago.

When Rose got to the hospital she asked Hank,

"Are you angry with me?"

Hank replied,

"Of course I am Rose. You should have been honest with me from the start. I left the number if you needed to contact me or you should have said something when I called."

Hank continued,

"I can't imagine what would have happened if I didn't come home when I did. I do know I'll never go away without Hannah again."

Rose had tears in her eyes when she repeated,

"Hank, I'm so sorry."

She knew Hank had every right to be upset with her.

Dr. Britt came in early the next morning. He examined Hannah and was not pleased by what he observed and heard. Hannah's breathing was more rapid, and becoming shallow. And, even with oxygen her lips were still blue. Dr. Britt decided it would be best to inform Hank of the seriousness of Hannah's situation. He requested Hank to meet him in the waiting room; he needed to speak with him.

"Hank I'm not going to lie to you. Hannah is critically ill. I'm not sure if Hannah's heart and lungs can withstand the strain of her illness. You need to be aware Hannah could die. I'm doing everything with in my power to prevent that from occurring. Maybe you should consider calling your priest."

Upon Hank's request, one of the nurses called the hospital's chaplain. Rose just arrived in Hannah's room, when the chaplain entered. Never in her wildest dreams did Rose believe Hannah was so sick.

"Please God, don't take my baby girl" Rose whispered.

Hank was also in the room and after the priest gave Hannah the Last Rights, he and Rose recited a few prayers. Hank realized Hannah had not opened her eyes in hours, and except for her breathing, she seemed peaceful. Rose and Hank both had tears in their eyes, each were lost in their own thoughts.

By evening Hannah still had not opened her eyes but her breathing seemed less labored. Hank persuaded Rose to go to the waiting room and try to get some sleep. While he was alone, Hank held Hannah's hand resting his head on her bed so she could feel him. Alone with Hannah, Hank would tell her everything they would do once she was well. He would mention Mandy and how much she missed her mother. Other times Hank pleaded with Hannah,

"Hannah, you need to get better, Mandy and I need you."

Hank couldn't imagine his life without her. Hannah was Hank's best friend, wife and lover. All during the night, Hank remained by Hannah's side. Sometimes lying his head on Hannah's bed. Everything Hank did, he felt meant nothing because her condition remained the same.

The next day Dr. Britt came in, surprised Hannah was still alive. He was sure she would have passed during the night. Dr. Britt said to Hank,

"There is no improvement, you should not expect her condition to change, and I'm sorry Hank."

Throughout the day, various nurses were in and out of Hannah's room checking her intravenous and oxygen tent.

Hank was exhausted but refused close his eyes. He wanted to be by her side no mater what. Hank knew she could sense him there.

He recalled what the patients use to say at the Homer Folks,

"Fight the Tuberculosis, don't let it win."

Hank then said to Hannah,

"Fight my love, don't let the pneumonia win."

Rose came in with relief to see Hannah alive. Rose insisted Hank to try and rest in the waiting room, but Hank said,

"As long as Hannah is with us, I will not leave her side."

Edmund Jr. and Harry came to visit Hannah, but were not permitted in her room. They waited in the waiting room, eager for Rose's updates.

It was another long night. Hank sent Rose home, as he returned to his nightly routine. Hank began with sitting next to Hannah's bed, holding her hand, and resting his head on her bed although tonight, he had his head touching her side. Hank kept his eyes on Hannah, talking to her, expecting for her to open her eyes and respond to what he was saying.

The next morning, Dr. Britt came in saying to Hank,

"She sure is a fighter."

But, he never gave Hank any sign of hope.

Through the next night, Hank swore Hannah's breathing was better, not as labored and her breathing was less rapid and shallow. Hank refused to close his eyes during the night, he had a feeling deep in his gut, that Hannah would open her eyes tonight. Hank prayed and spoke to Hannah most of the night; there hadn't been any change. Hank was beside himself, he knew he was right, she would open her eyes.

The following morning, Hank shared his observations about Hannah's breathing with Dr. Britt. Dr. Britt examined Hannah and said to Hank

"I agree with you her breathing is better, she has a long way to go. Don't get your hopes too high, not yet. Remember though, Hannah is a fighter."

Rose brought Hank food and milk. He doubted he could eat, but he ate everything Rose brought.

Before the meal from Rose, Hank had been surviving off the coffee the nurses brought him throughout the night.

Rose had Harry stop by Hank's house and bring him his razor, toothbrush, and change of clothes. Rose said to Hank, "At least you'll be presentable for Hannah when she wakes. Hank knew Hannah was still critical; he couldn't shake that gut feeling he had.

"You're going to make it, Hon." And Hank kissed her hand.

Hours slowly went by and Hank began pacing the floor in Hannah's room. A nurse came in and said to Hank,

"I have some good news, Hannah's temperature is down to 100 degrees."

Hank became overwhelmed with excitement, realizing he no longer felt tired.

Dr. Britt said to Hank the following morning,

"I think Hannah's getting better. Although, her heart and lungs are still beating too fast, her pulse rate slowed to 98. These are positive signs, Hank."

Hank turned to Dr. Britt,

"Thank you doctor, I knew my Hannah was a fighter."

Later that afternoon, while Rose and Hank were talking next to Hannah as she lay in bed, she opened her eyes, smiling. Hannah tried to say something, but her mouth was too dry. Thrilled, Hank ran to the nurse's station telling them Hannah was awake. Hank told them,

"Hannah tried to speak but her mouth is too dry. Could she have some water?" The nurse replied,

"Dr. Britt would have to order water for Hannah but, she could have some ice chips for now."

Once the ice chips moistened her mouth, very weakly she asked if Mandy was all right.

"Mandy is with my sister, Maria and her family. I've spoken to Maria every couple of days and Maria says Mandy is fine. She has all her cousins giving her so much attention, she probably won't want to leave."

Hannah finally took a hard looked at Hank and told him,

"Go and get some rest."

Hank stood firm on the topic of going home. He said to Hannah,

"I'm not going anywhere, I'm not leaving until Dr. Britt says there's no chance of relapse."

Hank wanted Hannah to close her eyes and rest,

"You need all the rest you can get right now."

When Dr. Britt came to see Hannah, she smiled and said,

"Hello."

"Hello to you too, my miracle patient," said Dr. Britt.

As soon as Dr. Britt saw Hank he said,

"Go home and get some sleep or you will be admitted."

Just as Hank was getting ready to leave, Rose entered Hannah's room. She said to Hank,

"I will call you if there is a change."

When Hank got home, he called Maria and filled her in on the situation. He said he didn't know how long it would before he could picked up Mandy, but he would stop by later to see her.

Hank slept soundly for about five hours. As soon as he woke up he called the hospital to inquire about Hannah. The nurse at the desk said,

"Mr. Schmidt your wife continues to improve. Dr. Britt was by and he seems pleased with her recovery."

Satisfied with the report from the hospital, Hank dressed to go see Mandy. He called Maria to inform her he was on his way.

Hank pulled up to Maria's, he noticed, he hadn't felt happy in quite some time, that was until now. When Hank knocked on his sister's door, the door flew open and there was Mandy. She hugged his knees as Hank picked her up giving her a big hug and kiss. While Hank held Mandy he told her,

"Mommy will be coming home soon and we will all be together again."

Hank knew that Mandy didn't understand except when mentioned the word Mommy. Mandy starting crying, Hank knew Mandy missed Hannah. To quiet Mandy down, he sat with her on his lap, and rocked her.

"Maria do you have a book I could read Mandy?"

"Here is Peter Cotton Tail. Will that do?"

"That's fine, thanks."

Hank started reading to Mandy, when one of Maria's little ones came to hear, Hank scooped her up and read to both of them.

When Mandy calmed down, Hank spoke to Maria,

"Maria I can't thank you enough. I am going back to work Monday, and when I get paid I will give you some money for taking care of Mandy."

Before Hank left, he gave Mandy another hug and kiss promising her,

"I'll be back soon and read you another book."

Hank went straight from Maria's to the hospital. Hannah beamed, when she saw him. She had so much to tell him.

"I ate food today and it tasted so good. As you can see they have taken me out of the oxygen tent. Dr. Britt was in and said they were going to do a chest x-ray when I can stand, and test sputum, and then a bronchoscopy. He said when someone is so sick it can reactivate the tuberculosis. Dr. Britt started to explain what the bronchoscopy procedure was to me when I told him I had many done at the Homer Folks. Hank was thrilled with everything Hannah told him, also he was delighted to see her spirits were up. Hank could see his Hannah returning.

Hannah wanted to know about Mandy and how she was doing throughout this ordeal. Hannah missed her so much she could feel her heart ache.

"I saw Mandy today. She looks wonderful and is growing like a weed. I told her you'd be coming home soon and we'd all be together again. I don't know if she understood anything but when she heard

Mommy, then she started to cry. That little girl definitely loves her mother."

"You don't seem to be coughing as much today. What did Dr. Britt say?"

"He told me I'm still running a low grade temperature. Dr. Britt did upset me when he told me to expect to be in the hospital for two more weeks. I so much want to be home with you and Mandy. I'm going crazy here with nothing to do, would you bring me my knitting and a few magazines to help pass the time?"

Hank replied, "No problem, my love."

Hank now had Hannah's attention to share his news.

"I talked to Mr. Singer about returning to work and he agreed, I can return on Monday. He also informed me I would not be losing any pay for the days I needed to take off. He said while I was out, the state sent in a large order. They are an account I've been working so hard to close; I've been talking to them for weeks. Now that they have made their order, I'll be receiving a substantial commission check. Isn't this fantastic?"

Hannah was so thrilled, she was proud of her husband. She wanted to ask him about the hospital bill, but she didn't want to ruin his good mood. Hannah decided to just ask,

"Hank I hate to bring this up, especially since you are so excited with your commission, but how are we ever going to pay all of the medical expenses

Hank explained to Hannah,

"I've spoken to both Dr. Britt and the hospital, both have agreed to let me pay so much per month. I also thought if I use the commission checks from the state, both bills could be paid off more quickly."

Hannah felt so guilty, it wasn't fair Hank couldn't enjoy his commission check; rather he would use it to pay her expenses. Hannah didn't feel right but she knew Hank would see it differently and insist she as more important than anything he could do with the check.

Hank spent the day with Hannah. Rose and Harry came by and Harry was carrying a large bouquet of flowers. Hannah's face lit up with delight.

"Oh Harry they brighten up this dull room, thank you so much. I absolutely love the flowers."

On Saturday morning Hank ate breakfast while he made a grocery list. He was not resentful toward Rose any longer and gave her a call to see if she wanted to go to the store. Rose's reply made Hank happy,

"Hank that would be wonderful. I can be ready in half an hour, and Hank, I can't tell you how sorry I am."

"Forget about it Rose, there is no need to apologize each time you see me. I know how much you love and adore Hannah. It was an accident and that's the end of it."

Sunday Hank visited Mandy. She smiled, wide, from ear to ear. She was so happy to see Hank, but she continued to ask for "Ma-Ma." Mandy was much too young to understand where her mother was, rather he tried distracting her. He read Mandy a book, making funny faces and strange sounds as he read. Mandy giggled and laughed and when they were done, Hank told Mandy he would be back very soon. Hank picked Mandy up, giving her a bunch of kisses and a bear hug. As he closed the door, he could hear his daughter begin to cry. As distant as he had been with Mandy, this time he could feel his heart ache.

Hank, then went to see Hannah, she seemed melancholy.

"What's wrong?" Hank asked.

"I'm just concerned how will we manage once I'm home. I won't have the strength I had prior to the pneumonia; Dr. Britt said I would need to rest frequently. I told him about the three-prong approach, used in treating tuberculosis, that I follow and he thought it sounded perfect."

Hank reassured Hannah,

"I'm positive your mother will be more than happy to come over and help you out until you've regained your strength."

Hannah seemed to relax some when Hank made the suggestion. She was sure Hank was still upset with Rose, but obviously they had made their peace.

Hank reminded Hannah,

"Remember, I return to work tomorrow. Therefore, I probably will be here around six o'clock."

Hannah knew Hank returning to work would be good for him and his sanity.

Hank then told Hannah about his visit with Mandy. He said, "Mandy keeps saying only two words, "Ma-Ma.""

With that, Hannah began crying. Hank held her, telling Hannah,

"It won't be long now, you'll be at home and so will Mandy."

Early Monday morning Hank arrived at work. He had to admit, it felt good to be back. His friend Bob gave Hank a big welcome and even Mr. Singer, the boss, greeted Hank warmly. Everyone asked about Hannah. Hank told them Hannah was recovering nicely and thanked them for their concern.

At six Hank arrived at the hospital, happy to see Hannah smiling.

"Oh Hank, I've had such a wonderful day. My temperature is back to normal and I was out of bed sitting in a chair. The nurse said, it is possible in a couple of days, I could walk around the room. If I can manage the room, next I'll be walking the halls. Once I've conquered the halls, home will surely be the final step."

Hank was so excited for Hannah. She definitely was his miracle. He knew he couldn't survive without her. Around eight pm, Hank gave Hannah a hug and kiss, saying goodnight until tomorrow. By the time he reached home, he was exhausted, but he knew he needed to eat. He fixed himself eggs and toast then collapsed into bed.

The following day Hank realized he would need help for Hannah. He knew he suggested Rose to Hannah, but giving it more thought, he knew Mandy would be too much for Rose at her age. When he arrived at the hospital that evening he brought up the need for help to Hannah, at least until her strength returned. Hannah said to Hank,

"I thought my mother was going to help." Hank replied,

"I've been thinking about that and I honestly don't think Rose could handle Mandy at her age."

Hannah agreed, but then suggested,

"What if Harry came with Rose?"

Hank thought about it briefly and said,

"I think we need a housekeeper, someone dependable, who can be with you and Mandy every week day."

They both knew it would be expensive, but they needed someone reliable to help Hannah during the week. Hannah suggested Hank call Rose, she would know someone.

When Hank returned home that evening, he immediately called Rose. He explained they were looking for a housekeeper and Rose told Hank she would be more than happy to help Hannah. As tactfully and compassionately as he could, Hank thanked Rose, but explained with Mandy he was afraid she would wear Rose out. Rose understood and agreed to make some calls. Rose returned Hank's call a short time later and gave him the name of Mrs. Sheridan. She told Hank a little about her and said Mrs. Sheridan was interested in the position.

During one of Hank's breaks, the following day at work, he called Mrs. Sheridan, explaining the job and what would be expected of her. Specifically, Hank stressed,

"Your hours would be from eight in the morning to six in the evening, Monday to Friday. You would be responsible for housework, wash, and looking after Mandy when Hannah needed to rest. The job would begin the day Hannah comes home from the hospital."

Mrs. Sheridan thanked Hank for the opportunity and to let her know when Hannah would be home.

Every day after work Hank went to the hospital. By now, Hannah was walking in the halls. She had the chest x-ray and the results showed great improvement with her lungs healing. The bronchoscopy results were negative and the deep sputum had no signs of the tuberculosis germs. Both were overwhelmed with such positive news.

Most of all, Hannah said to Hank,

"I'll be discharged on Saturday, I can't wait to go pick up Mandy and the three of us go home to our flat."

Hank was so happy he wanted to yell at the top of his lungs how much he loved his wife. Hannah smiled and said, "You do that, and they'll lock you up on the psych. ward."

TWENTY-FOUR

he Friday prior to Hannah's release from the hospital, Rose insisted on cleaning Hank and Hannah's flat. Not only did Rose clean every square inch, she washed and hung out the sheets, Hank and Hannah's and Mandy's. When Hank came home, he drove Rose home. Before returning he made a quick stop, picking up groceries. After putting the food away, Hank retrieved the sheets from the clothesline. For Hank making the bed was quite a challenge. After the third try, Hank was finally happy with the job he had done. Hank managed Mandy's bed, which turned out to be much easier.

Saturday morning Hank was up by six, his excitement to have Hannah home made it impossible to sleep. As he prepared for her homecoming, Hank shuddered at how close he came to loosing her. Now with Hannah coming home, his mission was to do everything in his power to ensure she remained healthy.

By eight, Hank drove to the hospital. When he arrived at Hannah's room, he noticed she was dressed, packed, and ready to go. She told Hank,

"We have to wait for Dr. Britt, he needs to discharge me. As soon as he gives the ok, one of the nurses will bring a wheelchair in, they will wheel me downstairs, and I'll be free to go."

Shortly after Hank arrived, Dr. Britt entered Hannah' room with some instructions for her. He said to Hannah,

"If you should develop a cough or run a fever call me immediately. It's important you don't wait to see if it gets worse or goes away. I'm serious, Hannah, contact me immediately. Until you are completely healthy, I don't want you around anyone who is sick or has a cold. If a member of your family becomes ill, I insist you wear a mask. You can purchase them at any drug store, and buy them on your way home. Do you have any questions?"

"Yes", Hannah replied, "I go on the porch in all kinds of weather. The porch is enclosed in glass windows, but they open. May I continue to sit there so I can get fresh air?"

"Yes that's perfectly fine. Maintain your the routine before you became ill, my only restriction, other than staying away from anyone sick, is absolutely do not do anything strenuous. Best of luck to both of you."

Hank shook Dr. Britt's hand and said,

Dr. Britt, I can't thank you enough for saving Hannah's life. I'll forever be indebted to you."

As Dr. Britt left the room, a nurse entered pushing a wheelchair. When the nurse stopped, Hannah hopped in, ready to go. Hank carried Hannah's bag and went ahead so the car would be directly by the entrance to the hospital. At the doorway, Hannah thanked the nurse, jumped into the car and said,

"Home, please, mister."

Laughing at Hannah, Hank reminded her they needed to stop first,

"Hang on, first we must go to the drug store. I'll be right back, I need to buy some masks just incase and you remain in the car."

Finally, as they drove away from the drugstore, Hannah thought,

"Now we are on our way home."

While driving, Hannah looked at everything, the trees, streets, and the lawns thinking how wonderful it all seemed. Shortly they arrived at their house. As soon as Hank turned off the car, Hannah was out of the car. Hank yelled,

"Wait a minute Hannah, there's no rush."

Hannah stopped and as they approached the stairs, Hank swept Hannah in his arms, caring her up the stairs. Hank was shocked at how light she was since being sick. As he carried her, Hannah could do nothing but laugh. At their front door, Hank put Hannah down. Hannah rushed into their flat. She inspected each room, looking at everything closely. Hannah said to Hank,

"I can tell my mother's been here."

Hannah had to admit to her self, it did feel good to be home.

Shortly after Hannah got settled the phone rang, it was Jack, Maria's husband. He was calling to let them know he would be bringing Mandy home after lunch. Hannah was thrilled to have her baby home but waiting until after lunch seemed unfair. To take her mind off her wait, Hank asked Hannah,

"Are you hungry, would you like a sandwich?"

Hannah replied,

"I'm starved, I'll come and help."

Hank immediately snapped,

"I will bring your sandwich and something to drink."

Rather than respond to how Hank ordered her to remain seated, Hannah let it go, knowing he was still concerned about her health.

Hank brought the sandwich and said,

"Enjoy this, then I suggest you rest because once Mandy's home everything will become hectic."

Realizing Hank was right, Hannah finished her sandwich and closed her eyes when the doorbell rang. They could hear Mandy coming up the stairs. Hannah opened the door expecting Mandy to run in her arms but Mandy stood there staring at her. Then tears started streaming down her face as she said,

"Want Da-Da."

Hank came over and picked up Mandy and thanked Jack. While in her father's arms Mandy kept peeking at Hannah. Hank said,

"Mandy Ma Ma's home aren't you happy?"

Mandy wouldn't answer.

For the rest of the day she clung to Hank while glancing at her Mother. Hannah wasn't sure how to react, then she remembered the times Mandy was teething or had a cold and the only person she would allow to hold her was Hannah. Hannah figured, Mandy would come around shortly she just needed time.

Hank insisted he would prepare dinner. He placed Mandy on one of the kitchen chairs. Hannah decided to quietly sit in a chair next to Mandy. Hannah put her hand on the table near Mandy's.

She wouldn't look at Mandy and shortly after she felt a little finger rubbing her hand. Still Hannah refused to look. Next Mandy put her whole hand on Hannah's. Hannah turned toward Mandy and smiled. The little hand remained on hers, Hannah placed her other hand on top of Mandy's. Without warning, Mandy said Ma-Ma and started to cry. Hannah scooped Mandy up placing Mandy on her lap. Hannah kissed the tears and said,

"Ma Ma loves Mandy."

Hank had watched the entire interaction, saying,

"Looks as if I've lost my job."

Hank kissed both his girls. Throughout dinner, Mandy remained on Hannah's lap.

As they finished eating, Hannah suggested a bubble bath. The three were in the bathroom. Hannah was bathing Mandy and Hank was there to lift Mandy in and out of the tub. The evening seemed to be going smoothly, but the real test was about to take place, putting Mandy to bed. Mandy was dressed in her pajamas, Hank lifted her into the crib and Hannah read her a book. When she finished the story, Hannah turned the light off and hummed a lullaby until Mandy fell asleep.

Hank and Hannah were enjoying the radio when they decided Hannah had a long day and it would be a good idea to go to bed. They just became settled, Hank with his arm around Hannah, when Mandy started to cry,

"Ma-Ma, Da-Da".

Hannah said,

"I'll go in to her and sing her back to sleep."

As Hannah entered Mandy's room, she saw Mandy standing in her crib sobbing. Hannah tried comforting her, humming her favorite lullabies trying to get her back to sleep. Mandy only continued to cry. When Hank came in and Mandy stopped crying, but still said,

"Ma-Ma, Da-Da."

Hannah and Hank each tried everything they knew and nothing worked. Exhausted Hannah said to Hank,

"Let's bring her in bed with us. When she falls a asleep you can carry her back to her crib."

Hank, by now was willing to give anything a try. Thus the Schmidt family, climbed into bed with Mandy between Hank and Hannah, pleased as ever. When Mandy was asleep Hank put her in her crib and she slept there for the rest of the night.

The weekend flew by and before anyone realized it was Monday. Usually Hank leaves by seven thirty, but today he wanted to meet Mrs. Sheridan. Hank and Hannah discussed what her duties would be. Hannah insisted the biggest chore would be the washing and hanging it outside.

By Eight o'clock sharp, the doorbell rang and Hank opened the door greeting Mrs. Sheridan. He introduced her to Hannah and Mandy and then left work satisfied Hannah was in capable hands

Initially, Hannah was shy, but Mrs. Sheridan was easy to warm up to. Hannah told what she would like her to do. Hannah was insistent,

"Taking care of the wash is a priority."

Immediately Mrs. Sheridan cleaned the living room and dining room. She looked in the bedrooms but the beds were made and everything appeared neat and in place. Next, she cleaned the bathroom and kitchen. Hannah showed Mrs. Sheridan how to use the washing machine. Mrs. Sheridan decided to get started with the wash right away. It was a beautiful day and the clothes would dry quickly.

While Mrs. Sheridan was busy with the wash, the doorbell rang. It was Rose. Hannah introduced Mrs. Sheridan and then Rose made small talk with Hannah. Rose fixed dinner at home and brought it for Hannah and Hank. Hannah smiled; she knew her mother was at the house to spy on Mrs. Sheridan. Hannah determined Rose's dinner was Rose's way of saying.

"I'm still useful."

Hannah realized Mrs. Sheridan proved to be an invaluable help surprisingly Mandy even was taken with her. When Hank came home that night, Hannah filled him in on her day with Mrs. Sheridan,

"Hank she is absolutely wonderful. She had the flat cleaned before lunch and did the wash beautifully. I know she will work out for the best because Mandy already warmed up to her."

"I gather she's worth cent, and then some more, she's great."

Gradually, Hannah gained her strength back, along with her spunk.

One night after Mandy was asleep, Hank and Hannah were cuddling while listening to the radio. Hannah said to Hank,

"I've been taking my temperature and tonight is safe."

"Are you sure? Do you think you're strong enough?"

Hank said,

"There's no harm in trying to find out, is there?"

Gently Hannah and Hank made love. Hank still felt as if she might break. They had the passion, but not the intensity yet. Neither cared, it was wonderful for both of them. Both thought aloud,

"Now life is back to normal."